A Startling Discovery in the Warehouse

It was really rather spooky, all alone between the rows of pallet stacks, nothing to see but shadows.

No, he wasn't all alone. There was whoever was wearing that bleeper, too—that insistent, nagging bleeper, bleeping on and on, unanswered. Why didn't the chap answer it?

"Oh, blimey!" Ted had rounded the corner of the stack in the farthest aisle, and now saw what had happened to his purloined load of fish fingers. It lay spread on the floor in an untidy heap, spilling soggily from burst cardboard boxes.

"Vandals! Oh, the—the buggers!" moaned Ted. *Who* could have done it—who in the Tesbury Warehouse was so spiteful?

The monotonous call of the bleeper broke through Ted's misery and confusion. Was the perpetrator hiding close by to gloat over his malicious joke?

And was he also deaf?

"Oh, blimey!" Ted had drawn closer to the wreckage and started to examine it. The owner of the bleeper lay underneath Ted's load of frozen fish fingers, crushed and squashed and, beyond any doubt, dead. . . .

D1012453

MORE MYSTERIES FROM THE BERKLEY PUBLISHING GROUP . . .

THE HERON CARVIC MISS SEETON MYSTERIES: Retired art teacher Miss Seeton steps in where Scotland Yard stumbles. "A most beguiling protagonist!"
—*New York Times*

by Heron Carvic

MISS SEETON SINGS
MISS SEETON DRAWS THE LINE
WITCH MISS SEETON
PICTURE MISS SEETON
ODDS ON MISS SEETON
HANDS UP, MISS SEETON

by Hamilton Crane

HANDS UP, MISS SEETON
MISS SEETON CRACKS THE CASE
MISS SEETON PAINTS THE TOWN
MISS SEETON BY MOONLIGHT
MISS SEETON ROCKS THE CRADLE
MISS SEETON GOES TO BAT
MISS SEETON PLANTS SUSPICION

by Hampton Charles

ADVANTAGE MISS SEETON
MISS SEETON AT THE HELM
MISS SEETON, BY APPOINTMENT

SISTERS IN CRIME: Criminally entertaining short stories from the top women of mystery and suspense. "Excellent!" —*Newsweek*

edited by Marilyn Wallace

SISTERS IN CRIME
SISTERS IN CRIME 2
SISTERS IN CRIME 3

SISTERS IN CRIME 4
SISTERS IN CRIME 5

KATE SHUGAK MYSTERIES: A former D.A. solves crime in the far Alaska north . . .

by Dana Stabenow

A COLD DAY FOR MURDER
A FATAL THAW

DEAD IN THE WATER

DOG LOVER'S MYSTERIES STARRING HOLLY WINTER: With her Alaskan malamute Rowdy, Holly dogs the trails of dangerous criminals. "A gifted and original writer." —Carolyn G. Hart

by Susan Conant

A NEW LEASH ON DEATH
DEAD AND DOGGONE

A BITE OF DEATH
PAWS BEFORE DYING

MELISSA CRAIG MYSTERIES: She writes mystery novels—and investigates crimes when life mirrors art. "Splendidly lively." —*Publishing News*

by Betty Rowlands

A LITTLE GENTLE SLEUTHING

FINISHING TOUCH

FROZEN STIFF

SARAH J. MASON

BERKLEY BOOKS, NEW YORK

The author is grateful to the agents A P Watt Ltd, on behalf of Jean Bell, for their permission to include the lines from *The Moving Toyshop* by Edmund Crispin on p. 30 of this work.

FROZEN STIFF

A Berkley Book / published by arrangement with the author

PRINTING HISTORY
Berkley edition / August 1993

ISBN: 0-425-13837-2

A BERKLEY BOOK ® TM 757,375
Berkley Books are published by The Berkley Publishing Group,
200 Madison Avenue, New York, New York 10016.
The name "BERKLEY" and the "B" logo
are trademarks belonging to Berkley Publishing Corporation.

PRINTED IN THE UNITED STATES OF AMERICA

10 9 8 7 6 5 4 3 2 1

One

DARK BLUE AND gleaming in the July sunshine, the car crept cautiously along the street. Its driver and passenger sank low in their seats as, with a discreet flick of the indicator, it turned through open gates and rumbled quietly towards the parking space in the shadow of a high brick wall. Breathing deeply, the driver spun the wheel, backed the car between the neat white lines, switched off the engine, and sighed.

A stealthy glance over one shoulder, a low murmur. "So far, so good. Don't forget to close your window. . . ."

A grunt of acquiescence, a strong grasp on the handle of the door. A warning cry from his companion as the burly man in the passenger seat prepared to climb out.

"Don't slam it! If anyone hears us now . . ."

The soft clunk of metal on rubber trim, the whirr of the central locking system. Another stealthy glance around.

"All clear, I think. Come on. . . ."

The double doors stood mercifully open: no fear that creaking hinge or rattling latch would betray the passage of these two furtive figures. They walked one behind the other, the burly man in front, the driver taking care to match footfall with footfall as they made their way along a grey-tiled corridor where every sound reechoed. There came a sudden rush of warm air from around a corner.

"Somebody must be coming," muttered the burly man, with a curse. His colleague frowned.

"We're almost there—we could make a dash for it—"

"The hell with all this pussyfooting nonsense!" The burly man squared his shoulders and strode out fearlessly. His colleague, with a shrug, followed suit, and mused on the workings of fate.

But the draught must have come from a newly opened window, not a door, for nobody came. And nobody saw the burly man's hand on the knob of a closed door, or heard the nervous chuckle with which the driver slipped through in his wake, or the sighs of heartfelt relief which greeted the successful outcome of the whole enterprise as, hurrying to the nearer of the two desks in the room, the burly man examined the blotter with an anxious eye, then turned to his accomplice.

"Nothing, thank the Lord! But it's all getting too much for me, at my age." He dragged out the chair and sat down heavily. "Good grief, girl, it's downright ridiculous that we have to go scurrying about the place like a pair of criminals just so Pleate doesn't see us. . . ."

People meeting Detective Superintendent Trewley for the first time could never decide whether he resembled a bulldog more than a bloodhound in appearance. A bulky man of late middle age, he had dark brown, mournful eyes, and features so corrugated that it took him twice as long as other men to shave. Humourists among the Allingham constabulary referred to him, in his absence, as the Plain-clothes Prune.

His sidekick and companion in crime, Detective Sergeant Stone—a small, slight young brunette whose looks gave no hint of the black belt in judo that she was, or the medical student she had once been—stifled a giggle as she took her own seat, noting with relief that her blotter, likewise, bore no reproachful message from the desk sergeant who ruled Allingham's police station with a truncheon of cast iron.

"I still think you ought to stand up to him, sir. Tell him straight that if you feel like sneaking—er, popping out for a pub lunch, that's what you'll do. The privilege of rank, sir, and all that sort of—"

"Stone, shut up!" Trewley buried his face in his hands and groaned. "Privilege be damned! If I was half as *privileged* as you make out, this office'd be air-conditioned, for a start."

"*And* have central heating that works—if it isn't a bit cockeyed to talk about radiators and hot-air blowers when the temperature hasn't dropped below seventy for the last three weeks—sorry, sir," as Trewley groaned again. The sergeant regarded her superior with some anxiety. It wasn't just her teasing that had made the restorative effects of the air-conditioned pub wear off so fast.

She jumped to her feet. "How about a cup of tea, sir? Nothing like a hot drink to make the body's cooling systems regulate themselves properly. Of course, if you're really desperate, I suppose I could try taking a look through Lost Property, in case anyone's handed in an electric fan. . . ."

Startled, Trewley stared at her. "Do I look that bad? You mean you'd be willing to risk life and limb and Sergeant Pleate and go hunting around in his blasted cupboards?"

"For you, sir, I might stretch a point." She chuckled. "Your need, in my humble opinion, is rather greater than Sergeant Pleate's. With the office being so small, even if we open both windows we never really have enough fresh air, do we?"

"Fresh air!" Trewley sighed, scowling about him at the four looming walls of the little room. "It's being indoors all the time that does it, girl. Sometimes I wonder if I'll ever breathe properly again. On days like this, I could do with a transfer to Traffic, I reckon. . . ."

Stone, who enjoyed (as the superintendent knew) a close personal relationship with a member of Allingham's Traffic Division, sadly shook her head. "I hate to disillusion you, sir, but you'd spend hardly any time at all zipping along the motorway with the windows wide open. Most of it's sorting out people parked on double yellow lines and idiots who run into the backs of cars at junctions, or shunt them on street corners and smash their rear lights . . ."

Green and glittering gold in the July sunshine, the container lorry came bowling along the street. The driver whistled a jaunty off-key tune through his teeth as he kept a careful watch on the cars parked either side of the road: one of the first things he'd been warned when he started his new job on Monday morning was that this was an area of potential ambush. At any moment, from between the vehicles ranged neatly against the kerb, an unexpected pedestrian might suddenly appear. If Ted was unlucky, such an appearance could lead to a licence endorsement, a fine, the sack, or worse. Since Tesbury's was one of the best employers in

Allshire, Ted was being very watchful indeed, nor did he want to blot his still-clean copybook by turning up late when he hadn't even collected his first week's wages yet. . . .

"Blast!" Now he'd gone and overshot the entrance. All through concentrating too hard on the driving, and not hard enough on the delivering. He swore again, braked, hesitated, glanced up and down along the road—and then began to reverse, the lorry's orange indicators flashing.

He almost made it. Creeping cautiously towards the gateway guarded by those inconvenient vehicular sentries, with the steering wheel on its tightest lock and a crick in his neck from peering over his shoulder . . . at not quite the right angle to do the job properly.

"Oh, blimey!" He stopped, braked, and climbed down from his cab to inspect the white BMW parked earlier by its owner—parked with a full complement of taillights—outside the Tesbury premises. "Oh, blimey!"

Another quick look round, then he was back in his cab, ready to straighten up and try again. And this time he made it through the gates in safety, carrying on down the drive, hoping nobody had noticed what had happened. Tesbury's might be tops when it came to groceries, but their security was pretty low-key. If he was lucky, he'd be able to—

He wasn't lucky.

"Next time, my son," growled Goods-In, as he emerged from his official cubbyhole to wave a menacing clipboard at him, "don't try to be so clever, all right? You take yourself arahnd the block and come in again if you find you're tight. Ain't no room for that fancy footwork you was a-trying, not with all them cars all over the show."

Ted grimaced. "Reckon there'll be much of a row? I'd sort of hoped as nobody'd seen me, but—"

"So who's seen you? None of *that* lot, for sure, up in their fancy office block." Goods-In scowled towards the nearby three storeys of gazing glass windows. "Use your common sense, boy. How many of 'em d'you reckon's got time to poke their noses aht to see what's happening dahn here, the way they're all being worked to death nowadays? Nah, you're safe enough—could of bin any old car or truck passing by what give it that little bump. Because it *was* only a little bump—right?''

"Right," gasped Ted, in great relief. "Hardly touched, it didn't—shouldn't cost a packet to put right, neither, not if they're properly insured."

"Yes, well, you won't say nothing abaht that, not if you use your loaf like I told you. What's a no-claims bonus to the likes of them in the office? But the likes of you, boy—ho, that's a different story!" Goods-In rolled his eyes, tapped the side of his nose, and winked.

"Nah see here, son. Best thing you can do's take yourself and your truck along to the garridge just as soon as you'n me've unloaded this little lot. There's a few scratches of white paint I can see from here, not to mention your bumper looking a bit bent—better get it fixed right after we've finished here, and I've signed for this lot. Signed for it, indeed!" He rolled his eyes again. "Bloody forms to fill in all day long, not a scrap of use to a soul, as I can see—but it's the new system, or so I'm told, and who am I to say I couldn't see nothing wrong with the old system? Done this job for years, I have—but do they think to ask me? Course they don't! Them cocky young buggers the Board's brought in, they think they know it all—but they don't, not by a long chalk they don't—and they'll find out one of these days as they should of listened to me in the first place, mark my words. Change for the sake of change, it ain't natural, that's what I say."

"Bin plenty of changes?"

"Too many, if you ask me." Goods-In scowled again as he leafed through the papers clipped to his board, hunting for those applicable to Ted's lorry. "Never does to go bringing in all them bloody foreigners, that's what I think. . . ."

For the traditional English villager, *foreigner* applies to anyone who hails from more than five miles away; for the town dweller, the distance is greater, and *foreigner* tends to attach to itself the dictionary definition of someone who comes from another country. In the present case, the other country was Wales, which was at least in the same general geographical area, but via America, which wasn't. Tesbury's

was one of the fastest-growing grocery chains in England—
too fast, in some ways. A transatlantic conglomerate, eager
to buy its way into the British foodstuffs market, rebuffed
by the larger, commercially more secure groups, had happened upon Tesbury's at a time of cash-flow crisis, and with
one generous financial gesture had effected both rescue and
entrance. Now the new Board was attempting to marry
old-fashioned English quality and understatement with fast-
moving innovation and technology; neither side doubted the
eventual benefits, but the honeymoon period was generally
felt to be rather bumpy for the indigenous partner.

"Just look at *that*, for a start." Goods-In glared in the
direction of the office block. "I ask you, who needs
it—another bloody great computer, taking up half the
bloody car park? So what was wrong with the computer
we'd already got? It was a bloody sight more peaceful"—in
a sudden bellow—"with just the one, believe me!"

Ted believed him. As Goods-In had been talking, a loud
and horrible drilling burst upon the summer air and made
further speech impossible. To one side of the office block,
and to its rear, holes were being dug and foundations laid for
the new, custom-built, air-conditioned Computer Wing
deemed by the new Board essential for the efficient future
functioning of Tesbury's. The architects (subsidiaries of
another transatlantic corporation) had pushed planning permission through official channels from the moment the
Takeover had begun to appear a foregone conclusion, and in
their enthusiasm had ruthlessly blue-pencilled away a good
fifth of the area where, from the opening of the Tesbury site,
the firm's staff had been able to park their cars in safety. As
soon as the new Computer Wing was completed, most of the
lost spaces would be replaced by an equivalent number on
the wing's flat roof; but Allshire builders were just like
builders from any other county, and belonged to the same
union, with its rules about never allowing themselves to be
hurried. Car-owning Tesburians expected to suffer the
inconvenience of an attenuated car park for several months
to come, and could be heard inveighing against the Takeover and the computer every bit as forcefully as Goods-In.

"Computers!" roared Goods-In, as the drilling stopped

and a cement mixer started up. "Nothing but extra work for them as don't need it, that's all they're good for—like this lot here," and he brandished his clipboard again. "Got to unload and sign on the dotted line before you can pop off to the garridge, that's the way of it now. . . ."

And, with another sigh for the peaceful past, Goods-In addressed himself to Ted's lorry, checking off delivery and advice notes against his clipboard list, grumbling under his breath as he did so.

Plump and Pickwickian, Amos Chadderton sat behind his desk in the House Services department and beamed a smile in the direction of Maureen Mossley, his secretary. Amos had recognised the box, lightweight cardboard and tied with thin string, which she carried in her hand, and he patted his paunch and smacked his lips in happy anticipation.

"Meringues, Maureen? A couple of Baxter's best, I hope. Or maybe—just maybe—four?"

Maureen opened the top drawer of her desk and slipped the box inside before turning to smile back at her boss. "Suppose I said it was macaroons—or Eccles cakes—or some of those new spiced ginger biscuits you like, instead?"

Amos, who was a keen reader of mystery stories in his spare time, wagged a ratiocinative finger at her in reproof. "It must be meringues, because macaroons and ginger biscuits come in a bag, not a box. And it didn't look heavy from the way you carried it—and we had Eccles cakes yesterday, anyway. So, as Sherlock Holmes said, when I have eliminated the impossible . . . I deduce meringues!" Amos sat back, folded his hands across his tummy, and chuckled.

Maureen smiled back at him: everyone new how much Mr. Chadderton enjoyed his food. A bachelor, whose housekeeper sister had been whisked into matrimony surprisingly late considering the excellence of her cuisine, he was never happier than when sharing a snack and a gossip with friends in congenial surroundings. Though House Services was open-plan in design, he took advantage of the screen which separated his desk from the rest of the department, and had long ago coaxed his secretary into indulging his epicurean inclinations—and into joining him in them, as well.

"All right, clever clogs, you owe me sixty pee." Maureen hunted through her purse. "I've change for a pound. . . ."

"I knew it!" Amos chuckled again as he pulled coins from his trouser pocket. "Meringues are thirty pence each, so that means one for elevenses and one for tea—"

A sudden yodelling scream rent the air right above their startled heads. Maureen dropped her purse, and Amos gulped. The expression on his face showed that all thought of confectionery had been driven completely from his mind.

"The fourth time this week!" He glanced at the office clock and groaned. "And Friday hardly started—it could be five times, or even six, before the week's properly over and done with. . . ."

As the yodel continued to scream its high-pitched three-fold message, Maureen, her eyes on Amos, picked up her telephone. At his weary nod, she began to dial. He watched her, sighing heavily, then opened the top drawer of his desk and took out a small black notebook.

Round the corner of his office screen appeared a grimacing head, bearded, with an expression of exasperation on its face. "Ready to go when you give me the word, Amos—and a thousand curses on that thing!" The head glared up at the screaming ceiling, then turned its attention to Maureen, now busy talking on the telephone. "Well?"

Maureen finished her brief conversation with the Switchboard, slammed down the receiver with a snarl, and took a deep breath as the beard emerged from behind the screen and proved to be attached to a tall, rangy young man. "Three guesses, Dick. They've checked every station, and where is it the light's up? Go on—guess."

As another series of triplicate screams echoed in their ears, Dick Slack shrugged. "Do I need to? Oh, hell—is that the blighters already?" And, sketching a salute to Amos Chadderton, he turned on his heel and hurried away, announcing to nobody in particular that one day he would buy himself some earplugs, then the whole boiling crowd could go to blazes.

A crisp female voice called out after him, but the words were lost beneath the ceiling's awesome battery of sound. The voice, on the far side of the screen, did not trouble to repeat its remarks, and fell silent. Amos and Maureen gazed glumly at each other.

"Oh, dear, how he hates having them all go on at him as if it's his fault. If only they would understand it isn't." Amos was consulting his black notebook, whose pages were filled with lists of dates and columns of figures. "I mean, it isn't *anyone's*, really—not anyone from this department, that is. There's nothing we can do about it—but at this rate, it won't be long before it would work out cheaper if we moved the entire office to a building that already had a new computer wing in it!"

He swiftly totted up the figures, which were sums of money. The earlier entries were relatively low in value, but as the date beside each entry grew more recent, the amount noted grew larger. When he had checked his running total, Amos sighed again. "Perhaps we should ask them if they'd give us a discount rate for buying in bulk. . . ."

Maureen wasn't sure whether or not this was supposed to be a joke. Before she could make up her mind, another voice—masculine, exasperated, wheezing slightly—spoke from the office entrance.

"Mr. Chadderton—sorry to spoil your day yet again, but we're stuck. Thought I'd better let you know we can't get through. . . ."

The man was bulky and perspiring in his helmet and shiny yellow oilskins, brandishing an axe and looking like a huge, gift-wrapped, homicidal canary. "Can't get through at all," said the fireman, "on account of vehicles blocking the road. Young Dick's already told us it's another false alarm"—as he spoke, the ceiling gave one final, cut-off shriek and lapsed into blessed silence—"but there's still regulations, you know. We've got to make sure as there's nobody burning to a crisp in here—so, as it's fifty-to-one them cars out there belong to your people, we'd be much obliged if you'd get 'em to move 'em all."

Amos looked in anguish at Mrs. Mossley. "Oh dear, everyone will grumble, I know, but it has to be done. Would you ask the Switchboard to put out a Call? Oh, dear. . . .''

As the fireman, having nodded his thanks, withdrew,
Mrs. Mossley slammed down the telephone she'd only just
picked up, rose from her desk, and marched out in his wake.
Amos blinked after her, too surprised to speak until she'd
gone, he presumed, beyond earshot. "Oh, dear. . . .''

He returned to a dismal calculation of the figures in his
notebook, which seemed no better the second time around.
Halfway through a still more dismal third calculation, he
was interrupted by the sound of yet another voice from
beyond the screen.

"Well now, Sadie!" It was a man's voice, charming,
with a light Welsh accent, mingling humour and resignation
in equal proportion. "A splendid finish to the week, isn't it?
Not five minutes have we been in the building, and—"

And then, as Amos felt his teeth begin to clench, there
came another interruption from the ceiling.

Two

"*Dingdong!*" The two-toned chime mercifully drowned out Ken Oldham, a newcomer to Tesbury's who was convinced he knew it all, and was never afraid to offer an opinion on any topic, whether asked or not. "*Dingdong!* Would any members of staff with cars parked in the road please move them now, so the fire engine can get through? All car owners to move their cars immediately, please. Thank you."

Muffled curses came from every corner of the building, as people sat trying to recall whether they'd been lucky enough to find an inside space that morning, and (if they hadn't) realising they'd have to make a rush for the lifts before everyone else filled them up, or somebody remembered to switch them off. . . .

"A splendid finish to the week, indeed." Ken Oldham was still addressing Sadie, his voice nicely calculated to reach the other side of the screen. Amos heard his teeth grinding as his jaw muscles tensed; he wondered whether Sadie and Ken could hear them, too. "Is that six times now, or seven?"

His jaw may have been clenched, but at the enormity of Ken's remark Amos felt it drop in surprise. He didn't have a chance to say anything, however, before Sadie Halliwell—*Ms.* Halliwell, defiantly divorced and with a subsequently low opinion of most men she met—replied in her most withering tones to the office bête noire:

"I'd always thought anyone doing your type of job had to be good at maths. Obviously I was wrong, though—you don't seem all that brilliant at keeping count, do you? Let's hope it isn't an indication of just how good at your job you are, or you could be redundant by the end of next week."

"Oh, Sadie!" Ken was determined not to be offended,

and his laugh sounded almost unforced. "Oh, Sadie, how very unkind you are this morning—and how wrong, too." The laugh became tinged with a harder edge. "Good God, do you still not understand it's mostly on my say-so that redundancies are arranged? And who in their right minds is going to arrange *themselves* out of a job—especially when it's as vital to the company as mine is!"

Sadie snorted. She wasn't going to give him the satisfaction of an argument, but it annoyed her to have Ken dropping such heavy reminders that he was a Board-appointed Management Consultant (ambiguous, infuriating term) and, technically, as free an agent in Tesbury's as anyone could ever hope to be.

Annoying though it was, however, argument would be worse than useless, as Sadie knew from previous experience; and she had no particular wish to listen (whether she argued back or not) any longer to Ken Oldham babbling about his uniquely powerful position in the department—in the company—in the very future of the Tesbury chain. Sadie was never slow to make up her mind. Since the only way of stopping Ken once he got going was to get going herself, she pushed back her chair and headed for the office where, behind his screen, her boss sat and listened to everything that went on in his department.

She popped her head round the corner of the screen and pulled an expressive face as she said: "Amos, I think I'll just go along to make sure my Little Lads didn't get stuck in the goods lift when the alarm went off. I wouldn't put it past them." This was not as ridiculous as it might, to the uninitiated, sound. Sadie's three Little Lads were honest but slow-witted souls renowned for always doing just as they'd been told. They could be trusted to run Sadie's section of House Services exactly as she'd instructed even when she went on holiday, for her instructions were clear and well-ordered—as was the Little Lads' routine—but the unexpected always unsettled them.

"And neither would I." Amos winked at Sadie's grimaces. It wasn't hard to guess why she was so anxious to be out of the department. . . .

The old Tesbury Board had carried its company passengers with tact and compassion, but the new Board, starting as it meant to continue, clearly had no intention of following the same style of management. The new policy, personified in the all-seeing, all-critical presence of Ken Oldham, was the best indication to the not-as-modern and not-so-lively that the risk of redundancy and compulsory early retirement was real and imminent as it had never been in the past. Mr. Oldham had been given a year to put things right. He carped and criticised freely, reported back to the Board on Tesbury shortcomings, and had everyone peering over their shoulders in a way they'd never done before.

Sadie, immunised by her divorce against Ken's personal charms, was by the same means, as she gaily admitted, protected against any serious financial threat. "I soaked that creep for every penny he had," she would boast when speaking of her former spouse. Yet, if she had no cause to fear Ken and his new-broom activities, neither did she need to stand up for her less fortunate workmates as she did. She could have weathered the storm by staying neutral, but staying neutral wasn't in Sadie's character. She never did things by halves: which was one reason she was so good at her job.

Dick Slack, too, was a valued Deputy Manager in the House Services department. Amos relied heavily on both of them to keep the place running smoothly, and to back him up in every possible way—as they did. There had been no need for Sadie to ask his permission before disappearing in search of her Little Lads; if she and Dick couldn't function as independent entities, they'd never get any work done. There were times when events moved so fast that, if everyone made a point of religiously reporting back to everyone else what they were doing and where they were going, a minor panic could develop into a major crisis.

So Amos smiled after Sadie's departed form, and was still smiling when Mrs. Mossley returned from the Switchboard. Maureen had stopped for a quick gossip with Veronica and Janice once the Call had been put out, and watched with them through the window as irate car owners emerged from the building to do their stuff.

"Oh, Amos, you should have seen it! Everyone falling

over themselves to get their cars out of the way, and the fire brigade cursing them for not being fast enough—did you hear them set their siren off?'' The smile faded from Amos's face, but Maureen was too busy chattering to notice. The disastrous start to the day—the disastrous end to the week—the confusion there was bound to be until lunchtime, while people settled down again—the chaos in the street, around the building, in the building, with empty desks and phones unanswered while the Switchboard girls rang and rang and tried to pacify the callers . . .

''. . . a *real* fire on the other side of town,'' she concluded, ''and the engine stuck here? Suppose by the time it managed to get away from us, it was too late?''

''Don't!'' Amos shuddered, and cast an anguished glance at his black notebook. ''The cash cost is high enough, but if I thought lives could be lost as well—and all because of our new computer—''

''And that's the reason,'' Ken Oldham broke into this lament, ''I'd like a word with you, Amos. Good God, even you have to agree now that things have gone quite far enough!''

Amos, sunk in gloom, jumped, while Maureen glared at Ken as she brooded on the significance of ''even you''. If that cheeky young know-all was trying to hint that her boss was falling down on the job . . .

On the other hand, the interloper was in a strong position, as he was never slow to point out. What was more, he worked in the same office. There were courtesies to be observed, even if it hurt to observe them. She took a deep breath, and spoke surprisingly calmly as she nodded at the sheets of paper Ken was holding.

''Looks like another report you've got there. It doesn't seem all that long compared to some I've had to type, so if you'd like to let me have it now, I might be able to give it back by dinnertime.'' And she tried not to feel like a traitor as she made the offer—she, Maureen Mossley, old Tesbury hand, volunteering to drop all other work in favour of Ken Oldham.

Ken glanced at his papers. ''Report? No, indeed, but thanks for the offer—I've no doubt I'll take you up on it

before many more days have passed.'' Porcelain whiteness
gleamed at her in a professionally friendly fashion, then he
switched off his smile and turned to Amos, dismissing the
secretary without so much as a nod. ''It was you I came to
have a word with, Amos. If I'm not interrupting?''

Amos was as incapable of ignoring Ken as Maureen had
been, and for more or less the same reasons. More, perhaps,
and understandably so. He was several years nearer retirement age than Mrs. Mossley. ''Come in, Ken.'' He tried not
to sound depressed as the younger man accepted the
invitation. ''Come in and sit down and tell me what's on
your mind.''

Maureen scowled as Ken took his seat and she returned to
her own. She couldn't decide which annoyed her more:
being on the end of the hollow charm the young man always
chose to project when he wanted something; knowing that,
when he was being charming, he was probably planning to
stab someone in the back; or being ignored, as he was
ignoring her now.

There were two chairs in front of Mr. Chadderton's desk.
Individual visitors usually took the one near the window, so
that they could turn sideways and include Maureen in the
conversation they'd come to have with her boss. After all, it
was an open secret in Tesbury's that it was Mrs. Mossley
who in fact did much of his job as House Services Manager,
since he never moved out of his office during working hours
if he could help it. Ken Oldham was one of the few people
who sat in the other chair on purpose, so that all Maureen
could converse with was the back of his head. She gazed for
a brief moment at that tempting target, let her eyes drift to
the paperweight next to her typewriter—Ken had made
noises about word processors almost since the day he started
work in Tesbury's, but Maureen would have none of
it—then pulled herself together, and went back to work.

Amos, his heart sinking, saw Maureen address herself to
her typing without even trying to join in whatever conversation Ken was about to start. His eyes behind their
Pickwick spectacles lost their normal sparkle; he had a fair
idea of what Mr. Oldham was going to nag him about.

He was right. ''Just how many times, Amos, would you

say this old alarm nonsense has happened this week—this month? I'm sure you've been keeping records as well.'' Ignoring Mr. Chadderton's reports, on which he'd been working until the fire alarm first sounded, Ken deliberately deployed his own documents in a careless spread right across the desk so that Amos could see how they were covered with neat and detailed calculations. He tapped his figures with a careless finger. ''Shall we compare notes, Amos?''

Ken Oldham excelled at psychological games. Poor Amos gritted his teeth at such deliberate overuse of his given name, but knew he would only sound petulant if he voiced any complaint. Ken smirked. ''Now, I'm sure you must have been keeping records of all the fire alarm calls, Amos. Here we are in the third week of July, and it must be fourteen times already this month there's been a false alarm—and fourteen times, to my recollection, that the fire engine couldn't get through.''

''Thirteen,'' said Amos quickly. Then he winced as Ken's grin showed him he'd fallen into the trap.

''There now, Amos, I *knew* you must have been keeping the score!''

Amos could practically hear the next sentence in his head: *You may be getting a bit past it, but you seem to have managed this little job, though I admit I'm surprised you're even this efficient. . . .*

''But never mind all that, Amos. Thirteen, fourteen—so what does it really matter, beyond the fact that it happens far too often? The company loses time—which means money, remember—whenever that fire alarm goes off, Amos. To say nothing of the risks to the general population of Allingham, as our Maureen pointed out just now.''

He spoke a little louder as he said this, to make himself heard above the clatter of Mrs. Mossley's typing. Amos had a horrid suspicion he was gearing himself up to say something dreadful and wanted none of the impact to be lost. Maureen had the same suspicion, and typed even harder than before, wishing she could bash the electronic keys with as much force as on her old-fashioned manual machine, long since gone to that great storeroom in the sky.

"Now, Amos, I expect you've been applying yourself to this problem—and I'm sure that, given long enough, you and Clem Bradshaw between you might come up with an answer." Ken's toothpaste smile didn't detract from the various not-so-veiled insults of his words. "But, Good God, Amos, we haven't time to wait for that happy day! The Board has given me one year to tackle the Tesbury problems in the way I think best, and I've already, as you know, come up with two possibilities for the car parking—which Clem Bradshaw has chosen to ignore, for reasons of his own." Ken's frown evinced scorn and suspicion in equal shares. The Transport Manager's reasons for taking no notice of Ken Oldham's ideas, his expression hinted, must not only be ridiculous—they could possibly be unethical or illegal, to boot. "Believe me, though, Amos, he won't be able to ignore my latest suggestion, no matter how hard he tries to keep out of my way." He smirked once more, and Mr. Chadderton ached to kick him. "Because it's brilliant, though I do say so myself. . . ."

He favoured Mr. Chadderton with a sideways look and a shrug. "Of course, Amos, I'm not suggesting for one minute that you haven't tried your best—but, well . . ."

Strange how a word of just one syllable could pack such a weight of challenge behind it. The startled House Services Manager blinked, and could find nothing to say; but his secretary rushed angrily to the rescue.

"If it wasn't for that wretched new computer the Board's saying we've got to have, and the building work, and all the plant and equipment being so heavy, and the vibrations keep on setting off the alarm—"

"My dear Maureen." Ken condescended to turn his head to address her directly, his smile not quite reaching his eyes. "You've no need to bother yourself with all this, honestly. I'm sure Amos can speak for himself! Besides, the decision to install a new computer was taken at the very highest level, and after very careful consideration—so this, Maureen, is really a rather pointless discussion, wouldn't you say? The real point is surely what's to be done about it."

Maureen felt her face grow warm, but held her tongue as Ken's gaze swept away from her and back to Amos, who'd at last found his voice. Even as he spoke, he was unhappily aware that it sounded like special pleading, but it was hard to think of anything to say except the truth.

"Well, Ken, as you know, plans were drawn up to re-mark the car park just as soon as we realised the difficulties. If the spaces are made just a little smaller, and if there's a special area for extra small cars like Minis, we ought to make room for another seventy cars, which should be more than enough by the time the roof's on. But surely the Board can't blame House Services—or Transport—for the weather? It's been remarkably fine these past few weeks, as you know. And, well, naturally the contractors have wanted to take advantage of so much sunshine to complete more, er, pressing jobs elsewhere, but—"

"Oh, Amos, Amos." Even as the older man spoke, Ken Oldham was shaking his head. "These are just excuses, not *reasons*—and certainly not the sort of thing the Board wants to hear, believe me." He contrived to looked as if he alone knew the Board's wants, and knew them better than any of its members. "Amos, all I'm trying to say is that you and Clem Bradshaw ought to be prepared to consider my solution—give it some serious thought, no more than that—instead of this senseless hoping something else will turn up, which is what it seems to me you've both done up to now. Unless . . ."

Ken leaned forward, his eyes piercing, and lowered his voice to its most solemn register. "Amos, is there some . . . particular reason why the pair of you—well, seem less than willing to do anything about the car park?"

———— Three ————

"OF COURSE, SIR," said Stone, doodling thoughtfully on the superintendent's blotter, "if it's a change of *scene* you fancy, rather than just a change of *air*, it needn't be Traffic. Have you considered the Fraud Squad, for instance?"

A frown creased the bulldog face, and suspicion danced in the dark brown eyes. "You're keen to get rid of me all of a sudden, my girl. Hoping for a spot of promotion when I'm gone, are you?"

"Perish the thought, sir!" And Stone looked genuinely shocked. "I was only trying to be helpful. I mean, if you only *think* about Fraud—the people you'd meet—the glamour, the excitement, the high life in the city set—"

"You've been reading too many trashy novels, Stone. I'd never have thought it of you." Trewley chuckled, then sighed. "Fraud work's a bit different from that, they say. The really clever crooks keep a low profile, and hardly ever get caught. The ones our lot meet are the dumb types who slip up because they're too bothered with keeping up appearances to take proper care—they're worrying all the time about are they going to get the key to the executive cloakroom, and what model company car they've got, and where's their reserved space in the car park . . ."

Everyone of Deputy Manager's grade or above had a space automatically reserved for them in the Tesbury car park, and not a soul in the company had grumbled about this until the present troubles started. Once they had, however, there was much clerical complaint along the lines of: *If you're so indispensable, you ought to be first in the office anyway!* As yet, nobody was taking this too seriously, but the arrival of Ken Oldham had decreased by one more the number of "free" spaces. Amos was at first urged by Maureen (whose own space had been unofficially obtained for her by Mr. Chadderton, custom having over the years developed the force of authority) to forget to remind Mr. Oldham of any possible entitlement; but Ken was nobody's fool. He had given Amos no chance to forget. Since Sadie and Dick could both claim the privilege, then a Board-appointed Management Consultant must definitely claim—and win— it, too, no matter how unfair this might seem to the fellow workers he inconvenienced.

Ken's monstrous insinuation against the integrity of not only Amos, but Clem Bradshaw of Transport as well, left Maureen seething and Amos, for a startled moment, speechless. While he spluttered and goggled at Ken, Mrs. Mossley felt her hand creep of its own accord toward the paperweight, felt her eyes fasten on the smug back of Mr. Oldham's skull. Coming to her senses, she knew she'd better take herself out of temptation's way until she'd calmed down again, and, with a muttered apology to Amos—who was just starting to frame an indignant denial— she pushed back her chair, bumped it into Ken's, and headed without apology for the sweeter air of the outer office.

Here, she found that, though Sadie Halliwell hadn't come back from wherever she'd gone, Dick Slack had. Wearing a haunted look, he sat slumped at his desk, reflectively chewing a pencil and—from the wry twist to his mouth— listening with indignation as great as her own to what he could hear of the conversation from behind the screen.

He grimaced at Maureen as she emerged, stabbing with the pencil toward the spot where Ken Oldham must be sitting, making a revolver out of its wooden length and squinting along the barrel to fire imaginary bullets through the sober hessian of the screen. Maureen nodded and made neck-wringing motions with her competent typist's hands. Dick grinned at her and rolled his eyes.

Maureen shrugged, rolled her own eyes, and felt a little better. She couldn't say anything much in case Ken and Amos overheard, so she hovered for a moment by Dick's desk, wondering whether she should pop outside to powder

her nose, or slip into the Switch Room for another chat—
anything to be away from Ken Oldham for a while.

Before she could make up her mind what to do, a third
and unexpected party presented her with a third and
unexpected course of action. Into House Services, her eyes
flashing and her face flushed, erupted five feet nine inches
of indignant female, clearly—from the purposeful manner
in which she marched toward Amos's office—bent on
confrontation.

"Is anything the matter?" Maureen didn't think her boss
could cope with a second confrontation when he was still in
the middle of the first. The thought did just cross her mind
that he might be glad to be extricated—but then again he
might not, if he was hoping to set Ken straight on a few
matters once and for all. Maureen couldn't be sure which he
would prefer, and accordingly spoke as loudly as she could
and still sound natural, so that Amos could hear what was
happening and make up his own mind.

She stepped forward to block Indignation's path. "Can I
help you? Are you looking for anyone in particular?"

Indignation—a young woman whose already plain appearance was not improved by anger—scowled at Mrs.
Mossley. "I want to see Mr. Chadderton. He *is* in charge of
the car park, isn't he?"

Maureen looked at Dick. Dick looked at Maureen.
Behind the screen, Amos uttered a little groan, and Ken
(they could imagine the smug look on his face) chuckled.

"Yes, he is, but"—and Maureen manoeuvred herself still
more obviously in the young woman's way—"he's got
someone with him right now. Shall I take a message? Do
you want me to ask him to ring you?"

"You?" Indignation swept Mrs. Mossley from head to
food with a burning gaze. "I want to talk to whoever's
responsible for the car park. And you're only the typist or
something, aren't you?"

Dick intervened before Maureen could explode. "I'm the
Deputy House Services Manager, so if—"

"Deputy's not good enough! I want to talk to the person
in charge—I'm going right to the top! The trouble with you
people in this office is that you don't seem to have any idea

of how—how maddening it all is that nothing ever gets sorted out when it's obviously wrong!''

''Oh, doesn't it?'' muttered Maureen, while Dick said:

''That's rather unfair, I think, because it does—most of the time,'' honesty made him add. ''But by and large we run things pretty smoothly, I'd say, though I agree it's a bit difficult just at the moment. But it *is* only a temporary hiccup—and we're working on it right now, love, so—''

''My name,'' interposed Indignation, ''isn't *love*—and you needn't try calling me *dear*, either. My name is Farnworth—*Miss* Angela Farnworth.'' She threw up her chin and glared at Dick as if daring him to comment on her spinster status. ''I work in Accounts. And, while my BMW was parked out in the road—*in the road*, because there was no room for it on Tesbury premises—some idiot of a Tesbury driver ran right into the back of it!''

This accusation rather threw Mr. Slack, but Maureen had found her second wind. ''How can you be so sure it was one of our drivers?'' She was stalling; she knew she wouldn't be able to keep Amos out of this, no matter how hard she and Dick tried to fend off Miss Angela Farnworth from Accounts. Car owners can be dangerous creatures when roused, irrespective of gender, and Angela's eye had a gleam that meant business.

''Yes,'' chimed in Dick, as Angela drew in her breath to reply. ''If the care was parked in the road, how on earth can you tell—''

''Don't give me that!'' The gleam looked more business-like than ever. ''You can't fool *me* into thinking it was an ordinary driver just passing by who hit my car. You may as well save your breath, because I won't believe you. I've got proof—scratches, and flakes of paint—green and gold paint! And my BMW's *white*. *And* he's smashed one of the rear lights and dented my bumper—and there's glass in the road, which someone's going to have to clear up unless you want everyone to get punctures when they drive in or out of this place. . . .''

''Yes, well, we certainly ought to be able to deal with that for you,'' said Dick, as she seemed to run out of steam for a moment. But she hadn't. She flushed an angry scarlet and scowled.

"I don't care about the stupid glass—that's your problem, not mine. I was simply saying it was another of the things you'll have to put right—but the most important is my car. Who's going to pay for the repairs? I don't see why I should lose my no-claims bonus when it isn't my fault. When I joined this firm, I was told there was ample space for everyone who worked here to park—nobody even hinted there was going to be a new computer block, or warned me there'd be all this muddle while it was being built. And I'm not leaving this office until I've got a sensible answer—until I've talked to Amos Chadderton, and not one of his—his useless underlings!"

Before either Dick or Maureen could stop her, she pushed Mrs. Mossley to one side and stormed past the barricade into Mr. Chadderton's sanctum. Poor Amos, who had listened with grim foreboding to her rising voice—she'd sounded so angry that even Ken Oldham had stopped trying to compete, and sat silent and startled—rose halfway from his chair as she appeared round the edge of the screen. Scooping up his notes, Ken also rose, though more (so Amos judged) as a preliminary to flight than from motives of chivalry. Angela Farnworth paused in the entrance, angry eyes focussing on the plump, bespectacled form of the House Services Manager.

"Are *you* Amos Chadderton?" Then, before he could reply, she turned from scarlet to sickly white, and crumpled in an ungainly heap upon the floor.

But the odd fainting female comes as no surprise to a department like House Services, accustomed throughout its working week to such emergencies as fire, flood, capricious air-conditioning and/or central heating, even the occasional power cut. Amos Chadderton, House Services Manager, coped with the current emergency in his usual inimitable way: he delegated it to his secretary. Even as Ken, muttering some inaudible excuse, stepped quickly round the unconscious figure on the floor and left the office, Amos sank back on his chair and raised his voice in a plaintive cry. "Maureen! Maureen—oh, thank goodness," as Mrs. Mossley came hurrying in. "My, er, visitor—she doesn't seem very well. . . ."

Mrs. Mossley sank to her knees, shook the recumbent form briskly, and reported to a quaking Amos that Angela appeared to be out cold. "And serves her right," she muttered, as she began loosening the buttons at Miss Farnworth's throat. Her blouse was prim, high-collared, and virginal; her skirt had a heavy waistband of a tweeded, schoolmistressy style normally only seen in sepia photographs and old movies. "It's a miracle she can even breathe, in all this," Maureen opined, as she deftly eased fortifications where she could. She was particularly pleased to have legitimate cause to slap those cheeks that continued as white as the blouse beneath which fluttered a visibly palpitating heart.

"Is—is she going to be all right?" came the nervous query from Amos, who sat rigid in his chair with a plump hand poised above the telephone in case this was one emergency where Maureen had to confess herself beaten.

It seemed an age before his secretary announced, with a note of regret—she would dearly have loved to administer a few more slaps to the no-longer-strident Miss Farnworth from Accounts—the news that Angela was coming round, and would live to fight again. "Here," said Maureen, giving her another shake. "Wake up, do. Wake up! Can you hear me?"

Angela's white face began to turn pink, and her eyelids gave fiction's customary quiver as she emerged from her swoon and uttered the customary enquiries.

"On the floor in House Services," snapped Maureen, who had little sense of the dramatic. "You fainted, that's what happened. Can you sit up yet?"

"I—I'm not sure." Angela swallowed and tried to push herself from the floor with a shaking hand: it shook so much that she slipped back, gasping, against Maureen's startled shoulder. "Oh—ugh!" She closed her eyes again and gulped. "Everything keeps going round . . . I—I feel . . . ."

"No, you don't." Maureen wasn't going to have her being sick and staining the carpet, tiles or not. Firmly, she redeposited Angela on the floor, and rose to her feet, ostentatiously dusting herself down. She looked at Amos and spoke with some reluctance. "I suppose we'd better try her with a drop of brandy. . . ." And she moved across to her desk with more speed than she'd heretofore shown, as Angela began turning pale again, breathing with deep, shuddery breaths.

In the outer office, Dick had buttoned Sadie Halliwell, back from her tour of duty. "Sadie—at last! Can you do first aid?"

"Sorry?" This was hardly the greeting she'd expected.

"First aid—kiss of life, that sort of thing. I can't, but I wondered—"

"If, being a *mere female*, I could? No. Never had any particular reason to learn. Why?"

Amos, listening hard to stop himself thinking about what might be happening on the floor on the other side of his desk, could imagine Dick's expression as he replied. "In there—some girl, barged in here saying she'd got to have a word with Amos, and just keeled over, bang, like that!"

"A girl? What girl?" Sadie's voice was wary. "One of ours? Do we know her?"

"Don't think so. Name of Farrington, or something—her first name's Angela. Accounts, she said."

Sadie thought busily. "Angela Farrington—no, I don't believe I've met her. Fainted, you said? And she's alone in there with Amos? Well, I could always take a look in case there was anything I could do to—oh!" Her surprise, as she rounded the screen and found Maureen in attendance, was almost comical. Her eyes flicked down to Angela's fallen form on the carpet at the foot of Amos's desk, then back up to Mrs. Mossley. "Oh, well, so everything's fine after all. I'll leave you to it, shall I?"

Maureen, who had retrieved the departmental brandy (kept for strictly emergency use or the annual Christmas party, whichever came first) from its hiding place, looked up and even smiled as the newcomer appeared. "Sadie, good. You might be better at getting her to drink some of this than me, though if we can't sort her out between us she'll have to go along to the nurses."

Sadie wrinkled her nose, but nodded, and reached for the brandy with a steady hand. "All right, if you think—"

"I don't want any brandy." A voice from the region of Sadie's waist made her jump. "I don't drink. And I don't want a nurse, thank you." Angela Farnworth scrambled shakily to her feet, brushing the demure skirt down below her drab nylon knees. "What I want is a sensible answer about my car!" She dragged herself upright, swaying and blinking, her face mottled, then scowled at Mr. Chadderton across his desk. "If *you* are in charge of the car park, I want to register a formal complaint. . . ."

Silently, Sadie handed the brandy back to Maureen (which made Angela scowl even more) and slipped from the office, leaving Miss Farnworth to face Amos unsupported. "There's never," said Angela bravely, beginning to turn red again, "enough room for all our cars nowadays—and if you don't get here early enough, which is what happened to me today, then you have to park out in the road. . . ."

Maureen poured the untasted brandy back in its bottle with great care, and as carefully didn't look in Angela's direction. "And today," went on Miss Farnworth, "one of the Tesbury drivers crashed into my BMW. . . ."

It was the same argument she had addressed earlier to Dick and Maureen. When she reached the bit about her no-claims bonus, Amos found himself nodding in sympathy even as he tried to find something to say that would calm her down. Angela leaned both hands on the edge of his desk and glared at him. "Well, Mr. Chadderton? What are you going to do?"

He shot a quick look at Maureen, but she wasn't playing this time. "Well, Miss—thank you, Miss Farnworth—well, yes, it's all rather—rather difficult just at the moment—but only temporary, I assure—"

"Difficult? Temporary? Why don't you people in this department change the record? And if all you can say now is that it's *rather difficult*, just how much worse will things have to get before you decide to treat it as serious?"

Amos, raising a desperately pacific hand, tried hard to look stern through his spectacles, and, to his (and Maureen's) surprise, this worked—for a while, anyway. Angela shut up, and stood prepared to listen, though it was clear from her expression she wouldn't listen for long to the ordinary fluff. Amos thought frantically.

"It's not just House Service, Miss Farnworth, but Transport as well that has problems—because, unfortunately, we none of us have any more control over company policy than we do over the weather. The Board, in its wisdom, has decreed that we shall have a new computer before we've had time to make adequate preparations, and . . ."

But the glitter in Angela's eyes told him that such talk was fluff of a woefully inadequate nature. He tried again. "Look, I promise to speak to Insurance about your car. Let my secretary have the details as you go"—he felt beads of perspiration break out on his forehead in case she refused to take the hint—"and, well, I'll be talking to Transport later, so I'll ask them if any of their lorries have been in recent collision with a—thank you, with a white BMW. . . ."

He quailed beneath Miss Farnworth's accusing glare and, with a gulp, fell silent. Angela's eyes narrowed to slits, and her face turned white with pure rage.

"Are you trying to tell me, Mr. Chadderton, that this is your final word on the subject?"

Maureen Mossley cleared her throat. Amos jumped, blinked, and rallied. "Well, yes, Miss Farnworth. For the moment, I am—I mean, it is."

And he exchanged a look of bright-eyed interest with Mrs. Mossley as Angela Farnworth, her face once more flaming, jumped from her chair and stalked, without a word of farewell, out of his office.

——————— Four ———————

As ANGELA DISAPPEARED, Amos turned in great excitement to Mrs. Mossley, stabbing a chubby finger toward the outer office. "Can you see her?" he mouthed frantically. "Is she still there?"

"No, she's gone," said Maureen, who had watched Angela's retreat with much satisfaction. "And good riddance!"

Amos sat back with a long, deep sigh, closing his eyes. The lenses of his spectacles were faintly fogged by steam, and his lips moved as if in silent prayer. His plump cheeks were pale.

Maureen shot him an anxious glance, felt herself shudder in sympathy, and hurried to her desk, her thoughts turning to the departmental brandy. Her hand groped for the drawer in which it was kept.

"Well, that was exciting, wasn't it?" Dick had eavesdropped shamelessly on events behind the screen, while not, of course, wishing to participate in them. Now that Angela was safely out of range, however, he couldn't resist the chance to discuss it all further. "You were lucky to get away with your life, I thought at one time, Amos."

Mr. Chadderton opened his eyes and blinked rapidly once or twice before remarking, in a plaintive tone, that Miss Farnworth certainly appeared to be a young lady of, well, of mercurial temperament.

Maureen snorted. "There's another word for carrying on like that, but I wouldn't sully my lips. Tantrums and fainting and carrying on—a fine way to behave, I must say!"

Dick chuckled. "Marched in here, took one look at you, Amos, and keeled right over, didn't she? What's the betting she's the relic of a youthful indiscretion and recognised you as her long-lost illegitimate father?"

Amos, to Maureen's started interest, turned as scarlet as any hue achieved by Angela Farnworth. "I—I don't," he babbled, "think that's very—very funny, Dick. Suppose"— with an anxious look at Mrs. Mossley—"someone should hear you and, well, believe such a story?"

"Calm down, Amos." Dick grinned as the spectacle lenses steamed up still more. "Nobody could ever imagine *you* with a misspent youth—take too much effort, wouldn't it?"

Sadie, out of sight at her desk, choked audibly at the idea of indolent Amos Chadderton treading the primrose path— treading any path, for that matter. She had seldom seen him take more than a dozen steps in any direction without stopping for a rest.

Maureen poured brandy into a paper cup. Dick's attempt at a joke had left Amos looking decidedly peaky. "Here," she said, thrusting the generous tot toward her boss. "A good swig of that and you'll feel better. As for you, young Dick, you ought to have more sense than to go upsetting people like that—"

"Come off it, Maureen. If anyone's been upsetting people around here, I'd have said it was that Farnworth female." Dick's eyes gleamed. "All right, so she's not Amos's guilty past catching up with him—but you're not telling *me* there wasn't more to it than just her perishing no-claims bonus. I mean, she *looks* the type to be a guilty secret, in those old-fashioned clothes doing penance for something or other—what's the betting she's Ken's long-lost sister, and if she hadn't been stolen by the Gypsies she'd have inherited the loot, and now she's seen him again she's going to claim her inheritance?"

Nonsense though such speculation might be, it pleased Maureen to observe that it—or perhaps the brandy—had brought a more normal colour to Amos's cheek, a less fraught glitter to his Pickwick eye. She was reluctant to bring an end to the fantasy that had played its recuperative part—but common sense must in the end prevail. "A bit too much of a coincidence, them ending up working in the same place," she said. "With him going to America, and all that. . . ."

"It's a small world," began Dick; but Amos, draining the paper cup, interrupted with considerable authority.

" 'Don't spurn coincidence in that casual way. You say the most innocent encounter in a detective novel is unfair, and yet you're always screaming out about having met someone abroad who lives in the next parish, and what a small world it is.' " He chuckled. "That, my dear Maureen, was Gervase Fen's view of such occurrences in *The Moving Toyshop*, and what's good enough for Fen is good enough for me—and for Dick, too, it seems." His eyes twinkled. "Although I can't help remembering that his interest was insufficiently great to allow him to, er, witness all the fun while it lasted—I thought at one time she was going to explode. People do seem to work themselves up so dreadfully about their cars, don't they?"

"And about car parks," Dick reminded him. Maureen scowled at Mr. Slack, but Amos took the remark at face value.

"Yes, you know, I felt sure I was in for a regular session over that wretched car park, but Ken just let it go. It isn't a bit like him to miss the chance to score a few Brownie points, is it?"

Maureen and Dick agreed that it wasn't, and there was a thoughtful pause. It was broken by the voice of Sadie Halliwell, crisper than ever as it signalled a warning to her cogitating colleagues. "Greetings to our wandering boy, Mr. Oldham. And just where did you disappear in such a hurry, if it's not a silly question? Is something the matter?"

Dick nodded his farewells and retreated to his desk, Mrs. Mossley began a barrage of typing, and Amos shuffled papers with glum foreboding. Sadie, having noted that her warning had been duly received, started to rummage in her own desk so that she wouldn't have to talk to Ken if he bothered to answer her—which he didn't. Clipboard in hand, he hurried straight past her, back to Mr. Chadderton's office.

"Well, Amos. As we were saying just now . . ."

He appeared to have found his second wind and harangued the House Services Manager at considerable length about the car park, and the computer, and the fire risk. He quoted facts and figures, explained his calculations and drew lines in coloured felt-tip on sheets of paper, and insisted that a speedy decision had to be reached.

"If Clem Bradshaw can't—or won't—make up his mind, then you'll have to help him, Amos. Now that I've explained it all to you, it shouldn't be too difficult. . . ."

And he went through every argument again—and again.

The excellence of the Tesbury canteen, despite the Takeover, was questioned by nobody. Even Amos Chadderton, noted gourmand, ate there almost daily, returning to his office afterwards for a digestive snooze. Sadie Halliwell was one of the very few who never bothered with a change of scene, preferring to bring a packed lunch to eat at her desk, having first rerouted the telephones for privacy's sake.

She was sitting now in the empty room with a selection of neatly wrapped packages in front of her, looking forward to opening them at last after a whirl of activity which had left her feeling hungry and irritable. She dusted out the inside of a plastic beaker with a large paper handkerchief, and gazed greedily at the array of assorted whole-food salads (homemade that morning rather than shop-bought) and fresh fruit which she always bought.

"It keeps me healthy," was her invariable reply when her workmates teased her. "I can't bear to think of you eating your lives away with cream cakes and sugar—all that cholesterol, all those calories, no proper roughage. . . ."

"But we enjoy it." This was unarguable, though Sadie still looked for a thoroughly squashing response. So far, she hadn't found one; and she was beginning to feel that there was a limit to the amount of time, breath, and effort she was prepared to expend in trying to reeducate the palates of others. Let every one of them eat his or her way to ill health at their own pace!

In view of her colleagues' opinions of her chosen diet, it came as a considerable surprise to Ms. Halliwell when Mr. Chadderton, trotting back replete from the canteen, did more than wave a well-padded hand in her direction as he passed through the office en route to his desk and his postprandial nap. He saw her—hesitated—smiled—and diverted his course towards her visitors' chair, which, with a questioning look, he made to pull out.

Sadie nodded, but did not stop eating: it was her lunch hour, after all. "Okay if I carry on? You wouldn't believe the fun and games I've just had. One of the notice boards on the top landing fell off the wall and nearly brained somebody. I, er, take it you haven't invited yourself to share my meal?"

"I've eaten, thank you." Amos regarded the red kidney beans, sweet corn kernels, sunflower seeds and wild rice with a shudder. "Yes, do carry on, Sadie. Enjoy yourself—if you can." Which Sadie, grinning, did.

He watched in some fascination as she speared an errant raisin with her fork then turned to smile at him. "I gather you wanted a private word," she said, when he seemed unable to say anything more. Her immediate hunger assuaged, she was prepared to be sociable. "Is it anything especially important?" Her eyes grew suddenly wary. "Is there something wrong?"

Amos looked quickly over his shoulder, then forced a laugh. "Oh, no—no, not really. It's just that, well, I hardly like to discuss it until I've told Maureen, and yet—well, as it concerns you, Sadie . . ."

"Me?" Sadie dropped her fork and sat up. "Have I been given the sack? Don't tell me Ken Oldham's arranging the House Services redundancies and I'm his first victim!"

"Good heavens, no." Amos blinked. "No, nothing of that sort, I assure you. . . ." And he sighed. "If Ken proposes to axe anyone from this department, it's far more likely to be me. After all, it's only another couple of years until my retirement—if they let me stay that long. . . ."

"They've heaved out a good few people they *didn't* let stay that long, remember—but I imagine they'd have to pay so much to let you go they'd rather lose two or three younger ones who haven't been here as long as you." Sadie eyed him with suspicion. "People like Dick, or me. . . . Amos, *are* you trying to break it to me gently? On the scrap heap when I'm barely thirty!"

"No, no, I promise you. Quite, well, the opposite, in fact, because—oh, dear, I'm putting this rather badly, but the thing is, Sadie . . . you've been with Tesbury's more than four years now, haven't you?'' Sadie nodded. She said nothing. ''You've seen plenty of changes, particularly over the past few months—and you've coped very well with, well, with everything.'' Amos frowned. ''Dick, now—he's only had two years of grind, though he'd done a splendid job, there's no question of that—he's still doing it, of course . . . and you've done just as well as he has . . .''

''For a woman?'' supplied Sadie, the light of challenge in her eye. Amos waved his hands rather helplessly as he tried to find the right words.

''Oh, dear. What I mean is, Ken has started me thinking— and I was wondering, well, about who's to replace me in two years' time and . . .''

Sadie stared at him for a moment, thinking fast; then she nodded. ''You're wondering if I could possibly be up to the job?''

Amos blushed. ''Oh, Sadie, there's no doubt that you can do it—I'm sure you can. That's why I'm asking if you'd like me to put your name forward to, well, to whoever—''

''I'm not crawling to Ken Oldham for a job—to any man, come to that. And I don't want anyone else to, either.''

''Oh, no, nothing like that—a simple recommendation, that's all. I'm sure you could do my job standing on your head, Sadie. And you'd have Maureen to help you over any rough patches—she's been here a long time. . . .''

''She'd prefer Dick, you know.'' Sadie's smile was thin. ''The two of them get along really well together—she only tolerates me. And your job—the way you do it, which works well—needs pretty close cooperation between the House Services Manager and the departmental secretary. I take it I—or whoever—would have to do more or less the same as you do now?''

''Oh, yes, I think so. There'd be no point in altering the distribution of responsibilities just for the sake of it—I'd recommend that we bring in somebody else to do what you do now, and leave Dick as he is. There isn't so much, well, practical detail to be learned in your job as in his— understanding machinery, dealing with servicing and all that sort of thing—''

"Then I *am* an afterthought?" He couldn't tell whether the idea amused or annoyed her. "You can't really afford to lose Dick, so it saves trouble all round if you promote *me* instead. I see." Now she did seem to be smiling. "Tell me, Amos. How confident could you be that the Board—that any of the higher-ups—would deal happily with a woman in a job where they've always before dealt with a man? Believe me, the last thing I want out of life is a load of hassle from male chauvinist pigs! Once you've been married to one, you don't want it at work as well."

"Oh . . ." He peered at her through his spectacles as if noticing her for the first time. "I, er, can't say I'd ever thought of it as any particular problem—"

"You wouldn't, would you? You're a man."

"Er, yes. But surely, as long as the job is done nobody ought to complain? After all, if you've coped with cleaners and maintenance men for four years without any trouble . . ."

"Cleaners are mostly women, remember. And maintenance men go about their business without bothering me, thank you. Leave expert work to the experts! I don't include Ken Oldham, of course, but think of my Little Lads, who know their work inside out, and get on with it without people having to breathe down their necks every five minutes. That's the way I like it—things getting done as and when they need to be. But direct complaints from the Board all the time . . . Would it pay much more than I'm getting now?"

"Oh." Amos blinked again. "I couldn't rightly say, but I should guess twenty percent—maybe twenty-five, if they were feeling generous—"

"Which, if Ken had his way, they won't. Any minute now he's going to direct his attentions to House Services, and if he ends up saying we're underpaid, I'll be very surprised. The only people in the world who *are*, according to Ken Oldham, are Management Consultants!"

Amos glanced again over his shoulder. "Sadie, I know you don't have to worry about the money side of work as much as the rest of us, but please don't joke about how much we get paid. If Ken heard you . . . he's already caused such a lot of, er, upset around Tesbury's in the short time he's been here . . .''

"Fair enough.'' Sadie grinned at him. ''You're the boss, Amos—and is it honestly a serious suggestion on your part that *I* might be the boss one day? Because if it is—well, I'll certainly have to think about it—''

"But you won't mention it to anyone while you're thinking, will you? Maureen in particular would feel hurt, I'm sure, if she heard about it from anyone but me. And as for Dick, and Ken—''

"Ken Oldham, as far as I'm concerned, is a—a cipher, a nothing—a time-wasting snoop who ought to find himself a proper job instead of poking about in other people's all day long. We managed to get along fine before he came here, and I've no doubt we'll manage just as well once he's gone. You needn't worry, Amos. I won't breathe a word to a soul.''

"About what?'' Sadie, who'd spotted Dick's approach from the corner of her eye, didn't jump at all, but Amos most definitely did. When he realised who it was, he slumped back on his chair with a sigh of relief; then he sat up.

"Dick, you're back early. What's wrong?''

Mr. Slack goggled at the array of partly eaten salads on Sadie's desk and sank into the other visitors' chair with a groan. ''Have you eaten, Amos? Have you actually gone into the canteen and come out again unscathed?''

Amos turned pale. Food poisoning! ''Well—well, yes, I have—I did. Why? What's happened?''

Dick mopped his fevered brow and closed his eyes. "How you survived, I'll never know. It isn't *safe* in that place, not for anyone from House Services. Almost every department manager in the firm is gunning for us after that business with the fire alarm. As far as I can make out, everyone who had to move a car to let the appliance through only just happened to be the most vital member of staff around—and then they weren't around any longer, because most of them took it into their stupid heads to skive off to the shops! They were daft enough to think it would take longer to sort out than it did—so now *we're* the ones being blamed for loss of productivity, or some such rubbish.''

Sadie pulled a face as Amos shuddered. ''Ken Oldham,'' in her tartest tones, ''would know the correct term, of course.''

Amos shuddered once more and seemed to shrivel where he sat. ''I think,'' he told his deputies in an unhappy voice, ''I'd better go and check the costings again. . . .''

And he scurried away toward the hessian screen and the safety of his departmental desk.

───────────── Five ─────────────

"THEN HOW ABOUT the Vice Squad?" suggested Stone, carried away by visions of Superintendent Trewley, happily married father of three, as a member of the dirty mac brigade. "Not that there seems to be too much vice in Allingham since we raided that massage parlour, but I'm sure you could hunt out the odd dubious bookshop somewhere, if you put your mind—sorry, sir," as the bulldog brow furrowed in an awful frown. "It was just an idea."

"It'd be a far better *idea* if you hopped along for that cup of tea you were babbling about and never brought me." He passed a weary hand over his face. "It's not the weather for your nonsense today, girl. May as well bring two, while you're at it—and never mind the diet, I'll take sugar in both of 'em. I need the energy. . . ."

Stone shook her head. "Sorry, sir, no sugar. And talk about a real vice—well, there you are! You know what they say about pure, white, and deadly—besides, your wife would make mincemeat of me if she ever found out. I'll bring you a sticky bun, instead. The starchy carbohydrates in flour break down into complex, rather than simple, sugars during the digestive process, which means they're released into the bloodstream at a sensible, steady rate and not in the artificial surge generated by sugar in your tea, or a piece of chocolate, or sucking a boiled sweet . . ."

Once Amos had disappeared, Dick and Sadie looked at each other and grinned knowingly as the sound of an opening desk drawer was followed by the desperate rustle of sweet papers. Mr. Chadderton was at the barley-sugar again; he seemed to find in it some consolation for the many miseries of a House Services Manager's life.

"Nice work, if you can get it," said Dick, looking from Sadie to her salad display. "But *I'm* absolutely starving!"

These histrionics did not impress Ms. Halliwell. "You could always pop along to the shops like everyone else does—and did—and buy yourself a snack to see you through. We can easily cover for you till you come back."

"Walk all the way when it's so hot? What are you trying to do—kill me with heatstroke? And if I took the car instead, what about the pollution? To say nothing of the risk I'd have lost my parking space by the time I got back."

A lesser woman would have twinkled at him; Sadie merely allowed her eyes to register slight amusement. "Don't talk rubbish. You know perfectly well that people with reserved spaces don't have to worry about parking their cars. People who include you, and me, and Maureen— and Ken Oldham, too."

"And they've all had something to eat today, I bet. Oh, go on, Sadie. Pretty please? I promise I'll never make another joke about nut cutlets!"

Sadie sighed. "Sunstroke or noxious gases or death from starvation—there's no choice, really. If I'm to live with a relatively clear conscience, I suppose I'll have to make the offer. . . ." She waved her hand over the plastic dishes on her desk. "Go on, help yourself. I'm not all that hungry anymore."

Amos, sucking on the comforting richness of his barley-sugar stick, could guess why she'd suddenly lost her appetite. He must have given her a great deal to think about, with his suggestion she should succeed him as House Services Manager, a position he was sure she would admirably fill—fill better than himself, perhaps. *Sadie* would never have been so weak over the matter of reserved car parking spaces, for example. . . .

Amos shook his head for his frailty and reached for another barley-sugar twist as he listened to the sounds of Dick Slack's attempt to enjoy the far more wholesome food on offer on the other side of the screen.

"Sadie, you're a gem. Er—what exactly *is* this?"

"Poison, of course. That's why I'm trying it out on you first—to make sure it works properly before I feed it to

Ken—oh, Dick, do stop pulling faces! If the wind changes, you'll be stuck like that forever.''

A pause. "I can't see how on earth you'd ever persuade him to chomp his way through this lot. What the blazes are these wriggly white things? They look disgusting—like maggots with pale green heads. . . .''

An exasperated sigh from Sadie. "They're bean sprouts, idiot. And if you're going to spend the whole time moaning about it, don't eat it. You can starve to death inst—''

"*Dingdong!*" The ceiling interrupted what promised to turn into a heated squabble: nobody is so keen to advise the unconverted as the person on a health food kick. "*Dingdong!* Calling Mr. Ebenezer Morecambe of Grocery Buying—would you please return to your office? Mr. Morecambe to return to Grocery Buying as soon as possible, please.''

Dick snorted, Sadie choked, and Amos chortled behind his screen. Dick sobered first.

"*Mr. Ebenezer Morecambe!* If I were Janice, I'd take care to keep out of Ben's way for the next few weeks. Everybody knows how daft he thinks his full name is, and here's Janice Blake gone and shouted it for the whole world to hear!''

"Come on, Dick, be fair. You can't blame Janice. Correct Switchboard procedure is to give the message exactly as the operator receives it, and that's what she's done. It's not her fault she's a bit . . . a bit slow in the uptake, is it? Far better to be conscientious than, er, slapdash, in my opinion.''

"Slapdash and slow? That's the understatement of the year!'' And Mr. Slack snorted again. "If you're referring to Julie, that is. You couldn't call Julie *slow*. One of the fastest little pieces for miles, she was—and if you count Veronica—''

"Which you shouldn't, not if you value your health and safety. Remember, Veronica's married now. And besides, she was very young at the time. . . .''

Necessarily the first link between outside callers and the Tesbury chain, Switchboard girls were always agreeable and outgoing by nature, warm of voice and welcoming. For some reason which nobody had ever worked out, these characteristics almost invariably accompanied a marked susceptibility to masculine charms. The notorious Veronica's fall from grace had been, as Sadie suggested, more in the nature of a misfortune: Julie's, infinitely more dramatic. She had so far succumbed to the attractions of one of Sadie's Littlie Lads as to elope with him; for, as a requirement of his job (mornings spent clearing wastepaper and rubbish from the three-storey office block, afternoons spent shifting furniture) he was, like his fellows, a splendid specimen of muscular and youthful virility. The sudden flight of Julie and her swain had resulted in a bemused husband, a bereft fiancée—and two vacancies in House Services.

An accident had transferred young Steven Bamber from Warehouse to Post Room duties, the latter being lighter in nature; and Steven had a cousin who was looking for a job. His uncle and aunt asked him if there might be a place for their Janice where he could keep a cousinly eye on her; and so, not one month before the stirring events narrated above, Janice Blake had come to work as a Post Room sorter. But the Post Room girls were a high-spirited crew; and Janice was the sole prop and stay of elderly parents—a friendly girl, and willing enough, but unworldly, and with a complete lack of understanding of all the practical jokes and ribaldry she was now encountering for the first time. Once news of Julie's elopement was confirmed, Steven spoke again to Mr. Chadderton on his cousin's behalf, pointing out that Janice was fully trained, and might it help if, in this emergency, she assisted Veronica on the Switchboard? Which Amos had gratefully assured him it might. . . .

Right now, Sadie wasn't going to let Dick sneer at any fellow female, no matter how less well-equipped mentally than herself. "You may think Janice is a—a bit dim, but she has a lot going for her. She has a pleasant speaking voice—she's hardworking, and friendly, and likeable, even if she's not quite . . . if she's different from some of the other girls in this department. She gets on very well with Veronica, too—"

"But she's nowhere near as good-looking." In common with every other Tesbury male, Dick thought red-haired

Veronica from the Switchboard one of the most attractive girls he'd ever seen.

"Which is just the sort of remark I'd expect from a man. You make excuses for the fact that Veronica's no brighter than Janice simply because of her appearance, for which she has nature and heredity to thank, and not—oh, what's the use? Here, have a drink, and let's change the subject."

Sadie snapped the ring-pull from the can of fizzy drink she'd never opened, so interested had she been in what Amos had to say, and poured half its contents into her plastic beaker. "You'll have to drink your share straight from the can. Not afraid of aluminum poisoning, are you?"

"Diet cola instead of mineral water? You're letting the side down, Sadie."

"Nobody's perfect." She chuckled at Dick's expression: he'd been expecting her to start blustering about it, and she hadn't. Sadie liked to keep people guessing. "Besides, who wants gallons of benzene sloshing round inside them? Not yours truly!"

He sipped slowly and pulled a face. "Watching your weight, are you? It's your only possible excuse—"

"If you don't like it, don't drink it. And prevention is better than cure, remember."

"Remember? I was a Boy Scout, believe it or not— Be Prepared and camp-fire sing-songs and good deeds every day, Bob-a-Job Week and collecting newspapers for recycling—"

"So don't throw that away!" She made a grab as he idly picked up the discarded ring-pull and seemed about to toss it into her wastepaper basket. "You ought to know better than that, being such a keen follower of Baden Powell. And when you've finished with the can, I'll take that, as well."

Dick had been cautiously sampling the contents of the salad trays as they talked and felt that he had at least taken the edge off his hunger. He took the hint and drained the last dregs of cola, then handed Sadie the empty can.

"Wow!" He gazed at her in awe. "Do you always flatten them in your bare hands like that? Amazing!"

"Space saving." She shrugged. "I'm not going to the save-a-can any more often than I have to—as you said yourself, think of the pollution when people use their cars. And, talking of saving space . . .''

With a paper handkerchief, she dusted out the now-empty plastic trays, stacked them one inside the other, smoothed and refolded their discarded wrappings, and tidied everything into the largest bag left to make one neat package. She put this into her capacious handbag, then leaned across her desk and switched her telephone back from its lunch-hour rerouting.

Dick was already halfway to his feet before she turned her gaze on him and seemed about to speak. He smiled.

''Sadie, you've saved my life. I was so hungry I think I'd have eaten almost anything, but that was much tastier than I'd ever have thought. You could convert me yet, if you worked at it. Er—maybe we can do it again sometime?''

''Maybe.'' Ms. Halliwell didn't hold with mixing business and pleasure. Lunch hour was over, and the time had come to start work again; but she, too, had enjoyed herself—the second half of her meal, anyway. Before Dick's arrival, Amos had given her plenty to think about. . . .

''Maybe we could.'' She returned his smile with a rather less austere twist of her lips than she might have affected on previous occasions. ''But now, here come the workers. . . .''

Maureen Mossley, slightly breathless, came hurrying in with shopping bags in either hand, heading for her desk. From behind his screen, stretching, yawning sounds suggested that Amos was waking from whatever brief snooze he'd managed to snatch. Ken Oldham, emitting boundless charm, was making his triumphal progress through the neighbouring Post Room to a chorus of giggles and girlish titters of admiration. . . .

House Services was once more back in operation.

The Tesbury internal postal system was very simple. Each department had a chosen desk to which, four times daily, was delivered the flat, zipped mailbag containing whatever had previously been sorted by the Post Room girls into its appropriate pigeonhole. Whoever sat at the appointed desk—usually the departmental secretary—would exchange the incoming bag for one bulging with outgoing mail: which, on completion of the delivery round, would be sorted in the Post Room either for distribution about the building or for dispatch outside it.

All this made it hardly a demanding job. The only qualifications needed were that you should be willing to walk for the greater part of the working day pushing a bag-laden, rubber-wheeled trolley around a predetermined route and (given the variety of departments into which your travels would take you) should possess an inordinate love of gossip. Delivery and collection of the Tesbury post was always a long-winded performance, though without doubt interesting.

Because of its importance as the department to which (and about which) all others would complain at the drop of a Lilliputian's hat, House Services learned and passed on (embellished as necessary) more scandal more quickly than anybody else. Maureen Mossley had one of the fastest tongues in Tesbury's, and always spoke up loud and clear so that Mr. Chadderton, sitting nearby, didn't miss out on a word of the news he loved to hear. His position as departmental manager rendered him in theory above the mudslinging indulged in by the lower ranks, but never stopped him enjoying, courtesy of Maureen's clacking tongue, the very wildest flights of speculation and surmise once whoever had brought the post had passed out of earshot—and occasionally before they did.

All good things, however, come to an end; in all smoothly running systems the eventual hiccup will occur. Let your post be brought by someone who positively disapproves of gossip, and your communications system is in jeopardy. . . .

The first time Steven Bamber (now married to the Switchboard's notorious Veronica) had passed Mrs. Mossley the black mailbag and been asked how things were in Grocery Buying, he had shaken his head at her in reproof.

"The words of a talebearer are as wounds, Mrs. Mossley, and they go down into the innermost parts of the belly."

"Oh," said Maureen, almost dropping the bag in her surprise. "Well, yes. But I only wondered if you'd heard—"

"A fool, when he holdeth his peace, is counted wise, Mrs. Mossley. And he that goeth about as a talebearer revealeth secrets. . . .'' He frowned, shook his head again, put a finger to his lips, picked up the outward-bound bag from her desk, and went quietly about his business.

When he'd gone, Maureen turned to Amos with an expressive shrug. ''And what do you make of that?''

''They say he never talked much over in the Warehouse, if you remember. And now we know why—it's against his principles.'' He sighed. ''I suppose we'd better not ask him anything again, in case it upsets him,'' for Tesbury policy (on the part of the old hands, anyway) had always been to work with everyone as happily as possible, fostering that family feeling of which Old Jem Tesbury had been so proud.

Steven had mellowed, in time—but not much. He might, if allowed to ponder his replies, cautiously discuss company matters with those he deemed to have legitimate interest in them; it had been the Takeover which had prompted this slight relaxation of his principles—to most of which he still, however, held firm. It was generally accepted that he was prepared to chat about events, but not about individuals; and he would still come up with suitable scriptural quotations if anyone tried to engage him in idle gossip.

It was Steven who brought today's first afternoon delivery into House Services, the bag heavy with envelopes and papers for Ken Oldham, plus a smattering of less vital documents for Amos, Sadie, Dick, and Maureen. Ken's eyes gleamed as Steven passed him, pushing his trolley.

''The post, at last! Good—I'm expecting some stuff about photocopiers and microfilming. Hope it's arrived.''

Dick's ears pricked up at this; and Sadie (who tended to treat with indifference anything Ken said about work) shot a quick look at her fellow Deputy Manager. How would Dick react to this declaration of Ken's intent to interfere, somehow, with the way Mr. Slack ran his part of House Services?

''Sounds like a good read,'' said Dick, as Maureen swapped bags with Steven, and Ken watched impatiently. ''Another of your pet projects in the offing?''

Ken laughed his merry, confident, infuriating laugh.

"Good God, Dick, would I dream of interfering in the way you run the Tesbury photocopiers?"

Dick thought he certainly would, but had no time to tell him so. Before Mr. Oldham could enlarge on the innocence of his actions, before he could (as he was almost sure to do) bring in some careless mention of the Board who'd appointed him, there was a rushing, angry movement, and Steven Bamber stood in front of him, eyes blazing.

"Thou shalt not take the name of the Lord in vain, Mr. Oldham, for the Lord will not hold him guiltless that taketh His name in vain."

Ken goggled at him. "Now, what the hell—?"

"Swear not at all, Mr. Oldham. Neither by heaven, for it is God's throne, nor by the earth, for it is His footstool."

And Steven Bamber stood and glared a few moments more, until he could see that Ken was sufficiently subdued; after which he departed in his usual quiet fashion, radiating disapproval as he went.

"Good God," said Ken again in tones of bewildered amusement, once Steven was safely gone. He looked round at his colleagues, ready to share the joke; but Dick and Sadie had their heads bent over their desks as if nothing was more important than their work, and did not reply.

Six

AMOS PICKED UP the telephone, dialled, and waited. On the other end of the line, a wary voice at last announced that it was the Transport Department: how could it be of help?

"Clem—Amos Chadderton. Are you, er, busy?"

"Busy? Not really. A couple of lorries broken down on the motorway, a pile of expenses claims to check, I'm pretty sure the diesel pump's leaking water into the tank—but no, I'm not busy. What little problem did you feel like adding to my already abundant supply just to make my day?"

"Oh, dear." It didn't sound as if his old friend needed anything else to worry about right now, but Amos knew that he owed it to Clem—to the memory of their school days, to the spirit of Old Tesbury—to sound him out, at least, concerning those veiled allegations made by Ken Oldham. "You, er, didn't say anything about the car park, Clem. Does that mean you've found a solution? Because if you have, after this morning—"

"No, I haven't, and at this rate I doubt if I'll even have time to think about the damned car park until next week. . . . Yes, I *know* that's what I said last week, *and* the week before—but there's enough routine work on my desk without having to go into some—some bloody in-depth project. . . ."

Amos recognised the influence of Management Consultancy and sighed. "Look, Clem—any chance of a few words? I'm being pressured as much as you are, and—"

"You needn't tell me—Ken Oldham, right? I hate the very sound of that cocky young blighter's name!"

Amos reflected that he wasn't the only one, but thought it wiser not to voice the sentiment aloud. "He isn't here right now, Clem. He's gone off on some new project he's just thought of—the photocopiers—and if you could spare the time for a quiet chat, well, we ought to be able to come up with a few ideas, if we could only settle down to talking the whole thing through sensibly. Two heads are better than one, remember.''

''All right, Chad, if you promise our mutual friend isn't going to turn up in the middle of it all and start badgering me, I'll come—but I won't stand for Ken Oldham telling me what to do. Nobody tells me how to run my department!''

''Well, of course, Clem. But I can't say for sure how long he'll be gone—although if he's checking out every copier in the building, it should take an hour, at least—''

''I'll be right down, then,'' said Clem, who thought the anxiety in his friend's voice was due to his inborn dislike of physical action. He'd once watched Amos miss a bus rather than run for it. ''I'll be glad of a bit of peace and quiet away from this madhouse, I tell you. There's been some damned woman ringing me up about one of our lorries she says hit her car in the road this morning. . . . Oh, have you? *She* won't be there, will she? . . . Good—then I'll be along soon. Don't run away before I get there!'' And Mr. Bradshaw chuckled as he hung up the telephone.

His face wore a more serious aspect when it hove a few minutes later into Mr. Chadderton's view. He nodded a greeting to Maureen Mossley, dropped into the more convenient (for Maureen) visitors' chair, and let out a tormented sigh.

''When I die—which at the present rate won't be long; if the blood pressure doesn't get me, the ulcer will—don't anyone be surprised if they find the words *Tesbury Car Park* engraved on my heart. You know that BMW woman actually came into my office just as I was leaving to come here? If Mary hadn't had the wits to make out I was somebody else looking for me—you know what I mean— she'd have started nagging me on the spot! That secretary of mine's worth her weight in gold—I'd never have escaped without her. 'I'll tell Mr. Bradshaw you were looking for him'—that's what she said to me, and fooled the baggage nicely.'' Clem grinned and mopped his brow with a large cotton handkerchief.

Amos frowned. The deductive powers he'd honed on a

diet of detective fiction hadn't prepared him for this sort of thing. "But how did Mary—how did you, come to that—know who it was? If the BMW girl didn't recognise you, how could you recognise her? Surely you never had time to—"

"Use your loaf, Chad! If a woman's been phoning you every ten minutes all day, you know the sound of her voice, no question. Besides, she *looked* like an angry motorist, so that was enough for me—and for Mary, too."

"Any good secretary would do the same for her boss," Mrs. Mossley assured him, one ear open for a reaction from Sadie Halliwell on the other side of the screen; but Sadie wasn't in the office at the moment. "Don't worry, Amos, I'll keep an eye open for her—and Clem, too, in case she's found out where you are. If I suddenly start to call you Mr. Smith, it won't be because I've gone bonkers. . . ."

The two men chuckled, and Maureen returned with a smile to her typing. Amos and Clem regarded each other carefully, and found themselves speaking in low voices.

"You've probably gathered that we've had our own trouble today over the car park," Amos began. "But Miss Farnworth and her BMW are only the tip of the iceberg—we have to find an answer soon, or the Board'll be breathing down our necks. In fact, I'm surprised nobody's yet made a formal complaint to them—but they can't have done, or we'd have heard all about it."

"Yes, from Ken Oldham!" Clem scowled. "Chad, the very thought of that young upstart and his fancy job makes my flesh creep—coming here telling everyone what to do and how to do it, getting poor beggars the sack if they don't toe the line. . . ." There had been many redundancies which hadn't met with approval from an already apprehensive work force as Old Tesbury gave way to New.

Amos nodded unhappily. "But let's be fair, Clem. Ken does seem to come up with ideas—which is more than either of us has been able to do, unless you count the re-marking, and the weather keeps ruling *that* one out, doesn't it? I'll admit I can see that if this latest brain wave isn't put over properly it could cause a few, well, problems—"

"Yes, it could! And who's going to get all the stick? Not

Ken Oldham, you can bet on that. Me! The years I've spent working for Tesbury's, rubbing along well enough with most folk though I say so myself—and then this young half-pint suggests a load of rubbish that'll take weeks to work out properly—and not only expects *me* to do the working out—as you can be sure he'll want—but to take the blame, too, when they all start complaining. What right has he to ruin my last couple of years in this job? Even if I managed to explain how it was him that thought of it, how does that leave me looking? Like some silly old fool who can't come up with a single idea for himself! Or else they'll say I'm using him as an excuse, and that it really was my own idea, and I'm too bothered by what they'll say to admit it. I've not forgotten that I'll still be here when Ken Oldham's gone—I hope. And I'll have to work with everyone his damned *ideas* have upset. . . ."

Amos was not convinced. For a moment, as he'd listened, the truth of what Clem said was obvious; but then the words of his old friend began to sound hollow—almost as if he'd been acting out a preselected part, hoping to confuse and conceal the truth.

Ken Oldham had suggested something of the sort. . . .

Amos leaned forward across his desk and spoke in tones even lower than before. Even Maureen, near as her desk was to Mr. Chadderton's, couldn't hear a word. "Clem," Amos murmured, feeling a traitor as he spoke, "are you . . . well, are you quite sure there's no other reason for—for being so adamant you're not prepared to consider Ken's plan? Is it really just because you want to sort it out without having to accept any help from a younger man, or—or . . ."

Clem Bradshaw sat silent in his chair, staring.

Amos held his breath as Clem sat, and stared, and then seemed to understand what his friend was saying, and opened his mouth to reply.

"*Dingdong!*" carolled the ceiling. "Calling Mr. Bradshaw of Transport—would you please ring your office? Mr. Bradshaw to ring the Transport Office at once, please."

Was the expression that now flickered across Clem's face one of relief at having been saved by the bell? Amos didn't have time to make up his mind before Mr. Bradshaw, raising a questioning eyebrow for permission, reached for Mr. Chadderton's telephone and picked up the handset, his fingers dancing a lively tango on the buttons. Thoughtfully, Amos studied him as he talked.

"Yes, it is—what's the matter? Bound to be trouble, of course. . . . Oh, no! From *where*? . . . Never heard of it. . . . Oh, did he? And now he's found out he was wrong? . . . The *what*? . . . So because this young idiot isn't driving a Range Rover or an amphibious vehicle or a blasted submarine, he's stuck in the middle of this flaming ford, is he? And what the blue blistering blazes does he expect *me* to do about it—hire a helicopter and drop him a frogman's outfit by parachute?"

This sounded so fascinating that Maureen stopped typing to listen. Strain as she and Amos might, however, to hear the other side of the conversation, they could make out nothing but a high-pitched electronic gabble. Clem Bradshaw was holding the receiver in a white-knuckled hand, unusually close to his ear. . . .

"Never mind his samples spoiling—you can tell him from me that it's *him* who'll be spoiled once I've got my hands on him! Hasn't he got the sense he was born with? Tell him to get the local garage to pull him out and check the car over before he moves another inch—if there *is* such a thing as a garage in a benighted spot like—oh, I give up!" Clem said something quite unprintable, and the telephone squeaked in surprise. "Tell him to stay right where he is and hold on, because I'm coming right now to give him the biggest bollicking he's ever had in his sweet life!"

With a bang, he hung up, then turned to Amos. "Sorry, Chad. One of our new buyers out on a cross-country trip—found a tree across the road, took a shortcut one of the locals recommended—and you heard the rest, I suppose. The idiot's car phone didn't work with all the water in the electronics, and he's in a telephone box this minute bleating to us, running out of change and without the sense to reverse the charges here so he can call a garage with the cash he's got left—I despair sometimes, I really do! So I'm off to make him sorry he was ever born. . . ."

Amos looked at Maureen as Clem barged his way out of the office. He couldn't help himself—he took a deep breath, and tried to sound casual as he asked: "If that buyer was on an outside line, why didn't Mary just transfer him through to my phone? Then Clem wouldn't have had to go dashing off like that—and we could have had our talk out properly."

Maureen shrugged. "I suppose she didn't realise he was here—she can't have done, or she'd never have put out the Call. He was probably in such a rush to get away from Miss Farnworth he never told her where he was going."

It was logical, yes, but the deduction failed to satisfy Amos Chadderton. All day he'd been worrying, at the back of his mind, about what Ken Oldham had said: and the short—all too short—deliberately short?—visit of the Transport Manager to House Services only served to fuel his vague anxieties. Hadn't Maureen said it was a matter of pride for a good secretary to protect her boss by scheming and conniving and dissembling when she must? He wondered whether it had really been necessary for Clem to be called back to his office before he could become involved in too deep a discussion on the problems of the Tesbury car park. . . .

Amos silently cursed Ken Oldham for having poisoned his mind against his old friend—with unworthy suspicions, Mr. Chadderton was sure.

Or—*was* he?

Seven

THERE CAME A bump and a rattle outside the office. Trewley looked up to see a small foot hook itself around the door as it drifted open, and Stone appeared with a metal tray in her hands, a wicked grin on her face.

"Two for you, sir, and one for me." She dealt the china mugs about his desk, put a chipped plate with two iced buns on his blotter, and flopped into his visitors' chair. "And you don't know how nearly I sugared mine, despite my awful warnings just now—for shock, you see. I was nobbled, sir. I barely escaped in one piece!"

Trewley, wrapping his hands gratefully around his mug, gave an anxious chuckle. "Pleate, I suppose? He doesn't"— he tried to keep his voice steady—"know we didn't have our dinner in the canteen, does he?"

"I don't think so, sir. He didn't say anything—about the pub, that is, though he had plenty to say about everything else. He did keep giving me those *looks* of his—but if he'd known about our ploughman's lunch I'm sure he'd have done more than look. And I can't believe anyone would have been mean enough to tell him we sneaked out of the station for an hour or so. . . ."

"They know I'd be after 'em if they did," muttered Trewley. "Self-preservation, that's what it is, when Pleate's on the warpath. . . ."

"All for one," Stone agreed, "and one for all. United we stand, against the tyranny of the ruling class as personified by Desk Sergeant Pleate—goodness, I sound more like a shop steward than a serving member of Her Majesty's constabulary!"

"Don't even mention the Unions," moaned Trewley; and a brooding silence filled the little room.

• • •

There were others besides Amos Chadderton with the
Tesbury parking problem very much in their thoughts.
Several members of the clerical staff, whose untimely
(though temporary) absence from work had so roused the
wrath of their departmental supervisors, had buttonholed
one of Tesbury's two Union representatives and were
expressing their grievances with enthusiasm.

". . . not fair we should keep getting an earful every
time something like that fire alarm makes us leave the
building to move our cars . . ."

". . . used to be ample room for everyone before the
Takeover, not stuck out in the road . . ."

". . . insisted on bringing in the new computer, didn't
they—and who knows where it's all going to end?"

"Ladies, ladies." Charley Marks had a very thoughtful
look on his face as he tried to soothe the excited little group
about him. "I only wish I knew what was happening—
you're not the only ones to be a bit bothered about what the
computer might do. Like losing jobs, maybe, once it's up
and running—"

"Never mind when it's up and running—what about our
jobs *now*?" demanded one discontented young person.
"The way my supervisor spoke to me, it was as much as I
could do to keep my temper—and it wasn't even my fault to
begin with, was it, having to stop work like that—but catch
Them letting you stand up for yourself and argue back.
You'd be out on your ear if you did!"

"Which is what your Union rep's for," Charley reminded her. "You've come along to me and expressed, er,
certain worries about, er, certain aspects of your working
conditions—worries with which the Union has every sympathy. We intend to express these worries to Management
just as soon as we've had a chance to look into it all
properly—"

"Properly? When's *that* going to be?" And a chorus of
loud agreement drowned out Young Discontent's final snort
of derision. Charley squared his shoulders and coughed.

"Just as soon as we've had a chance to look into it all
properly," he repeated firmly. "I know you don't want to

put up with, er, all this sort of thing any longer than you must, but *we* don't want to rush into discussions without we're absolutely sure of our facts, in case—''

An even louder chorus, indignant and incoherent, presented Charley with quite as many facts as he could wish to know, if he'd only been able to distinguish them. ''Yes, girls, yes—of course—but what else can I say for now, except that we, er, sympathise and understand? We—''

The chorus switched from indignation to derision, making the point that the Warehouse started work at least an hour earlier than anyone on the clerical side. If Charley took into account all those staff who work flexi-time, there were (the chorus reminded him) people who arrived at Tesbury's a good couple of hours after himself and his colleagues—who couldn't possibly understand the bother the clerical staff had to undergo to find a parking space. . . .

''If you ask me,'' put in Young Discontent, whose boyfriend read Sociology at Allingham Polytechnic, ''it's all part of a Management plot. If they make it so hard for us to come to work late because of worrying about parking our cars, then we'll end up coming in earlier and earlier every day, won't we? And then, once we're here, what's to stop them expecting us to get on with out work just because we *are* here—and you can bet they won't pay us for it, either. It's—it's slave labour, that's what it is!''

Charley could hardly conceal his shock and dismay as she finished speaking. Exploitation of the workers was one aspect of the matter which hadn't occurred to him before, but—now that she'd put the idea in his head . . .

''Look, girls, let's not try to get too steamed up about things and imagining what's not there, eh? Suppose you just leave it with me and Freddie, and we'll get back to you as soon as, er, there's something to report.''

Sooner than that, they told him. There had been talk of docking their wages for the time lost—and was that fair? Of course it wasn't! It was (came the parting shot from the sociologist's girlfriend, as everyone realised Charley had nothing more to say at present) a further example of Management's exploitation of the workers. (Charley jumped: it was unnerving to have somebody read his mind.) Since the Takeover, there were Management spies everywhere, weren't there? That Ken Oldham, for one. If all this sort of thing went on much longer, nobody would be able to call their souls their own. . . .

And, for the first time in his whole long, happy career at Tesbury's, Charley Marks very much feared that this could be the case.

Until recently—until the Takeover—the post of Union representative had been more or less a sinecure. Everyone working for the Tesbury family felt confidence in that family, most of whose members were seen more as friends and colleagues than employers. You might run across Old Jem Tesbury walking round the headquarters of his empire, stumping with his stick up the stairs, scorning the lift, wheezing and pausing for a breather on the landing and a chat with whoever passed by at the time. You might see Young Jem driving a forklift just to keep his hand in, or gossiping with Goods-In as a load arrived or departed. Assorted Tesbury cousins and in-laws and collaterals pottered in and out from time to time, each one approachable, recogniseable . . . each one both trustworthy and trusted.

Everyone had pulled together in the days of crisis, lamenting the inevitable doom as the Takeover drew remorselessly nearer. And it was only then that Charley Marks, with his fellow Union man Freddie Seraphim, saw the writing on the wall: they were going to have to fight for their rights now as they'd never even dreamed of having to do before! Gone were the good old days of amicable get-togethers in the local pub, of wages adjusted or time sheets altered over a pint or two and a game of darts. This new Board brought tough, streamlined policies into a company that barely knew what the words meant. They would have to be fought with their own chosen weapons— which Charley, for one, wasn't sure he could do. . . .

Retreating to the comparative safety of the Warehouse, Mr. Marks came upon the other half of the Union double act deep in conversation with an irate Goods-In. Freddie Seraphim, who had rashly chosen to enjoy some fresh air during his tea break, was working himself up into a fine temper. When he spotted Charley, he beckoned him furiously across, and said, in thrilling tones:

"You just listen to this, Charley Marks—you just listen! The beginning of the end, that's what it is—and something'll have to be done!"

"About what?" Freddie's quick-fire nature was a Tesbury byword. Nine times out of ten it was no more than histrionics—but there was always the tenth time. "What," enquired Charley Marks warily, "are you talking about, Fred?"

"*You* tell him." Freddie glared at Goods-In. "You saw him, didn't you?"

Goods-In spat on the ground. "Oh, I saw him—that Ken Oldham and his perishing clipboard—always said we'd have trouble with him, didn't I, and wasn't I right?"

"Were you?" Charley looked at Fred for guidance. "Why, what's he been doing?"

"What's he been doing?" Goods-In spat again. "Only come trying to sneak his way in here for a look-rahnd, that's what! I ask you—if it wasn't bad enough before, with his new bloody systems and hardly a penny extra for the extra work—"

"Yes, yes." This grumble had been heard on many previous occasions. "We did the best we could, and you know we're still working on it—but what's happened *now*? What else is he doing?"

"It's all the fault of this bloody new computer, that's what." Goods-In spat in the direction of the nearby mud and excavations of the proposed new Wing. "Isn't it bad enough there's to be clerical jobs lost once the thing's working, answer me that—"

"I told you, we'll be talking to Management," interposed Mr. Seraphim, stern and certain. "They won't get away with it as easy as they—"

"Later, Fred—please." Charley knew better than to let Freddie Seraphim start speechifying. "What I want to know is, what about *now*? What's with this Oldham bloke that's so much worse than what he's been doing all along?"

"Trying to sneak in here with his clipboard and a pen," reiterated Goods-In, with a growl. "But I soon saw him

•

off—give him the real rough edge of my tongue, I did, when I found out what that young man was after, believe me!''

Charley drew a deep breath. "What *was* he after?'' Goods-In goggled at him. "What—was—he—doing? For crying out loud, tell me!''

"He wants,'' said Freddie, hoping that by repeating the dreadful news he might lessen its impact, "to—to *utilise the resources of the new computer to the full*, isn't that right?'' He glanced at Goods-In, who nodded grimly. "Says he wants to make it pay its way as soon as possible—wants to use it for monitoring Warehouse security, and for stock control—*that's* what he wants!''

Charley felt himself turn pale. "You—you're kidding.''

"I'm not.'' Freddie nodded at Goods-In. "*He's* not. Ken Oldham's going to get that damned machine of his to count everything that comes into this place, and everything that goes out. And you know what *that* will mean!''

Charley's voice trembled. "Oh, I know. And I know another thing, too. If we don't put a stop to Ken Oldham and his smart-ass ways—and fast—then we're never going to know a single minute's peace again.''

His companions concurred with this view, Freddie adding that they ought to go off to besiege the Board that instant until a meeting could be arranged to talk it all over. Mr. Marks shook his head and held up a pacifying hand.

"No use going off half-cocked like that—there's nothing we can do that's any use until we know for sure what's what. We don't want to give 'em warning what our argument's likely to be, *or* have them say there's nothing to talk about before we've properly started. We need to ask a few people to keep their eyes and ears open and find out exactly what the plan is—which shouldn't be too hard, considering.''

The others agreed that it shouldn't. Tesbury's had been a family concern for more than just the Tesbury family: the generation of employees which had started out with Old Jem now had, like himself, numerous nephews and nieces, siblings and offspring and ramifications by blood and marriage and illicit liaison working in head office. Not a department but knew someone in another department who could tell them, in due course, whatever they might want to know. . . .

"Meantime," said Charley, "we've got something else to be getting on with. This car park business—I've promised the girls we'd look into it, so suppose we have a word with Clem Bradshaw—or Amos Chadderton—and find out what the hell's going on?"

"Have a word with them both," suggested Freddie. "They wouldn't be able to keep passing the buck to each other, if we were all of us there together."

Charley stifled a sigh for the good old days when not even Freddie, effervescent as a firework about workers' rights, harboured such suspicions against his fellow workers. There hadn't been any Us or Them, any opposite sides: they'd all been Tesburians, working together. And now, here he was saying that the only way to get an honest answer out of two of the company's longest-serving employees was to set up a formal meeting. . . .

Still, times changed. He sighed again. "We'll give 'em both a bell now to ask when we can pop along to talk things over—give 'em fair warning so they'll have time to come up with a few answers. I can't believe they won't have found *some* sort of solution after all the fuss there's been!"

But Clem Bradshaw proved to be out of his office, and—despite Freddie's whispered urgings—Charley didn't insist that Mary should have her boss paged over the tannoy. They would, he said, try again later; and he rang Amos Chadderton instead.

As Mr. Chadderton was known to spend nearly all the working day in his office, Charley could be sure that, if the line wasn't otherwise engaged, it would almost certainly be Amos who answered his telephone. He might well have in Mrs. Mossley an efficient and capable secretary, but (since she *was* so efficient) she was always busy with the business of actually running House Services, with (in consequence) better things to do with her time than answer the telephone all day long. Amos and Maureen were both happy with this system, which had been honed to perfection over many years and was known to the whole of Tesbury's as the way in which the department was run—to the whole

Company, that was to say, except the new Board (who had
never asked about it) and Ken Oldham (who had never been
told).

"House Services: Amos Chadderton speaking. . . . And
hello to you, Charley Marks. What can I do for you? . . .
Oh. Yes, well, if you insist—though the car park will be the
death of me one day, I'm sure. . . . Well, perhaps it's a
little late today"—in thankful tones—"but if you'd like to
pop along on Monday morning—how about having elevenses with Maureen and me?"

And so it was arranged. "We'd best forget about Clem
for now," said Charley, after a second phone call had failed
to connect with the Transport Manager. "If there's anything
to be known about this place, Maureen Mossley will know
it—and if *she* knows, then Amos ought to know as well. So
we'll find out what's going on and take it further once
we've got a proper answer. . . ."

Eight

MONDAY MORNING, THE Union duly went into action. Shoulders squared, spines straight, minds bent on saving the Warehouse from exploitation and Management deceit, Mr. Marks and Mr. Seraphim marched into House Services to confront Amos Chadderton.

There were two extra mugs beside Mrs. Mossley's larger-than-usual thermos and a Baxter's bag which hinted at ginger biscuits. Charley and Freddie weren't sure whether to be pleased by the apparent welcome, or to worry that its warmth might be intended to divert attention from the matter in hand—but it would be bad manners not to accept the invitation to join Amos and Maureen for early elevenses and a gossip before starting the week's work: so they accepted it.

Charley Marks dunked a gingersnap in his mug. "Young Steven getting along all right, is he? He hasn't been over our way for a while, except when he's delivering the post, and he doesn't say much then—just in and out again so's not to waste time."

Amos nodded. "He's a good worker. Reliable—we're all very pleased with him." His spectacles twinkled. "Though I'm not so sure he'd say the same about some of us!" And he told them of how the punctilious Mr. Bamber had rebuked Ken Oldham on Friday afternoon for bad language and blasphemy. Steven's two former colleagues chuckled.

"He'll think twice about speaking out of turn in front of Steve again, that's for sure. But"—and the grin was wiped from Freddie's face—"talking of Oldham—"

Charley broke in quickly, as Amos groaned. "Let's leave him out of this for the moment, shall we? Until we're sure we know just what he's up to. We're only here to talk about the car park."

Charley's insistent tone puzzled Mr. Chadderton. "Well, I know you are. That is . . ." He fidgeted on his chair and frowned as his two visitors eyed him with interest. "Well, I didn't realise, you know, that you'd heard Ken's latest, er, scheme. Clem Bradshaw wasn't exactly, er, keen to talk about it last time we spoke."

Freddie shrugged. "We'd no idea Oldham had anything to do with the car park—always excepting, of course, that he's the one behind this whole damned computer business in the first place. All I meant was what Goods-In told us—"

"Skip it, Fred!" Even among friends, Charley knew you couldn't be sure nowadays that your words wouldn't go further than you'd like, or be misinterpreted, at the very least. "Let's just wait till we know for certain, shall we? And as the subject of the car park's come up sooner than we meant, what say we talk about it now, while we're having coffee?"

On the other side of the screen, Sadie Halliwell gazed at her desk, as if expecting to see the papers on it wafted to the floor by the force of Mr. Chadderton's sigh—a sigh clearly audible as Charley finished speaking. Dick looked across at her with a rueful grin. He'd suffered as much as Amos in the matter of the car park, if not more; but this current complaint was being made to the department's nominal head, and it amused Mr. Slack to hear someone else struggling, as he had struggled, to explain away the apparently insoluble problem of the Tesbury parking. Just as well Ken Oldham had gone off on another of his investigative forays about the building—photocopiers again, probably— or he'd have been there behind the screen with the others, shoving his oar in where it wasn't wanted and infuriating everyone. Charley and Freddie had been delighted to observe his absence when they first arrived, and had remarked on it as they passed through the office to Amos's sanctum. Dick and Sadie had rejoiced with them, and promised to start a barrage of coughs if the Management Consultant returned before the business of the visit was concluded.

"The car park. Yes." Amos sighed again, recognising

that ginger biscuits and hospitality could only put off the moment of reckoning. "Well . . ."

Once more he rehearsed the sorry saga of the fine weekend weather and the thwarted re-marking, but his heart wasn't in it, and in the end he ran out of steam, sighed heavily, and nerved himself to the Big Admission. He didn't like to make trouble for his old friend, but if it was a question of Clem Bradshaw's nerves or his own, he rated Clem's as considerably more robust. He drew a deep breath.

"I, er, have to tell you that a—a solution, well, *has* been proposed—but I should warn you," as they greeted this announcement with a chorus of *why on earth didn't you say so before?*, "That is was proposed by, er, Ken Oldham, and—"

"Oy!" cried Freddie, going red in the face. Charley was almost as put out by this news as his friend.

"Oldham? Then it's fifty to one we won't like it, whatever it is."

"Oh, dear." Amos blinked several times and tried not to sigh. "Well, I'm afraid that, er, if what he suggests is accepted—as official policy, you know—by the Board, it may not, er, please a great many people—unless it's very carefully explained first, that is. . . ."

Charley muttered about plain speaking and honesty, but Freddie was more forthright. "Are there *any* people who're pleased by that young smart-ass's suggestions? Every five minutes he's come sneaking round the Warehouse trying to find out—"

"Freddie!"

But this time Charley's warning went unheeded. "Just give him half an excuse," stormed Freddie, "and he's right in there checking up on us, asking questions all the time, trying to tell us what to do and how we can do it better—"

The telephone rang. Maureen answered it: it was a wrong number, but its ringing had served to dampen Freddie's outburst a little, and for Charley to mutter sideways at him. He scowled and fell silent.

Mr. Marks took up the thread of the original conversation as if it had never been lost. "This idea, then. You don't think anyone'll like it, but you think—at least Ken Oldham thinks—it might just solve the parking problem. Perhaps it might, at that. Suppose you tell us, then we can be the judges of how upset everyone's likely to be.''

Amos wriggled on his chair again and picked up a pencil from beside his blotter, jabbing with the point into the imitation leather corner. "It isn't my idea, remember—or Clem's either. We'd never dream of anything so . . . well, I suppose *divisive* would be the nearest word, but . . ."

"Divisive?" Charley recalled the sociologist's girlfriend. "You mean Them and Us—exploitation of the workers—is that what you're saying?"

"Er," said Amos, looking unhappy. "It all depends on how you look at it, of course. But, er, he's suggesting—that some members of staff could . . . well, could . . . use buses.''

The sky didn't fall in on Amos, for which he was thankful, even though he realised it was probably because Charley Marks and Freddie Seraphim hadn't entirely taken in what he was saying. As they stared at him, he nerved himself—now that he'd made a start—to explain the rest.

"Buses." He jabbed with his pencil again. "Part of the problem, you see, is that parking's always been on a first come, first served basis—apart from people with reserved spaces, that is. It always *has* been like that . . ."

"And it's never been a particular problem," Charley told him. "Not until this ruddy computer came along. If you'd heard the way those girls from the second floor were bending my ear on Friday—"

"I know!" It wasn't like Mr. Chadderton to interrupt: but then, Tesbury's wasn't like Tesbury's anymore—and he was more nervous than ever. "Yes, well, Ken's plan should stop the necessity for, er, that sort of thing, if it works. And how it would work," he went on, as the Union men opened their mouths to enquire, "would be if some of the spaces now in use were no longer used by the people who use them. . . ." He blinked, frowned, but soldiered gamely on. "And then the people who still came to work in cars could use the spaces the other people, er, didn't. Because they came on the buses, you see."

To Amos, it sounded confused even as he said it, but the

Union men got the hang of it quickly enough: and they didn't much like it. Freddie took a deep breath.

"So which people might they be, just as a matter of interest, who're not going to be let drive their cars to work anymore? Who's going to be—to be herded together in buses like a lot of cattle going to market? That Ken Oldham and his suggestions! Neither you nor him'll ever make me believe it's to be Management, never in a million years!"

With Charley scowling at his side, Freddie turned a furious face to Amos, who quailed. Maureen stared desperately at the telephone, willing it to ring. It didn't.

Amos gulped. "Oh, dear. You see, Ken suggested . . ." And a sudden brain wave struck him. "Look, why don't you talk to him about it when he comes back? I'm sure to make mistakes over the, er, finer points, and . . ."

"The basics will do," Charley snapped. Freddie sat back on his chair, folded his arms, and glared again. Amos found himself trying not to sound guilty as he began:

"The suggestion is for . . . certain—certain categories of staff working, er, more regular hours than, er, others—categories such as, er, the clerical grades . . ."

"Class distinction!" cried Freddie Seraphim, before his colleague could call the suggestion divisive. "It's Us and Them, all right—and if anyone had ever told me Tesbury's would try such a—such an infringement of liberty—"

"It's only a suggestion!" Amos found himself breaking in, in a manner which was quite foreign to his normally easygoing nature. "Nothing's been, well, decided yet—Ken said he's only made a few preliminary, er, costings—it'll be up to Clem Bradshaw to—to make the final . . ."

He couldn't go on. Ken's hints about his old friend—Clem's attitude when they'd discussed the car park . . . What secrets did the Transport Manager have to hide?

"It'll never be stood for, you know." Charley Marks was shaking his head. "Not in a million years! Half of Tesbury's told they're—they're second-class citizens and can't come to work in their cars? This company's turned into a rum sort of place over recent months, Amos. Redundancies and rationalisation and all sorts of upset we've never had dealings with before—and we don't like it one little bit."

He rose to his feet. ''There's obviously no use talking to you about it—you're as stuck with young Oldham as the rest of us. But someone's got to have a word with him before too long, just to let him know it's high time he tried to fit in with us, not keep expecting us to be modernised out of all recognition just to keep him happy. What's the happiness of one man worth against an entire building?''

And on this magnificent exit line—giving nobody else the chance to cap it—Charley beckoned to Freddie Seraphim and strode out of House Services with his face set, and an almost visible thundercloud upon his brow.

Nine

Dick was studying a hyperbolic brochure from an ever-hopeful photocopy paper merchant when he became aware of a hovering form on the other side of his desk. Stifling a sigh—the end of the week seemed a long way off—he looked up.

"Oh, hello, Ken. Back so soon? Want something?"

The welcome was hardly ecstatic, but Ken Oldham was happy enough. He felt sure that, if he presented his case in the right way, he'd soon have Dick eating out of his hand. Once won over, he'd be moral support for the more audacious plans the Management Consultant was in the process of making. He reached for Dick's visitors' chair, sat down, and spread an impressive fan of documents on top of the various papers his reluctant host had been examining.

"Now, what do you make of all this, Dicky boy?"

Mr. Slack stared at the baffling array of loose-leaf charts and tables before him. It would be galling to give an honest answer ("Absolutely nothing, if you really want to know") so he compromised by asking curtly what Ken *supposed* he ought to make of it.

Sadie shot him a quick glance of warning. She always thought it wise to know the enemy's plans in as much detail as possible before taking action: she did not think it wise to antagonise him by showing your hand—in this case, your opinion of his character—too soon, so that he told you nothing. Dick saw the glance and modified his tone:

"It all looks . . . pretty impressive, Ken." He thought of his mortgage, and the high cost of running a car, and the convenience of working in Allingham. "In fact, it's so very impressive, I haven't a clue what it all means!"

Ken was delighted to have to explain, as he'd intended from the start, how much more clever he was than the majority. "Well now, Dicky boy, just you read this . . ."

Mr. Slack peered across at the neat printed heading on the sheet of paper Ken held up just far enough out of range for him to have to lean over his desk. It was another of the little games Mr. Oldham played, altering people's perceptions of themselves in relation to himself. He had others: walking round to their side of the desk (invasion of personal space) to unnerve them, leaning on their shoulders (ditto), perching on a corner of the desk to expound his point of view (ditto yet again). He'd started very well on this occasion by proving how much more important his papers were than Dick's by scattering them on top of Mr. Slack's . . . and Sadie (who had watched it all), who'd read a few books on Assertiveness Training, felt her jaw clench in sympathy. But, much as she hated the type of psychological tricks Ken so adroitly employed, there was little she could do about them now. Dick would have to fight this battle on his own.

He did his best. "*Projected Savings from Reclamation of Silver Used in Microfilm Development Process*," he read, and paused. "Savings? Savings of what?"

Ken laughed his merry laugh, indulgent, tolerant, amused at the denseness of others. "Good God, Dick, savings of money—what else? You people are pouring a fortune down that drain every day, boy! But there's a little machine we could install that would pay for itself in no time at all, so long as you increase the number of films processed by just seventeen percent, Dick. Seventeen percent—think of it!"

Dick thought of it. "Seventeen percent? We couldn't increase the processing by even seven percent without increasing the number of documents we filmed, as well."

"So what's wrong with that? Think positive, Dick. Why not increase the number of documents you film?"

"Because I don't have the staff, for one thing—"

"Good God, Dick, you're missing the point, boy! We'll get you extra staff as you need them—simple. Clever, eh?"

It was extremely clever. Ken had baited his trap well. Who is not averse to a quiet spot of empire-building? The slightest hint of a larger department and Dick, tempted, was ready to fall. Sadie sat listening in dismay; behind the screen, ears alert, Amos wondered where in this proposal was the threat to himself he felt sure must exist. If Ken

Oldham won Mr. Slack round to his way of thinking . . .

"About how many extra people d'you suppose I'd need?" enquired Dick, golden visions before his eyes. Ken smirked.

"I've done the calculations, of course, and my estimate is for a minimum of two—one to work the camera and prepare documents for filming, one to process the films through the developer and reclaim the silver. But," said the voice of the serpent as he studied Mr. Slack's expression, "to be on the safe side, I'd recommend three—illness, holidays, and so forth. Three more people, Dick—and then we could think about buying another camera—to do even more microfilming than before!"

Maureen Mossley tore a mistyped letter from her type-writer with a savage gesture and hurled it, carbons and all, into the wastepaper basket. She'd heard Amos sigh and could guess why he'd done so. How dared these bright young newcomers barge into the department and make everyone feel out-of-date and useless?

Dick was asking where they were to find all the additional documents for filming and processing. Ken laughed once more, seeing the fish almost hooked.

"Come on, Dicky boy, use a little imagination—from the Archives, of course! There's piles of stuff there taking up room and hardly ever looked at—some of those invoices have to be kept for seven years, by law, yet who bothers with them except the accountants, once in a blue moon?"

It made sense. Dick found himself nodding, seduced into agreement despite his original doubts. "We could buy one of the new continuous feed cameras for filming cancelled cheques and things like that. I wonder how much they cost?"

This time, smirking, Ken happily pushed his paper right across the desk. "Here's the preliminary figures I worked out, Dick. You'll notice I've been looking very carefully into *all* our expenses—Ken Oldham doesn't do things by halves! Capital tied up in equipment—depreciation—general purchasing outlay on consumables—"

Sadie could bear it no longer. "Do I gather—from what I could hardly help overhearing—from these proposals that, if you go ahead with them, there will be more space in the Archives than is at present the case?"

Amos sat up, his eyes beginning to sparkle: he could see what was coming. So, smothering a grin, could Dick. Ken Oldham, however, couldn't.

"More space? Sadie, of course there'll be more space—what else would you expect? If you store documents on microfilm, you've finished with them for good. They can just be thrown away—they're nothing more or less than wastepaper." He eyed her condescendingly. "Do I gather it's the thought of the wastepaper bothering you, my dear Sadie?"

"Certainly not!" The ears of everyone within eavesdropping distance began to flap as the fat was flung well and truly in the fire. Sadie Halliwell didn't much care for being told how to run her department. "Depending on how much extra work there was, I might have to think about getting another Little Lad—though that's isn't your problem, Ken," very pointedly. "It's mine—and I can cope with it, should it come about." Maureen and Amos exchanged delighted grins; Dick choked and looked hurriedly away as Ken gazed at him in some surprise.

"And I wouldn't say," continued Sadie, "that it was so much bothering me as interesting me, greatly—your plan to microfilm the archival material and clear some space. When you were talking about equipment just now, it struck me—"

"No, Sadie!" Dick broke in before Ken had time to work out what she was really saying. "It was a good try—better than usual, I've got to hand it to you—but the answer's still a very loud *no*." He turned to Ken. "Our Ms. Halliwell is a born opportunist—you may have noticed."

"That," retorted Sadie, "is a matter of opinion. For my part, I think of myself as being . . . practical. If there's a weakness anywhere in the system, I exploit it—as anyone with any sense of self-preservation is bound to do."

"You're dead right there," said Dick, as Ken was still trying to understand the point of the little exchange which—from the chuckles audible behind the screen—had amused everyone except himself. "Self-preservation" said Mr. Slack firmly, "is very important, I couldn't agree more. I apply the principle myself—so the answer is still *no*!"

As Sadie, with a rueful shrug, remarked that it had been worth a try, Ken had to ask. "No to what?" he enquired;

and the combatants regarded each other, and then Mr. Oldham, with that air of sharing a joke which can be so uncomfortable to outsiders.

"Sadie," explained Dick, as Ms. Halliwell smiled with the air of a good loser who knows she will win in the end, "says I should let her take over part of my Archives for her Furniture Store—she's been trying to pinch a few feet extra for ages. The slightest encouragement, and she's after me again. Predatory, that's the word."

Sadie raised cool eyebrows. "You know very well I have hardly enough room as it is, and with extra staff joining the company all the time, and the modern equipment they ask for—to say nothing of desks and chairs being put in storage for repair—"

"Those extra members of staff," said Dick, "send documents for filing in the Archives just the same way everyone else does. The floor space we manage to clear by filming will soon have to be used for them, the rate we're going." Now the idea had been put in his head, he wasn't going to surrender without a struggle: he was carried away by thoughts of future glory. "Besides, what use is a larger store to you unless it has much stronger walls and a better lock than you've got right now?"

That was below the belt. Sadie's breath hissed through gritted teeth as his words forced her to recall the recent disappearance of a rather handsome swivel chair and two anglepoise lamps, mysteriously spirited away from her usually efficient charge.

"But how," had cried Amos, whose own office was graced by a similarly noticeable item of seating, "could they have taken the chair? I can see the lamps would be easy enough—but something this size?"

"Oh, that would be easy as well," Dick had assured him, rubbing salt in Sadie's wounds. Mr. Slack's full complement of microfilm machines and photocopiers had made him smug, and his smugness had driven Ms. Halliwell wild. "When was the last time anyone ran a spot-check on people coming in or out of this place? Our security's laughable— and you just can't trust anyone nowadays, can you?"

He'd been so amused by the whole affair that Sadie had

refused to speak to him, unless absolutely necessary in the course of her job, until the advent of Ken Oldham had united the entire House Services management against him. Now she wasn't sure who annoyed her more, Ken or Dick. Better, perhaps, the devil you knew . . . and she deftly turned Dick's taunt to her own ends.

"Doesn't that only go to prove my point? I need plenty of room for a proper, organised, *secure* Furniture Store, as well as a separate one for office equipment—"

Ken realised they were so busy arguing with each other that he was about to lose his advantage. "Given enough time," he interjected smoothly, "I'm sure we could work out something which would suit both of you. I'll think about it," he promised, and Sadie scowled. He smiled and turned back to Dick. "But first things first, and we were talking about these figures here, weren't we? You know, there's a good deal more we could be doing, if we took things to their logical conclusion. Sadie"—she looked at him without responding to his smile—"be honest, now. Are you quite sure the wastepaper doesn't worry you?"

"Quite sure, thank you." Her voice was sharpened ice. "Are you suggesting I am failing to carry out my duties— that my Little Lads are inadequately supervised or working insufficiently hard? If *that* is the case—"

"Oh, Sadie, perish the thought! You misunderstand me, I'm sure. My fault, no doubt," and he smiled again, "for not explaining properly. All I meant was, with the extra staff and the increase in wastepaper—of *any* paper, if we take Dick's Archives into account—well, there are bound to be problems of storage and disposal."

"Good gracious, so there are. How silly of me not to have noticed, after all my experience in this job. Thank you, Ken, for reminding me—but if I can't cope for any reason, I'll let Amos know—he is the House Services Manager, after all. Just for the moment, however, I need no help—or interference—in my job, Ken."

"I'm sorry if you think I'm interfering. *My* job, you see, is to make life easier for everyone in every way I can. The paper, for instance. Suppose there was a paper-free office? Think how your job—both your jobs—could be made so much easier if all the routine work could be done away with. Wouldn't you both be pleased to have time to spend on more important projects? Oh, we'd have to look into the exact costs and potential savings, but that's *my* problem— it's what I'm trained for. You needn't worry over that side of things. For example, Dick, most of your archival storage is paper originating from outside Tesbury's—invoices and receipt notes and confirmation of orders . . .''

This was a definite score for Mr. Oldham. His ability to snoop with success could no longer be doubted, with such obvious proof of its results. There were some people who had been employed by Tesbury's for decades without even having heard of the Archives, let alone knowing what it was for or what was kept there.

''. . . computer linkup, eventually, from buyer to supplier direct, with no paperwork at all! But that's still some time in the future, when more of our larger contacts install computers as sophisticated as ours, and with compatible systems. I might well be monitoring the position and dropping a few hints in the right ears . . .''

Listening hearts sank. How far in the future did Ken Oldham plan to be employed in Tesbury's? They'd hoped it was to be for a year or so only. . . .

''. . . cost-effective—but for now, Sadie, why don't we take a look at *your* involvement in the Tesbury paper mountain!''

''Why?'' It irked her to observe how Ken's enthusiasm could sway people into paying him close attention, but she knew that for the sake of departmental unity she might as well go along with him, to find out all she could. ''What, from your no doubt expert point of view, am I doing wrong?''

''Why, nothing,'' said Ken, in tones which suggested he, the expert, could list a hundred things, but was too polite to do so. ''Nothing—but don't you have three Little Lads working flat-out every morning to clear away all the bulky forecasts and orders and computer printouts of price lists? And when the only paper we're likely to need in the future is general office stationery—scratch pads for notes, envelopes, and so on . . . we'll be finished forever with those great wodges of paper taking up so much room and needing to be shifted round the building all the time—finished forever, Sadie! Think of it!''

She thought of it. ''How?'' she enquired, and waited.

It was Ken's big chance. ''The new computer,'' said that machine's awestruck acolyte, ''won't need to print out on paper at all! Computer paper's pricey stuff—it must cost a small fortune every month, judging by the amount lying around on people's desks and in their filing cabinets—but Sadie, Dick—once the computer is up and running, anyone who requires particular information will be able to call it up directly from the mainframe to their own personal terminal—they'll work from the screen, *not* with paper! Though there is always,'' he admitted, in grudging accents, ''if they *really* need it, the facility to turn what's on the screen into hard copy—paper, I mean,'' as Dick and Sadie stared.

He could see that Sadie, at least, was about to dispute this concept of two different types of paper replacing one and hurried on before she could open her mouth:

''But of course, the times when anyone will actually *need* hard copy will be far, far fewer than at present—most people only want to check the occasional figure, or price, or date—yet at the moment they work with a complete printout because this computer can't cope with issuing it in sections! The new one, of course, could, if we wanted it to—but we won't. Those one or two members of staff who need to juggle with more than just a few pages, and who can't learn how to do it on screen''—Ken's tone suggested that he had no sympathy with such a Luddite reaction to this twentieth-century technology— ''will end up with standard letter-sized A4 paper, not huge sheets with perforated edges. And,'' he went on, as his audience still seemed unconvinced, ''for anyone whose job doesn't involve dealing with information on the computer— who works with documents generated from outside Tesbury's—there will be the new facility of *microfiche*. Fiche are hardly bigger than postcards, but you can fit sixty A4 sheets on just one of them—invoices, delivery notes, you name it! Just think of the potential there. . . .''

They all thought—Sadie, Dick, Amos, Maureen—and were convinced, for the moment—though in varying degrees. Sadie frowned, Amos sighed, Maureen wished she could stuff a gag in Ken's mouth—but Dick's eyes gleamed as Mr. Oldham played his masterstroke.

"You, of course, Dicky boy, would be responsible for all the new microfiche readers which would need to be issued to each department for individual use. . . ."

Which, on top of an already fraught discussion, was too much for Ms. Halliwell. "If these—these microfiche readers are to be used in individual departments instead of being a centralised facility as micro*film* is, surely they must count as Office Equipment? And the same must apply to the computer screen terminals you're talking about. Office Equipment is *my* responsibility, not Dick's. Besides, isn't he going to have quite enough extra work with the silver reclamation, never mind—"

"Microfiche," Dick broke in, "are just microfilm in a different shape, as Ken said—postcards instead of rolls. They're exactly the same principle, so naturally they would belong to *my* department—"

"Now, now." Ken was delighted to have divided and conquered so cleverly, but didn't want them to become so caught up in their quarrel that they'd stop paying attention to him. "No need to fall out over a little thing like this! I'm sure that once we've talked it over with Amos"—the plump little man behind the screen was startled to hear his name coupled with a technological miracle he knew he'd never understand—"he'll agree it's at least worth a try. I'll arrange to hire a reclamation machine for, say, a month—cost of hire to be deducted from the subsequent purchase price, of course, if we decide to go ahead. Which I'd take a sizeable bet we will." He preened himself. "I'm not such a bad hand at arranging this sort of deal, you know. I told you, I always check my figures carefully before I start any new project—and you see if I'm not right about this. . . ."

And, from the firmness with which he spoke, nobody in House Services could doubt that Ken Oldham, confident and keen, meant eventually to alter the way everything in Tesbury's was done . . . to alter it beyond recognition. The old days were gone forever.

Ten

"FEELING BETTER, SIR?" enquired Stone, as Trewley finished his last mouthful of sticky bun and looked hopefully at the half she'd left on her side of the plate. Hot weather never made her as weary as it did the superintendent, but she lost much of her appetite, nonetheless.

She grinned and pushed the plate across. "Go on, sir, you know it would be a shame to waste it—and I'd hate to deprive you of your fix. The blood sugar," she explained, as he paused with his hand above the vivid pink icing and stared at her.

"*Fix* be damned! You'll be saying next you think a job in the Drugs Squad's what I should be trying for. . . ."

Stone looked shocked. "Drugs, sir? Not in Allingham! You'd have to go up to London for that, thank goodness. You know as well as I do that our usual cases are far more likely to involve fools who've had too much to drink than idiots who've been sniffing disgusting powders or sticking needles in themselves. . . ."

Toward the latter part of Ken's conversation with Dick and Sadie, a distant hubbub had been gradually growing louder, sometimes even drowning out odd words which had to be guessed at from the context. The Post Room was celebrating. Young Tracy, electing to come of age at eighteen instead of the still-more-traditional twenty-one, had (with the wary permission of Amos) brought to work six bottles of cheap wine, a selection of paper plates and plastic cups, and a most elaborate cake, baked and iced by her mother.

"Provided the work gets done," Mr. Chadderton had decreed, "and provided, of course, that I'm given a decent slice of cake—then by all means celebrate, my dear. Only don't, for goodness' sake, let them all get tiddly and start chasing each other round the office. . . ."

One employee of the Post Room to turn his back with resolution upon this mildly intemperate merriment was, as might have been expected, Steven Bamber. When Tracy, already giggling in anticipation of his reply, offered him a beaker of plonk in exchange for a birthday kiss, Steven shook his head with the remark that wine was a mocker, and strong drink was raging—and took his share of the afternoon's postal round out for one of the earliest deliveries that route had ever known.

"Shouldn't think Veronica will say no," someone said; and everyone chuckled, though not unkindly. Veronica's fall from grace was legendary among Tesburians, even if it was rarely mentioned—at least, never in front of Steven, and certainly not in the presence of Veronica herself. "Shall we take some in to her at the Switchboard? Oh, and Janice too, I suppose. She can always say no."

Janice Blake, overshadowed as ever by the more sensational Veronica, was the quieter of the two girls, more often than not tacked on as an afterthought. Her family background made it unlikely that she would regard alcohol as a respectable beverage any more than Steven did; but, though the Post Room might tease, it was never ill-natured, and the idea of leaving her out of any fun that was going seemed very unfair. As they recognised, she could always (unlike her colleague Veronica) say no.

"Veronica and Janice," said Tracy, setting beakers out on a tray. "And there's Mr. Chadderton and Maureen, and Dick—and Miss Halliwell . . ."

"And Mr. Oldham!" The suggestion made everybody giggle. The boyish good looks of Ken had quite won their hearts, for they saw only the surface charm, never having had to face the sheer ruthlessness which lay beneath. It was easy for Ken to be affable with his inferiors, since it cost him very little; but as he intended to score whenever possible over his equals, and (in time) over his superiors, he could never afford to relax with them. Of this sexist and self-seeking policy, however, Tracy and her lovelorn cronies were happily unaware.

"Oh, yes. Mr. Oldham, too." Tracy sighed dreamily as she filled a generous beaker and cut an extra-plummy slice of cake. With a loaded tray and a simpering escort, she headed for the House Services management area.

Ken's desk was the first to be reached. "Oh, Mr. Oldham, it's my birthday, and . . ." Blushing, Tracy gushed her way through an explanation, and made a point of handing him the most generous serving. Ken, refreshed by his intellectual skirmish with Sadie and Dick, didn't disappoint his expectant admirers.

"Why, how very kind of you, Tracy—it *is* Tracy, isn't it? Now, am I allowed to give the birthday girl a kiss?" And Tracy's face as he saluted her was rosy with more than the effects of cheap red wine and mere birthday excitement. "Many happy returns of the day, my dear!"

Tracy tittered as her companions uttered little squeals of envy. "Oh, Mr. Oldham—oh, Mr. Oldham!"

She missed the look of scorn on Sadie's face, as that emphatic divorcée observed proceedings at the neighbouring desk. The girl, she reasoned, knew no better—but Ken Oldham did, and could not be excused for having taken advantage of a silly and flattered teenager who'd had a drink or two and was in an exalted mood.

"Miss Halliwell—it's my birthday . . ."

The gesture touched Sadie, though common sense told her Tracy could hardly have left her out if she was distributing goodies to the rest of the department. But it is a pleasant feeling to be liked, even in so routine a display; and Sadie smiled, and made a little joke, and forgot for a few moments her annoyance with Ken Oldham.

"Why, Tracy, how kind—thank you. It all looks lovely, but I do hope you've remembered to bring flasks of coffee for afterwards!"

"Oh, that's all right, Miss Halliwell. My boyfriend's driving me home."

Sadie's unguarded tongue was about to remark that men could, after all, have their uses, when she was saved from this indiscretion by the ringing of her telephone. With an apologetic nod to Tracy, she picked up the receiver, while the girl took herself and her tray off to Mr. Slack's desk.

"Oh, Dick, it's my birthday, and—"

"I know, Tracy, I know. And anything Ken can do, I can do, too!" This welcome was much appreciated by Tracy, who soon found that Mr. Slack could suit action to words.

She was blushing more than ever as she picked up her tray
and started to make for Amos Chadderton's office . . .
and stopped in surprise as she heard Sadie Halliwell slam
down her telephone and emit a few choice curses in a loud
voice.

"And I think," she added, as everyone turned to stare, "I
might scream, as well. So anyone who wants to had better
ask Maureen for some earplugs from the first aid kit—or
maybe," as her eye fell upon the plastic beaker, "I'll turn to
drink, instead. Tracy, cheers—you've saved my life!"

Remembering Sadie's toast, Tracy was giggling again as
she went over to Maureen and Amos with their cake and
wine; but Sadie herself was far from cheerful.

"That damned ladies' loo on the second floor is blocked
again, and would I please do something about it? That's the
third time this month! It's not as if I haven't done my best
to sort it out, though you'd never think so from the fuss
they're making—I've had the plumbers look at it, and they
can't find a thing wrong."

"Poltergeists," suggested Dick, as she pushed back her
chair with a groan and prepared to set off on her sanitary
expedition. "Gremlins of some sort, anyway—want me to
come with you to get rid of them?"

If Ken Oldham hadn't been listening, Sadie might have
allowed herself to weaken and accept Dick's kind offer; but
she had no intention of letting the Management Consultant
think her a helpless female. "Thanks a lot, but I think the
good old plunger routine should see me through. Ugh! How
I hate these messy jobs. . . ."

She took another gulp of plonk, grabbed the large rubber
plunger from the box of assorted tools she kept in readiness
behind a potted palm, brandished it in salute, and was gone.

The titters and sniggers from the Post Room never grew so
loud that Amos felt he must interfere by sending Maureen to
quieten them. Frequent loud shushings drifted in the direction of the screen, and Amos smiled. He knew the girls to be
good-hearted, their youth notwithstanding, if inclined to
high spirits: not hard to see why Janice Blake hadn't been
able to settle there. She was far too staid and decorous,

mentally more of an age with Sadie Halliwell than with the giddy youngsters who were her true contemporaries. Veronica, on the other hand . . . But that, he reminded himself, had been before her marriage. Hadn't she seemed far more steady than she used to be, now that Steven Bamber had given her a legitimate share in his own respectability? Amos wondered idly whether Steven had come back yet from his post round, then applied his deductive skills and decided he couldn't have done. Nobody was quoting scripture anywhere within earshot, and the sounds of merriment continued unabated.

One of the wandering House Services staff returned to the fold. Sadie Halliwell, breathless and damp, greeted Mr. Slack with a rubbery clunk as she dropped her plunger on the desk in front of his startled nose.

"Honestly! Why can't people get their facts straight? It wasn't the toilet that was blocked, it was one of the basins. I've given it a good squelching and cleared it, as far as I can tell, but there's gallons of water all over the floor. I'll bleep Biddy Hiscock to go and mop it up, or the idiots will be slipping and sliding all over the place and breaking their daft legs—I stuck a notice on the door, but you know half of them never bother to read anything. . . ."

"While the other half," supplied Dick on cue, "*can't* read anything. Was it that lot from the Visual Display Units chucking their sweet papers down the overflow again?"

Sadie dropped into his visitors' chair and picked up his phone, punching out the well-known number as she replied that she didn't know and didn't care, just so long as it was cleared. Ken Oldham, observing the little scene, was irrationally annoyed that, though he hadn't volunteered to help her in the first place, she had managed nonetheless to cope.

"Congratulations, Sadie, on a job well done. How do you manage to deal so efficiently with all the excitement? It's too much for me, so early in the week—I'm going to stretch my legs for a while. . . ."

No sooner had he appeared in the Post Room than he was gleefully buttonholed by Tracy and her friends. "Ooh, Mr. Oldham—would you like another drink? Or some cake? There's plenty left, if you would!"

"That's very kind of you, ladies. But why so formal?

We've been getting to know each other pretty well this afternoon—and the name's Ken, remember?''

Sadie, waiting for her bleeper call to be answered, raised despairing eyes to the ceiling as delighted giggles floated from the Post Room. Dick, watching her, pulled a face and shrugged. He—his look made plain—would never behave in such a fashion. Sadie grinned at him.

Then she frowned. She jiggled the handset up and down, and dialled again. "Damn—somebody else is using the system now. Why couldn't the wretched woman answer the first time?"

"Maybe she's forgotten to wear her bleeper," suggested Mr. Slack. "Though she's pretty good about it, isn't she?"

"Biddy?" Ms. Halliwell jumped from her chair and headed for her desk. "Reliable as they come, though I suppose I'd better check. Now, if it had been one of the Lads . . ." She jerked open her top drawer and rummaged inside. "No, she's wearing it. So, if she doesn't answer next time . . ."

Which, to Sadie's annoyance, she didn't. ". . . then I'll just have to put out a Call for her. And won't everyone grumble when I do! Still, they'd grumble a good deal more if they started breaking bones on the washroom floor—it's the lesser of two evils. And, if a thing has to be done, the sooner the better. See you!"

She was gone, leaving Dick (who had checked his trouser waistband and found his bleeper in its proper place) feeling virtuous, and Amos feeling guilty. Overhearing Sadie's comments, he had opened his own desk drawer to see if his bleeper had, by some strange chance, disappeared—which, of course, it hadn't. As he rarely moved out of the office, he seldom bothered to wear the thing, though he knew that he really should. In an emergency, clipping his bleeper to his belt was bound to be low on the list of priorities. . . .

His barley-sugar lay next to the bleeper. Absently, he unwrapped a stick and popped it in his mouth, closed the drawer again, and smiled as the sweet juices began to run down his throat. He sucked happily for a while, then crunched the last golden sliver to oblivion, and smacked his lips. He reached for Tracy's plastic beaker and prepared to drain it . . .

When the peace of the office was once more shattered.

"*Dingdong!* Calling Biddy Hiscock of House Services—would you please telephone your department immediately. Biddy Hiscock to call House Services at once, please."

Ten minutes later, Sadie was back at her desk, having left the cleaner mopping away for dear life in the second floor ladies' washroom. "Flat battery," growled Ms. Halliwell. "I've given her mine for the moment. . . ." And with a steel nail file she deftly unscrewed the small panel at the back of the bleeper and removed the metallic cylinder. "Why doesn't the silly woman check it every morning?"

Dick levelled his own bleeper like a ray gun, squinting ferociously down his outstretched arm at his victim. "Ex-ter-mi-nate! O-blit-er-ate! E-rad-i-cate!" he chanted, in a Dalek's tinny tones, and pressed his thumb upon the test button. The bleeper duly bleeped.

"Hands up, or I fire," responded Sadie, testing Biddy's bleeper in her turn. With its new battery, it worked. "And what a lot of bother would have been saved if I hadn't had to fix this. . . ."

Dick grinned. "Not everyone has the same mechanical skills as you, remember." He was thinking in particular of how, one chilly autumn evening, his car had refused to start—and how Sadie, who'd enrolled in Car Maintenance classes at night school ("So what if I can afford to pay for service and repairs? All the alimony in the world won't change a flat tyre for me in the middle of Hannasyde Heath or replace a broken fan belt, will it?") had happened along, fiddled under the bonnet, and within minutes made the engine run as sweetly as ever. Dick had brooded on this phenomenon all night, and the next morning accused her of having doctored his car herself, just to prove a point. Sadie laughed at him and told him he should learn to do things for himself as she'd had to do—and even Maureen Mossley had chuckled.

"And I suppose," he said now, "you're probably one of the only people in House Services sober enough to change a battery," as a burst of laughter came from the Post Room. "Let's hope too many mailbags don't end up in the wrong slot this afternoon."

"Well, there'll be nothing wrong with Steven's," Sadie said, thinking back over who had and who had not been present at the Post Room festivities as she walked by. "I notice Veronica's slipped out to join the fun—did you hear it was Janice who put out that Call for Biddy?" She lowered her voice. "I hope nobody spikes her drinks this time. . . ."

Dick, for the benefit of the Post Room, said loudly that he was sure the girls would all be sensible about the party, and wouldn't abuse the trust Mr. Chadderton had placed in them. Amos, hearing him, hoped so, too—but Sadie wasn't so sure. Drink had been the occasion of Veronica's downfall; Ken Oldham was a personable, persuasive Lothario (to eyes of less experience than her own, at least); she hoped he would have sense enough not to go too far in his flirting, because some of the girls weren't as worldly-wise as they thought themselves to be. The giggles and chatter still sounded friendly enough, but you could never tell when a Situation might not arise. . . .

"Thou shalt not covet thy neighbour's wife, Mr. Oldham." The stern voice of Steven Bamber broke into the happy hum of conviviality. The Situation had arisen. "Woe to him that giveth his neighbour drink."

There was a pause, and a scuffle. Sadie, who'd jumped to her feet and hurried to see what was happening, was in time to see Veronica slip from Ken Oldham's embrace and stand, blushing, to face her husband. Steven looked gravely at her pink cheeks and dishevelled state, then pointedly at the door of the Switch Room. Not only had she been kissing another man—she had abandoned her post to do so. "Veronica," was all he said: but at his tone, Sadie shivered.

"A birthday salute—nothing more," blustered Ken, for once not certain how to react. "I assure you—"

"My wife's birthday," said Steven, fixing Mr. Oldham with a burning gaze, "is in January. Isn't it, Veronica?"

There was no reply from the errant spouse, who had taken his unspoken hint and slipped back to the Switchboard. With another long, suspicious stare, Steven Bamber turned away from Ken Oldham in a manner which said more than a thousand words would have done. . . .

And not even Ken felt confident enough to break into his silence, brooding and thoughtful and accusing as it was.

———— Eleven ————

"YOU KNOW, SIR, if you're really keen to work in Town," Stone told her sticky-fingered superior as he wiped his hands on a paper handkerchief, "how about Special Branch? Skullduggery and spies—MI5 and MI6—telephone tapping—"

"For heaven's sake, girl! Can you seriously see me bugging phones and eavesdropping and creeping about the place in disguise? That's no life for a career copper!"

After burning out the first few layers of deadwood, the initial conflagration of the Takeover had died down, though there remained a loyal core of Old Tesburians in certain key positions about the firm. A large proportion of this core consisted of members of staff who could have done as good a job as (if not better than) their bosses of running the company—the secretaries.

When, on Monday evening, one particular secretary spotted Ken Oldham acting in a manner more furtive than his sly and suspicious wont, she managed to type so many mistakes in a letter destined for immediate despatch that, brooding on overtime, her boss instructed her to stay on late to complete a corrected version. During the course of her labours—for it was a long and complicated document, and she had taken care to make the mistake on the first page—it happened that, by chance, her hand caught and flicked upwards the intercom switch linking her desk with the office of her boss. Her boss who was a member of the Board. . . .

Had Ken Oldham done such a thing, he would have been at once condemned as a snoop and a spy. In an Old Tesburian, such action was regarded as no more than family loyalty—an interesting example of the dual morality essential for survival in contemporary corporate enterprise. For the secretary in this case was Freddie Seraphim's niece. . . .

Tuesday morning found Freddie discussing the whole affair in graphic detail with Charley Marks, who hoped his more volatile colleague was exaggerating, but very much feared that he wasn't. He saw his task as twofold: to extract the basic facts from Freddie's diatribe—and to soothe his colleague's blood pressure to something approaching normal.

Having listened and made appropriate noises until the explosive Mr. Seraphim's face had faded from purple to scarlet, from scarlet to its customary brick-red hue, Charley decided he might now safely venture on comment and considered opinion.

"The trouble is, Fred, it's no more than hearsay evidence, if you think about it. *I* know she heard right, and so do you—but it'd never stand up in a court of law."

"Infringement of our liberties this way'd never stand up in a court of law neither. Suppose—"

"Suppose nothing, Fred—not till it's been checked out a bit more thorough-like. For a start, we need to find out if it's been put on record as official discussion, not just a—a chat after working hours."

Freddie winked. "A bit of luck, her having to stay on for that typing, and them talking in the other office. But as to official discussion—minutes of meetings, I suppose you mean?—she's not had *them* to type, that I know of."

There was a pause. Charley suddenly slapped his forehead. "Typing! Of course—that's the answer. Ten to one, if Oldham's put anything on paper, Maureen Mossley'll have typed it for him. She'll know, all right."

"If she does, why hasn't she tipped us the wink before this? It isn't like Maureen not to tell us if there's funny business going on."

Charley subsided. "You're right. She *would* have said, wouldn't she?" He thought again. Once more, he brightened. "He'll have it in notes somewhere, that's what, and not put in for typing yet. He'd never have been able to plan it all in his head—there must be something on paper somewhere—and Maureen's the one to find it for us. If we give her a ring—"

"We'll go and see her," said Freddie, man of action. "Now. And we'll ask her to have a look, if Oldham's not there—you know how he's never in the office half the time, sneaking around the place like he does, asking his bloody questions. . . ."

Charley knew. He also knew that Ken Oldham, despite the hopes of many in Tesbury's, was no fool. "We'll need a good excuse for dropping in, in case he's around. What say we make out we've come to ask how Steve Bamber's getting on? See if he still doesn't want us to apply for compensation for the accident. . . ."

And, Freddie concurring with this suggestion, they left at once for House Services: where they found a grim-faced Mrs. Mossley at work on the first page of the House Services Circular, and Mr. Chadderton, looking frail and hungover, sucking a restorative barley-sugar at his desk. Of Ken Oldham, there was no sign.

The shop stewards summed up the situation with the eyes of long experience, and, having nodded a greeting to Amos, turned their attentions to his secretary.

"Maureen, love. That Ken Oldham of yours—"

"He's no man of mine!" Mrs. Mossley glared at them, and thumped her typewriter with an irritable fist. "You can take him, and welcome!"

"No fear," said Freddie at once, while Charley chuckled.

"Of your department's, then." Amos, who'd emerged from this brooding to wonder what they wanted, thought about correcting this, but the moment was already lost. Charley spoke in urgent tones.

"Before he comes back to this office—by the way, d'you know where he's gone?"

She shrugged. "He could be anywhere. Probably checking on the photocopiers, from the way he's been moaning about them the last day or so—unless he's doing his usual trick of using it as an excuse to cover up something else. Your guess is as g—"

"The Warehouse!" cried Freddie and Charley as one.

"But surely he'd never dare"—from Freddie, furious—
"go prowling about in there without asking, would he?"

"He would, all right," said Charley; and Maureen nodded.

"You know what he's like. When you want him, you
can't find him, bleeper or not—and when you don't want
him, up he pops like a rabbit out of a hole." She sighed.
"Did you boys really come bothering me in the middle of
my work just to talk about Ken Oldham?"

"In a manner of speaking," began Charley.

Freddie was less circumspect. "Yes," he said, and
scowled at his more cautious colleague. "Has Oldham ever
asked you to do any, well, special typing? Extra work—"

"Huh!" Maureen thumped her innocent typewriter again.
"Has he! You should just read what he's ever-so-nicely
made me put on the front page of this week's House
Services Circular!"

Charley looked at Freddie. Freddie looked at Charley.
"He'd never," breathed Freddie, "do it as public as
that—would he? Not without fair warning!"

Charley looked at Maureen. "If he has, then there's a
warning gone missing, somewhere along the line. You'd tell
us if there was anything funny going on, wouldn't you?"

"I don't see you can call the buses *funny*, exactly—"

"Buses? What buses?" But Charley did not wait for an
answer. "This is nothing to do with buses—this is important." He glanced over his shoulder and lowered his voice.
"Look, has Oldham ever given you anything to type up
about—well, about the new computer—about using it in the
Warehouse?" He lowered his voice still more. "Secret
reports, Maureen—reports that he maybe asked you—you
know, not to mention to anyone else?"

She looked puzzled. "Heaven knows he's not shy about
giving me stuff to type—there's almost a whole shelf full of
just his files in my cabinet—but I can't say I remember
anything about the Warehouse."

Charley nodded. Freddie nudged him. Charley frowned.
"I don't suppose, love, you'd happen to know where
Oldham, er, keeps his reports before he hands them in for
typing? Or his notes, stuff like that—the rough work?"

Maureen gazed at her half-typed Circular. "When it's

notes, he mostly keeps them on that damned clipboard—the swanky black one he takes everywhere with him so he can get his ideas down on paper before he forgets them.'' She rolled her eyes. ''And don't we wish he would!''

''What does he do with them afterwards?''

''Before he works them up into reports, you mean? Puts them in one of the filing trays on his desk, I suppose—if it's not something he wants to use when he goes off round the building for a snoop.'' She sniffed. ''When he runs out of steam, he sorts them out and writes another of his damned reports, and yours truly has to type it—like all this rubbish about the car park and the buses—''

''Never mind the buses!'' The interests of the Warehouse were what concerned the shop stewards now, not this mysterious transport system which so obsessed Mrs. Mossley. ''So, if someone was to have a look at Oldham's desk-top files . . .''

It dawned on Maureen that they were perfectly serious. She looked from Charley to Freddie, and from Freddie glanced at Amos, who, still frail, had closed his eyes and retreated to his hangover. Maureen—as so often in the past—was going to have to trust her own judgement.

She frowned. ''If I know Clem Bradshaw,'' she said slowly, ''he won't be at all pleased about what Ken Oldham's got planned. Could be quite a nasty shock when he reads about it in the Circular—and I wouldn't like that. In fact, as soon as I've finished typing, I'm going to take a—a sort of advanced copy for him, before I send it along to Reprographics for printing. And if there happened to be anything you two wanted copying, while I'm at the machine . . .''

''Maureen, you're a star.'' Charley paused to clap her on the shoulder before heading for Ken's desk: Freddie, with a grin, had already reached it. Amos, as soon as they'd gone, opened one eye and favoured Mrs. Mossley with a reproachful look—but for once she ignored him, busy with her typing. Whereupon, with a quiet groan, he slumped back on his chair and dug in his desk for more barley-sugar.

Dick Slack and Sadie Halliwell, who'd hardly had time to greet the two Union men as they hurried through the office to speak with Maureen Mossley, looked on with interest as

Mr. Marks stationed himself on watch, and Mr. Seraphim began a systematic hunt through the sheaves of notes— paper-clipped, stapled, india-tagged—which lay in the high stacking trays beside Ken Oldham's blotter. The air was filled with a fusillade of typing as Maureen provided camouflage for the most public burglary the department had ever known.

"Found it!" Freddie's cry of triumph coincided almost exactly with the speedy zipping sound which showed that Mrs. Mossley had completed her first page. "But—oh, that devil of an Oldham—listen, Charley! *Some Proposals Concerning the Use of the New Tesbury Computer Facility for Improvement of Stock Control and Intensification of Warehouse Security*—bloody hell, this is dynamite!"

"Then stop waving it about like that, can't you?"

As Charley finished speaking, Maureen appeared behind him. "Freddie—here, give me that, quick, and I'll nip down to the copier with it. Let's hope he doesn't come back and spot it's gone—we want it back in place as soon as possible. You can read it through somewhere else—and for goodness' sake don't you ever let on it was me!"

For his pension's sake, Amos, behind his screen, shuddered. Charley and Freddie shuddered too, but for different reasons.

"A scandal—a ruddy scandal, that's the only word for it, Fred. After all these years, to be treated like this by a—by a blasted machine and a know-all paper-pusher!"

"The lads will never stand for it, of course." Freddie's eyes gleamed with the light of battle. "They'll say it's an insult, and they won't be far wrong. Repercussions, that's what there'll be, mark my words—"

"We'll have to study this perishing report very carefully before we tell 'em," cautioned Charley, as ever the voice of reason. "We got to be absolutely sure—"

"I read the first paragraph," Freddie reminded him. "You didn't. And I know what I read—and there's worse to come, see if I'm not right. It's all down there in black and white—and we've got to do something about it! And it isn't as if it's just losing the perks, neither. He talks about *rationalisation*, too—*losing jobs*, Charley. . . ."

Charley, shocked, was speechless. Even Dick and Sadie, puzzled onlookers, sympathised with the stricken Union men as they understood the full and terrible truth of Ken Oldham's intentions, and could find nothing to say. Only fiery Freddie Seraphim managed to give tongue as he said, his jaw jutting in defiance, his face purpling:

"Something's got to be done about him, Charley—quick." And Mr. Marks could do nothing but nod in fervent reply.

"Don't make such a racket—someone'll hear you!" Maureen was back from the photocopier, the guilty files in her hand. She passed one set, still warm, to Charley, and the other to Freddie, who replaced it among Ken's papers with a grateful wink and a relieved sigh. Her finger to her lips, Mrs. Mossley went back to her desk in silence; and in silence the two shop stewards stared at their bootlegged prize. Mr. Seraphim, impatient as ever, started to reread that first, damning page, while Charley Marks, fascinated, found himself peering over his colleague's shoulder. . . .

Sadie cleared her throat. "If you *must* read that here, I'd move away from Ken's desk, if I were you."

Charley jumped. "Hell's bells, she's right. From a distance, he'd never recognise this, but close to—well, he's no fool." He dragged his colleague across to Sadie's desk. "Mind if we take a seat? May as well know the worst as soon as possible. . . ." And knowing it first in a public place might dissuade Freddie from creating one of his more spectacular scenes, for which Mr. Marks did not feel himself at the moment ready.

The two Union men studied the document in a grim and speaking silence. Sadie could almost swear she saw steam coming out of their ears as she watched for Ken and watched her visitors in turn. She looked at Dick, who mimed frantic curiosity: if Charley and Freddie found out anything exciting, he hoped (as did Sadie) they'd share the excitement before they left House Services.

They did . . . in a way. Freddie scowled as he came to the bottom of the final page. "This won't do, you know, and we've got to tell the Management so—fast. We'll call the whole Warehouse out the minute we can, and tell 'em what our friend Oldham's got planned for changing their jobs—''

"How," enquired Dick, unable to bear the suspense, "are they going to be changed?"

Cautious Charley spoke before Freddie could let too many cats out of the bag. "We'll be off now, before Oldham gets back—we'd like to read it right through again, slowly, before we say anything. We don't want to run the risk of any misunderstanding the Management could latch on to later—"

"There's no misunderstanding about this, Charley Marks!" Freddie snatched at the report as his friend took and folded it and thrust it into his pocket. "If there's a man in the Warehouse," stormed Freddie, "who won't say it's a downright shame and scandal—losing our perks, losing our jobs, treating us like this after all these years—"

"We have to be sure of the facts!" Charley had a dogged streak in him. "We need to know *exactly* what it is that's wrong before we take action about it—"

"Action!" Freddie leaped to his feet. "We'll call the whole place out—twelve o'clock on the dot, that's when, and we'll tell them all about *that*!" And he pointed a dramatic finger toward Charley's coat pocket.

"Oh no, Fred. They won't want that—not twelve o'clock and mucking about with the dinner break. Make it half past eleven, if you like—then it won't matter so much."

"So we *are* going to have a protest!" Mr. Seraphim pounced with enthusiasm on the one vital fact in his more prudent colleague's advice. "Half past eleven, then, not a minute later—and we'll tell everyone what's going on!"

Charley sighed, nodded, and patted his pocket in a meaningful fashion. "Oh, yes, we'll have a protest— nothing else we can do, if this report's telling the truth. But we don't put the word round, mind, until we've gone through it all again—"

"Then," broke in Sadie Halliwell, efficient as ever, "it really would be more sensible for you to go back to the Warehouse to sort things out. If Ken comes in now—"

"You're right, love." Charley, preoccupied with his troubled, nodded absently, and didn't see her wince at this mode of address. "We'll be off—and thanks for the lend of your chairs. Come on, Fred—and thanks to you, too, Maureen,'' he called in the direction of Mr. Chadderton's secretary, as he and his colleague took their leave.

Maureen waved good-bye, but Amos groaned again as he contemplated the unorthodox behaviour of certain members of his staff, and how it would look if anyone ever found out, and of how serious the loss of his pension would be. . . .

But before he could force himself, from the depths of his misery, to speak a gentle word of reproof to Mrs. Mossley, Ken Oldham came bouncing back into the House Services department.

──────── Twelve ────────

HE GREETED DICK and Sadie with an airy wave of his clipboard, and they saw that the top sheet of the thick pad of paper fastened to it was covered with neat tables of figures and written calculations.

"Remember, Dicky boy, how we had that little discussion on Friday about the photocopiers?"

Mr. Slack nodded grimly: he'd ended that discussion with the distinct feeling that, for once, Ken Oldham had been successfully squashed. Something in Ken's manner, however, now gave Dick the distinct feeling he'd been wrong. . . .

"Well, Dicky, I took your advice, and I've been monitoring the situation around the building at statistically significant, although random, intervals—there are so many other claims on my time, you understand." The word *preen* might have been invented for Ken Oldham in his present mood. "But I should say that my three days' observation has resulted in sufficient data to make an educated guess at what the usage is likely to be during a typical working week. . . ."

Uninvited, he drew up Mr. Slack's visitors' chair, sat down, and prepared to argue the matter out in comfort. "Now then, Dick. If we extrapolate the mean average throughput from each twenty-minute period of observ—"

"Oh, do speak English." Dick was even less in the mood for Ken's jargon than usual. Sadie grinned at him sideways, and stuck out her tongue, unobserved, behind Ken's back. Mr. Slack stopped scowling.

Mr. Oldham noticed nothing. Full of new ideas for the streamlining of yet another Tesbury operation, he would probably not have noticed if Dick had tried to shout him down, instead of merely snarling. When Ken had a theory to propound, he concentrated on that propounding, and on nothing else.

"I've been to every copier in the building, Dick—two on each floor apart from the second, with three, right?"

"Well, apart from my monsters in Reprographics, yes."

"Never mind them—for the moment," he added, leaving Mr. Slack to wonder what the future might hold. "I'm talking about the casual copiers, where people can simply wander up as they please and copy whatever they want. Now, judging by what I've seen for myself—and what I've made a note of here"—he tapped his clipboard with a didactic finger—"at least one-third of the secretaries' time is taken up with what I call the complete photocopying experience: walking to and from the machine, queueing to use it, waiting for one of your staff to come and sort things out when there's a problem—jammed paper, empty toner drums, a blocked filter—"

"You're not telling me anything I don't already know by heart," Dick broke in, with a sigh. "Yes, the system's not perfect, but it's the best I've been able to manage in over two years of trying. And other people tried before me, with about as much success. It can't be done, that's all—as I thought," waspishly, "I'd made plain to you on Friday."

Ken waved his clipboard again. "Proof that it can, Dick—if you'd just listen to me instead of perpetuating all the negative feelings you've been conditioned to accept as true. Just take a look at my figures, Dicky boy!"

"I'd rather look at the real thing, thanks." Dick pushed back his chair and rose to his full height, goaded beyond endurance by this bumptious newcomer's insistence that he'd fallen down on the job. Yes, the photocopiers were a problem—he'd never denied it: but better men like Ken Oldham had wrestled with that problem and given up in despair. Mr. Slack's predecessor had departed Tesbury's, a broken man, for the relative peace of a North Sea oil rig. What did Ken Oldham know of the realities of the House Services department? All he seemed to know were figures and statistics and surveys and reports—and he was bright enough, Dick had to acknowledge, to be able to adjust every one of his calculations to prove whatever point he wanted to make. There was only one way to argue with him—face facts with facts.

"I'm going round all the copiers myself, right now," he told an astounded Ken, who'd expected the conversation to take a far different direction. "And I'm going to see just how many secretaries *I* find queueing up to use them—and I'm going to ask every single one of their bosses if they think it damned well matters!" With which, he stalked off past Sadie's desk, not even pausing to acknowledge her amused and sympathetic smile.

"Good God." Ken stared after Dick's disappearing form in apparently genuine surprise. "Whatever's the matter with him?"

Maureen Mossley stifled a snigger. Amos suppressed a chuckle. Sadie, hearing them, thought quickly.

"Take no notice—I think he had a heavy night of it in the pub yesterday. Or something," she added, for she was on the whole a truthful person. "But I expect, when he's had time to check things out for himself, he might be more, er, receptive to what you want to tell him. After all, it's in his best interests to do his job the most efficient way possible, isn't it?" Inspiration struck. "Suppose you were to explain it to me first—then I could try talking it over later with Dick, perhaps when you aren't here. I'm sure," with some asperity, "you could always find an excuse for not being at your desk for a while."

"Oh." Ken regarded Ms. Halliwell doubtfully. "I hadn't actually planned to go anywhere else today—now I've finished checking the copiers, I'm going to write up my notes into a preliminary report."

Honesty, in its place, was all very well, but . . . And Sadie ground her teeth in exasperation for a Management Consultant who, even in his own interests, didn't know how to conjure up a little deception and deceit. Surely these were the very foundations of his job? "Weren't you talking on Friday about checking the Archives?" She fixed him with a pointed stare, wondering whether the penny would drop. "But never mind that for now. Come on over and show me your sums—I'm sure we'll think of something, between us. . . ."

A gentle murmuring ensued, as together they began to pore over a ream of mathematical scribblings. Amos Chadderton drifted back into his doze, wondering how much longer it was until lunchtime. Maureen Mossley resumed her secretarial duties and answered the telephone when necessary. . . .

"I hope I'm not breaking anything up." Dick Slack had returned from his copier excursion, with less iron in his tone and less steam coming out of his ears than anyone would have expected. He appeared, indeed, almost smug. "Now I've had a look for myself, and talked to a few people, I don't mind taking a gander at these circulations of yours, Ken. Old boy. All right with you?"

The little consultation at Sadie's desk broke up at once as the Management Consultant seized his clipboard and prepared to do battle for his theories: he had the distinct impression, from Dick's air of triumph, that he wasn't going to have it all his own way.

Sadie seemed pleased about something. "I think," she remarked to nobody in particular, "I'd be interested to see what's happening for myself," and she hurried off without another word. Ken and Dick, plunging into a flurry of calculation and controversy, hardly noticed her departure, and were caught by surprise when she came cheerfully back to interrupt them by saying, with a broad grin:

"Ken, if I told you how many executive suits and middle management waistcoats were waiting around for cups of coffee out of the machine on the second floor, you'd never believe me. I'd make a sizeable bet with you that *they* cost the company more in wasted time than ever the copiers do!"

Ken gaped at her; and Dick grinned as she went on, nodding towards the wall through which, had it been windowed, the Warehouse might have been seen. "I saw *them*, too. Eleven-thirty on the dot, and the whole place coming out dead on time. But don't let my silly female chatter disturb you men from your all-important work, will you?"

Dick chuckled as she sat at her desk and buried herself in furniture catalogues. Good old Sadie: she hadn't defected to the enemy after all; and the thought inspired him to ever more forceful argument with Ken Oldham, who wasn't going to give up his theories easily. It was a fairly even contest. Both men were convinced they each knew what they were talking about. Ken quoted statistics by the dozen; Dick capped them with instances from real life. Ken reminded him that the exception proved the rule; Dick said that the only rule was that everything should work—that the old system did—and that it would be risky to alter it on the off chance of something better.

Amos was enthralled by the discussion as it raged to and fro. It was Old Tesbury versus New—it was proven practice against theory—it was—

It was interrupted. "*Dingdong!* Would any members of staff with cars parked in the road please move them now, as the traffic wardens are just about to inspect this part of their route, and police warn that obstructing cars are likely to be towed away. All car owners to move their cars immediately, please."

Muffled curses came from every corner of the building, most of them unprintable. In Accounts, Angela Farnworth raised her voice to express the sentiments of the majority of Tesbury motorists.

"If something isn't done soon about that car park, I shall sue—I really shall!"

In the Visual Display Unit section, operators switched off their machines and leapt for the lift without waiting for the supervisor's permission. "Bet they still dock our wages, no matter how quick we are," someone said, as the lift took its time in arriving. "That car park!"

"That computer," corrected her next-door neighbour. "If it wasn't for that, we wouldn't be having to sit staring at those horrible green screens hour after hour. . . ."

In House Services, Ken Oldham paused in his impassioned plea to Dick to *at least let me run through it once with you* as he cried:

"Half a minute, Dicky boy—I don't want my wheels clamped, do I? Be back in no time!" And was gone before Dick could think of a rude reply.

"I wish he hadn't taken that clipboard of his," he said to

Sadie, who'd looked up from her brochures and was smiling to herself. "I'd love a proper look at it without him there trying to confuse me—I *know* I'm right and he's wrong, but somehow he always manages to run circles round me. . . ."

"You ought," said Sadie, "to have the courage of your convictions. She thrust the brochures to one side and began to rummage in her toolbox. "If you're so sure he's wrong, why not do a proper survey of your own, to prove it? You virtually started one earlier, after all. If Ken and I can stand about for minutes at a time watching people use photocopiers and coffee machines, I don't see there's anything to stop you."

Dick regarded her with awe. "Brilliant, Sadie! Thanks—a proper survey of my own. And thanks for squashing him like that, too. Er—by the way, was it true?"

"About the coffee machines?" She sat up, brandishing a large spanner, and smiled again. "Of course it was. Would I be daft enough to risk having him pull me up on it later? But what I *didn't* tell him was that there was also a queue at the ladies' loo on the second floor!" She rose to her feet. "Why those idiot females can't comb their hair somewhere else except right over the basin, I'll never know—and why they haven't the sense to go to one of the other loos, instead of cluttering up the landing giggling and screeching like a load of parrots—"

"Sexist," he interjected, as she drew breath. She opened her mouth to deny the charges, then laughed.

"You could be right—no, you're not. I'm stupidityist, if there *is* such a word. There damned well ought to be, for that lot on the second floor! I stuck the notice back, and gave them all a piece of my mind, but I'd better go and fix it before Ken finds out. . . ."

Dick watched her go and sighed. That Call Janice had just put out was guaranteed to cause chaos. Any minute now the telephones would start to ring with complaints from car owners, departmental managers, and anyone else who felt like a good moan about the way House Services coped with things.

He went to let Amos know he was ready for the fray. Mr. Chadderton was speaking into the telephone. "You don't have any idea where he's gone? . . . Well, please ask him to ring me as soon as he gets back. . . . Yes, it is, rather. . . . Or he could come to see me, if he'd prefer. . . . Yes. Good-bye.''

He looked up, saw Dick, and waved him into the office. ''Clem isn't there—not that I blame him—''

He got no further. Replacing the receiver had left his telephone free to ring, which it now did. Amos groaned as he picked it up; and the subsequent discussion, whose sense was only too clear to the sympathetic ears of Dick and Maureen, evoked even more groans as it ended.

''I'm sorry, we have absolutely no control over the Allingham traffic wardens. . . . No, I should think it highly unlikely the company will pay the fines of anyone whose car is impounded. . . . Well, I really don't see how you can blame *me* for the weather!''

He dropped the receiver with a clatter and buried his face in his hands. ''Maureen,'' he moaned, ''*please* would—''

The telephone rang again. Mrs. Mossley snatched it up without hesitation. ''Mr. Chadderton? I'm afraid he's not available at the moment. . . . Car parking? I really think you ought to speak to Mr. Bradshaw of Transport about that.'' And she depressed the cradle, released it, and left the receiver lying on the desk, so that the line was blocked.

Five seconds later, there came a summons from Dick's telephone, beyond the screen. He winced and made no move to answer it.

''This, you know, is going to be a very long day. And if we haven't all been lynched by the end, it'll be a miracle.''

Amos raised his head, his eyes dull behind his spectacles, as Sadie's telephone, too, began to ring. ''Clem Bradshaw is probably outside this minute, watching everyone move their cars and feeling sorry for himself—but no sorrier than we feel here. Oh, dear. . . .''

''Feeling sorry for yourself isn't a lot of good,'' Maureen said, ''but if you ask me, Clem's found the answer, all right. Never there when you want him, is he? Leaves everything to Mary, like when you wanted to talk to him about Ken Oldham's piece in the Circular about the buses.''

''Ken. Yes.'' Amos sighed, listening to the rhythmic

scream of the telephones in the main office. "I wonder if it might just be worth trying, after all. The Board . . ."

"The Board," Dick reminded him, "will be in no mood for ideas unless they've been planned right to the last detail, after today, what with the car owners and the Warehouse both stopping work within half an hour of each other—"

"I heard Sadie say they were out." Amos sighed again. "But nothing to do with us, thank goodness," with a pointed look for Maureen as he remembered her illicit photocopying. "Charley Marks and Freddie Seraphim and the Union people and nobody else—except the Board, when the time comes. We've enough worries of our own, haven't we?"

And Maureen, listening like her boss to the telephones, nodded; and Dick, feeling guilty about ignoring that relentless ringing, pulled a face.

"We certainly have." He rolled his eyes. "Here we are, not yet halfway through the week—and how much worse can things possibly get?"

Before very long, they were to find out.

———— Thirteen ————

DICK HAD JUST announced his plans for escaping on the first
stage of his photocopier survey when Sadie came back with
tousled hair, damp hands, and a cross expression. "If
anyone with a degree in plumbing ever applies for a job in
this department, bags I first refusal!" Her eyes were bright
and her face was pink as she poured out her woes to her
colleagues. "That damned loo is still awash with water—
and for no earthly reason, as far as I can tell. Nothing seems
to be blocked—the toilets flush okay—I've cleared all the
sinks and basins again—and do you think I can find
Biddy?"

Amos duly applied his deductive powers. "That new
battery of hers must have been a dud, I suppose."

Sadie shook her head. "She's probably damaged it
without realising. Every time I dial the number, all I get is
the engaged tone. Call me irresponsible if you like, but I
really don't want to go rushing up there with a mop and a
bucket, slippery floor or no slippery floor. How the hell do
we find her?"

"Suppose," suggested Maureen, who'd been secretly
amused at the bandbox-neat Ms. Halliwell's dishevelled
state, "you pop along to powder your nose while we try for
you."

"Thanks—you've saved my life." Sadie, unaware of the
snub, smiled with gratitude. "I'll be back as soon as . . ."

Before she'd finished speaking, Mrs. Mossley was recon-
necting the telephone to feed the three-digit number into the
bleeper system. She frowned. "Engaged, all right, but I'll
keep trying. For one thing," she added grimly, "it'll stop
people ringing up about the cars, won't it?"

Amos was still chuckling quietly to himself when Sadie
reappeared at his office entrance. Maureen greeted her with

the news that she'd had no better luck raising the cleaner than Ms. Halliwell had had earlier. Visions of mops danced before Sadie's eyes, and she sighed. Maureen added:

"I think something must be wrong with the whole system. Remember it jammed once before, when someone knocked a telephone off their desk right in the middle of dialling? I bet that's what's happened—in all the rush to go and move the cars. . . ."

Sadie remembered: it seemed a likely enough explanation. "I'll go and check with the Switchboard," she said. "They can put out a Call for her at the same time—yes, I know everyone will moan, but it's better than broken legs and the company being sued for negligence, isn't it?" She was her normal unruffled self once more, decisive and efficient. "But thanks again for trying."

Maureen hung up her telephone as Sadie departed: and it rang. She cursed. With an apologetic cough, Amos picked up the other extension.

While he was still striving to excuse the shortcomings of the Tesbury car park to the irate voice on the other end of the line, the Call went out from the ceiling.

"*Dingdong!* Calling Biddy Hiscock of House Services— would you please telephone your department at once. Biddy Hiscock to ring House Services immediately, please."

Which then involved Mr. Chadderton in a prolonged explanation of why the working day seemed to be interrupted every five minutes by *those damned tannoy messages*—of how the resultant loss of (a) concentration and (b) productivity were hardly his department's fault—of how he had no intention of absorbing the cost of such losses into the House Services budget. . . .

Dick Slack reappeared in the middle of all this, muttering that nobody from the department was safe anywhere while all this was going on, and listened grimly as Amos spluttered—and eventually stormed—at the angry undermanager on the other end of the line. Sadie returned as Mr. Chadderton banged down the receiver to break the connection, then lifted it at once to stop other calls coming through. He groped for a barley-sugar stick and muttered as fiercely as ever Dick had done.

Sadie ignored the mutterings, "Any word from Biddy yet?" Maureen shook her head. Sadie frowned. "Odd— she's usually very reliable. She must have been waylaid somewhere—got stuck in the lift, perhaps." She shrugged. "Oh, well—it's mop-and-bucket time for yours truly, after all, and never mind what I said before."

Dick couldn't resist the chance to wind her up. "She's probably joined the other car movers and skived off for an early lunch. But if you need a hand, I'd be happy—"

"Biddy comes to work by bike," Sadie said, looking grimly at her mischievous colleague. "She wouldn't need to go outside to move anything. I'm sure," she said hopefully, "she'll be here soon."

Amos nodded, and said through mouthfuls of clear orange crystal: "Yes, I've always thought of Mrs. Hiscock as one of the most conscientious members of House Services. I'm sure there will be a good reason for—"

"And they say," broke in a cheerful voice from the other side of the screen, "listeners never hear any good of themselves! Just goes to show they're not always right. Thanks for the vote of confidence, Mr. Chadderton." Biddy Hiscock, mop and bucket in her hand, manifested herself in Amos's office looking as damp and dishevelled as Sadie Halliwell had been ten minutes earlier. "Sorry," said the cleaner, "not to have answered as soon as you put out that Call, but I was in the second floor ladies again—someone said there was a great puddle all over the floor, and when I saw your notice, Miss Halliwell, I thought to myself, *Biddy, my girl, you did really ought to get that there cleaned up before somebody goes tumbling*, that's what I thought. So that's what I did. And then I thought, *Well, I'm away for my dinner in a bit, and no phone handy to ring the office, so why not just ask 'em what they want when I pop in to say I'm off home. . . .*"

She waited, her head cocked to one side, for someone to explain why they'd put out the Call—and why, after looking at one another in silence for a few moments, they'd burst—all four of them—into hysterical laughter.

The protest meeting was over. Charley Marks and Freddie Seraphim had spoken with much eloquence of Management's duplicity, and the insult of Warehouse integrity, and the need to register strong disapproval in an atmosphere of worker solidarity. Then, as Freddie's oratory showed signs of encroaching on his colleagues' lunch break, Charley called a halt; and everyone, with loud cheers, agreed by the show of hands that this sort of thing wasn't to be put up with, and that the two Union men should discuss the matter with the Board as soon as possible. And then they all went off for something to eat.

Exactly on the hour, they returned to work. They had a fair idea of how long it would take, at a slightly forced but steady pace, for them to catch up on what they'd missed: old habits die hard when you can still recall a shirtsleeved Jem Tesbury joining in as the fancy took him, toiling as hard as any of the Warehouse men, approachable to the end.

"Jem would never have tried to put this one over on us," lamented loyal Old Tesbury. "Not without listening to what we had to say, at least!" And so, fired with the best of intentions, they resumed their abandoned tasks.

Some were able to do so much easily than others. Young Ted, still finding his feet among the close-knit community, supposed someone must be having a joke at his expense when he returned to where he'd left his forklift truck and found it gone. But the lads didn't mean it unkindly, he was sure. Every job has its initiation ceremonies, and maybe this was one of them.

"Lost something, son?" Ernie Oswald, longest-serving of the Warehouse team, had been enjoying a last few moments of sunshine before going back inside. "What's wrong?"

"Oh, well." Ted, the good sport, tried to grin, though he couldn't help feeling a little anxious. "It's my forklift, see—seems to have taken a walk. Won't be too far away, I expect. Someone's just having a bit of fun."

Ernie mopped his streaming brow as he gazed around the sheltered spot where no breeze, no matter how determined, on such a day could make itself felt. "Left it just here, did you?" Ted nodded. Ernie looked at him. "Just what was it you was working on, son?"

"Unloading a lorry—halfway through I must've bin,

when I heard about the walkout. That lorry over there," as Ernie looked at him again. The older man sighed.

"That lorry, you mean?" He jerked a scornful thumb toward a gleaming white juggernaut nearby. "Fresh 'N' Frozen Foodstuffs *is* the one you're talking about?"

"Well, yes. Just got another pallet down, I had—"

"And thought it might fancy a nice suntan while you was off having your dinner, did you?" Ernie sighed, but it came as no real surprise to him, after so many years, that some people could be so stupid. "You never thought it might not do it any good sitting around for a couple of hours when the temperature's in the eighties?"

Ted's guilty gasp and flush of dismay were answers enough. Ernie sighed again. "And what was on the pallet, if one may make so bold as to enquire?"

"Fish fingers," Ted told him, ashamed, turning pale at the realisation of what he'd done. "Jumbo packs—but honest, Ernie, I never thought!"

"You never do, you youngsters. Still wet behind the ears, most of you. No more sense than the day you was born, not even to work out what's happened to that truck of yours instead of getting yourself in a right old state about it."

"Oh. What—what *has* happened to it?"

"What's happened, son, is that someone with a sight more brains than you's shifted it out of the sun to stop it spoiling. A whole pallet loaded up—nobody's going to let that go to waste, never mind your job on the line, too, I should think. You oughter thank your lucky stars as somebody saw fit to do you a good turn. But it's not going to keep cool forever, not even inside—so you'd best get weaving and find it, hadn't you? What are you waiting for?"

"N-nothing, Ernie. Thanks!" And Ted was gone, questing into the bowels of the Warehouse after his errant forklift truck. Ernie grinned as he watched him scamper off. The lad wouldn't do too badly, once he found his feet. Not one of those making out they knew it all—seemed willing to learn, and not likely to make the same mistake twice. And didn't try to off-load the dirty jobs on other people. . . .

Inside the cavernous and echoing gloom of the Warehouse, Ted peered thoughtfully down every aisle for some sign of the vanished vehicle. Anyone could have moved it: the controls were pretty basic. A competent motorist could understand them in minutes. It needn't have been one of his mates who'd shifted the thing: perhaps a passing clerical worker, knowing the Warehouse to be busy protesting, had taken pity on both load and absent driver, and had moved the melting cargo out of harm's way. . . .

The aisles were full of activity as Ted's colleagues caught up their missing minutes. Ted asked, and asked, and always had no for an answer. He was laughed at (though not unkindly) and told that exercise was good for him, and sent trotting off down yet another wide metal aisle piled high with racks of pallets, dotted with small groups of men busy around the bottoms of towering columns of foodstuffs.

Now he was approaching territory he'd had no occasion to explore during his few days with Tesbury's: a deeply shadowed and rather sinister back area, where the slowest-moving and least-called-for merchandise was stored. Ted had no idea why he shivered amid the gloom, but as he walked farther from company and closer to the unknown, he was unaccountably relieved to realise he wasn't alone in such a strangely forbidding place. Somewhere in the distance, as yet invisible, somebody else was with him: he could hear the high-pitched sounds of a bleeper, and bleepers didn't go walkabout by themselves any more than did forklift trucks.

Probably this bloke with the bleeper was the one who'd moved his truck in the first place. Ted would thank him for saving the load, but ask him why he'd had to take it so far away. It was really rather spooky now, all alone between the rows of pallet stacks, nothing to see but shadows. . . .

No, he wasn't all alone. There was whoever was wearing that bleeper, too—that insistent, nagging bleeper, bleeping on and on, unanswered. Why didn't the chap answer it? Surely he could find a phone somewhere near and dial into the system to shut off that repetitive, pestering summons?

"Oh, blimey!" Ted had rounded the corner of the stack in the farthest aisle, and now saw what had happened to his purloined load of fish fingers. It lay spread on the floor in an untidy heap, spilling soggily from burst cardboard boxes.

The corner of the pallet seemed to have been caught on something, almost as if it had been raised up to the underside of the topmost shelf and, forced still farther, had broken, displacing its load, sending it smashing and crashing down about the base of the stolen forklift truck.

"Vandals! Oh, the—the buggers!" moaned Ted, as he saw bonus and wages and even job going down the drain with the slowly melting ice. Why had someone picked on *him* as the victim of this cruel trick? *Who* could have done it—who in the Tesbury Warehouse was so spiteful and destructive?

The monotonous call of the bleeper broke through Ted's misery and confusion. Was the perpetrator of this vandalism hiding somewhere close by to gloat over the success of his malicious joke?

And was he also deaf?

"Oh, blimey!" Ted had drawn closer to the wreckage and started to examine it. The owner of the bleeper was indeed close by—and deaf. But not in a way the youngster could ever have dreamed. . . .

The owner of the bleeper, hearing nothing now but the sounds of the eternal dark, lay underneath Ted's load of frozen fish fingers, crushed and squashed and, beyond any doubt, dead.

——— Fourteen ———

THE MUGS WERE empty, the buns no more than a memory. Stone tossed the last crumbs out of the nearest window for the benefit of the sparrows roistering in the dust-bath of the flowerbed that was normally Sergeant Pleate's pride and joy. Trewley watched her in absent approval. She was a good girl, for all her nonsense: she'd known he was hot and tired, and had done her best to cheer him up. Anything rather than have to face Pleate at his most indignant. . . .

The telephone rang. Trewley, who had been intent on his brooding, blinked, sighed, and reached out slowly. Stone's reflexes were faster.

"Mr. Trewley's office—Sergeant Stone speaking. . . . What? Are you sure? . . . Good heavens!" She stifled what sounded, to a suspicious superintendent, like a giggle. "Yes, we'll be there as soon as we can. . . ."

She hung up and turned to Trewley, her eyes sparkling. "Well, sir, if you're serious about wanting a—an unusual job, the very thing's just come up—at Tesbury's, of all unlikely places. That was—"

"I've no intention of becoming a store detective, my girl. This time, you've gone too far—" But even as he grumbled, he was rising from his chair; somehow, he didn't think she'd been joking.

"No, sir! That was Pleate on the phone. Tesbury's have just rung in to report a murder—the weirdest thing you ever heard of . . ."

They stood quietly together, staring at the soggy mess of tattered cardboard and torn plastic and slowly melting frozen fish on the Warehouse floor, watching the forensic team as they toiled among the confusion.

"Coshed first, then had this lot dumped on top of him,"

said Stone, the voice of experience. "A conscious man would have spotted the truck coming up behind him—they only go about five miles an hour, don't they? He'd have had plenty of time to hop out of the way if he'd been awake."

Trewley looked with disfavour upon the forklift truck, now surrounded by a welter of intense investigation. "Ugh. I always thought those things were supposed to be foolproof—and safe. But no cracks about how everyone's got to be wrong once, girl. It's far too hot, even in here. . . ." With a sigh, he tore his gaze away from the icy patches on the floor and looked about him.

"Mr. Oswald?" Ernie, who had been hovering in the shadows, duly approached. "Mr. Oswald—how did he do it? Not too technical, mind," as Ernie opened his mouth. "My sergeant here's been educated, you know. You'll have to spell it out in words of one syllable for her, or she'll never make out what you're saying."

Ernie, looking taken aback, closed his mouth again, but Stone winked at him, and he ventured the faintest of grins in reply. He wasn't feeling particularly cheerful. Still, the chance to hold forth on this expertise was always welcome. He cleared his throat.

"Didn't put his forks in." He thumped one of the pallets on a nearby stack with an expressive fist, then thrust an arm between the rough wooded struts. "One of the first things we tell our new drivers, about putting their forks in good and proper—"

He broke off, glanced at Stone, coughed, and cleared his throat again. Stone sighed faintly; Trewley frowned, just enough to warn Mr. Oswald he'd better watch his step. There was a pause.

It was broken by Stone. "So you're saying he left half the length of the fork sticking out? Then what?" as he nodded. Ernie pointed upwards.

"Then, if the front edge catches under anything—as it might be that top shelf, see?—with the fork not being able to support all the weight, the pallet'd tip, and the nails'd get pulled out—and down she comes! I reckon that's what happened here. Made enough mess, hasn't it? And that there shelf looks a bit dented, from where I'm standing."

Both detectives followed his pointing finger and agreed that it did. Trewley gave instructions for the shelf to be included in the forensic examination, then returned to his expert witness.

"Easy to drive one of these forklifts, is it?"

Ernie's professional pride was piqued. It meant higher wages when you were promoted from ordinary goods-handling to driving the trucks. "Need proper training, of course, can't just have anyone—oh." It had dawned on him that he wasn't exactly diverting suspicion from his workmates. "Not that an ordinary driver couldn't work out the controls for himself in a few minutes—the basics, anyway. I mean, stop, go, forwards, back, up, down—not with a load on, maybe, but they could *move* the thing, all right, given time."

"Which they had," Stone reminded him. "When did your protest meeting start—eleven-thirty? And the truck and the body not found for a couple of hours. Plenty of time to study the mechanics, especially in a place like this, miles out of everyone's way."

"Any chance," enquired Trewley, "it could have been an accident?"

Ernie snorted. "Those forks didn't get up there above that shelf without somebody raising 'em *after* they'd been caught underneath and broke the pallet—and there's no way he could've reached the lever from where he's lying *before* it broke. That weren't no accident, believe me. Nobody'd stand smack under that lot and let it fall on 'em if they'd got the choice of it. . . ."

Ernie shuddered at the memory of those tragic ten minutes which had been so unexpected an aftermath of the Warehouse's harmless protest. Young Ted's horrified screech had alerted his friends, who had rushed to the scene and begun at once to muscle their way through the revolting, malodorous, damp mess of part-frozen fish and squelching cardboard under which was buried whoever-it-was whose bleeper bleeped remorselessly on, ignoring its wearer's inability to heed the summons.

"Can't somebody shut that bloody thing off?" someone cried in frustration, as they struggled to free the prisoner, and received a nerve-racking reply. The bleeper-wearer was dragged clear, and Ernie (First Aider as well as Oldest Inhabitant) was feeling for the pulse he gulped to admit he couldn't find . . . when, at his words, the bleeper hesitated, hiccupped, and faded into silence with a wail. More than one man himself looking upwards, as if following the escaping spirit on its supernatural flight.

Ernie gulped again. "The melting water's short-circuited the thing—or its battery's gone flat—or dried out—or, well, something," he said, finally working out a likely explanation. "But—but he's dead, all right. Stone cold, so he is," and he offered a limp and lifeless wrist for a second opinion.

There were no takers. "You'd be cold, if you'd had this lot on top of you," a quavering voice answered him from the surrounding crowd; and a general muttered consensus faded to an awkward silence, broken only by the sound of backward-shuffling feet.

Ernie squared his shoulders. "I'll stay here till help comes," he said, accepting that he'd already been volunteered for the job whether he wanted it or not. "Better ring for the nurse as well as the—the police . . . and if I've got to stay here, I could do with a cup of good strong tea—and one for the youngster, too." For poor Ted had collapsed, as soon as rescue arrived, upon an upturned crate, from which he had not stirred. He sat slumped and shivering, eyes shut tight in a pale green face, horrifying images in front of them.

Ernie clapped the wretched body-finder on the shoulder, and under cover of this kindly gesture managed to swing him round on the crate so that, once he'd been coaxed into opening his eyes, he wouldn't have to face the grisly wreckage of his forklift load and what lay underneath it. Mr. Oswald began to chat bracingly about star witnesses and newspaper interviews, maybe even the telly; and young Ted began to come gradually back to life. He flicked open a wary eye—opened the other—and was licking pale lips in readiness to speak when, in the distance, he heard the sound of an approaching bleeper.

It was the final straw. Ted's eyes opened wide, swivelled round up and under their lids, then closed as he crumpled forward in a dead faint—just in time for Nurse Joan (drawn thither by the repeated summons of numerous nervous bleeper calls) to see him fall as she arrived on the scene.

"Which," concluded Ernie, as he brought Trewley and Stone up-to-date, "as there wasn't much as could be done for *him*, poor basket"—indicating the site of the fish fingers' revenge—"it was lucky for Ted, poor kid. Green as grass he was, if you believe me—"

"We believe you." Trewley shook his head glumly. "Very nasty, I must say. You'll be wanting to get along, I don't doubt, Mr. Oswald—but before you go, I suppose you couldn't give us an idea of this chap's name? There'll be official identification later, of course, but my sergeant's a terror for keeping her records straight right from the start."

Ernie glanced towards Stone, who was pulling out a notebook and pencil. She winked at him again. He hesitated, not sure how far he would compromise himself and his fellow Warehouse men by being papered in this way. "Well . . ." he began, and stopped. Trewley glowered at him; Stone arched surprised eyebrows. Ernie coughed. "I do know him, yes. But wouldn't it be better if somebody from his own department told you who he was?"

"Would it?" Trewley looked as surprised as his sergeant had been. "Better than you telling us, now. Fancy that." And Stone made a couple of shorthand squiggles to remind herself to find out what it was Ernie Oswald had to hide. Her action made him nervous, as she'd intended it should. "I know him," he said again, quickly, "even though he didn't work in the Warehouse—always poking and prying where he'd no business to be, he was. His name's Ken Oldham—and he works for the House Services department."

"Strictly speaking, Mr. Trewley, he doesn't. Didn't." Amos, now the shocking news had been broken, had recovered his wits and was eager to help with police enquiries every bit as much as anyone would be when their regular bedtime reading is detective fiction. "Ken certainly worked *from*, and sometimes *in*, this department—but he didn't work *for* House Services. His was"—he couldn't help a sigh escaping him at the thought—"an outside appointment, direct from the new Board. They just put his desk here, I've always supposed, because we had slightly more space than some of the other departments—and also because all the facilities he would need were here, too.''

One of those facilities stifled a snort of disgust at this ingenuous explanation, drawing the attention of Trewley and Stone away from her boss to herself. Maureen, busy with teacups and milk, answered their unspoken question.

''Hadn't been in the place five minutes and he was giving me more typing than Amos—Mr. Chadderton—would in a year! You'd never believe the length of those reports of his—he must have spent all his spare time at home writing up the notes, and then expect it ready yesterday.''

Amos shot her a look of mild reproach—speaking ill of the dead wasn't what he'd have expected from Maureen—and, though Trewley saw that look and wondered if it contained a warning, it was the first part of her snappish little speech to which he responded.

''New boy, eh? How long exactly had he worked here?''

Amos and Maureen silently consulted each other. ''Three months, all but a week or so,'' said Maureen at last, and Amos nodded. ''He arrived just after the Takeover.''

''I remember.'' Could anyone living in Allingham forget? The local paper had been full of the news of the financial difficulties in which Tesbury's had found themselves. Rumours and counter-rumours of massive redundancies, receivership, and corporate buyouts were rife. Trewley's next-door neighbour had asked if there was an age limit to joining the police force; his wife's cousin had taken after-hours employment as a barmaid. ''I remember. So he's been with the firm nearly three months. And what exactly did he do during that time?''

Make a nuisance of himself snooping would be an honest, but uncomfortable answer—as well as being, Amos told himself, too vague to be of much use. He blinked and frowned.

''He was, well, a Management Consultant. Which meant he had a very wide, er, range of activities. . . .''

Maureen snorted again. Amos hurried on before she had time to commit further indiscretions. ''Well, basically, you could say he was brought in to, er, look over general company practice—efficiency, and, er, so on. He, er, had a brief to go wherever he wanted and to look at whatever he liked—with a view, you see, to, er, bringing things more up-to-date. Streamlining. Which is why"—with an apologetic glance at Maureen—"he wrote so many reports."

"So he could wander about all over the show asking questions all day long—and nobody could stop him so long as it was to do with work?" Trewley's bulldog face looked more glum than ever. "Sounds like a right recipe for trouble—the whole building's probably full of people with reasons for wanting to do him in."

"He, er, *was*, a Management Consultant," Amos reminded the superintendent, with a twinkle in his eyes: the possibilities raised by Trewley's remark had cheered him. "Wouldn't you say that spoke for itself?"

Trewley couldn't bring himself to twinkle back. "Don't know much about the breed, but from what I can make out—yes. The very nature of this chap's job would make folk hate him even before they'd got to know him well enough for what you could call the more personal kind of motive—and you've got upwards of eight hundred people working here, Mr. Chadderton! It's not going to be easy to treat 'em all as suspects—downright impossible, to tell you the truth. So I won't. I'm going to narrow this murder down to manageable proportions, and if you ask me, the only way to do that's to concentrate on the ones he worked most closely with."

Amos nodded. He'd known that was the logical thing to do, but he'd hoped against hope that Trewley would already have some clue leading him straight to the . . . to the . . .

"Are you—certain Ken was—was . . . murdered?" But he had no real expectation of hearing they were not.

They were certain. The police doctor had assured them that a man does not hit himself on the back of the head and then arrange himself face upwards on the floor in order to tumble a great number of hard and heavy objects on top of his unconscious person. Trewley had grunted, and told Stone not to get too big for her boots.

"He was murdered, Mr. Chadderton, no question. And

we'll want to examine the documents in his desk sometime soon, to give us a few pointers, you understand. We've got to start somewhere. But they're bound to be on the technical side, so how about you giving me a run-through of who does what in House Services, to begin with?''

Amos removed his Pickwick spectacles and gently rubbed the tip of his nose with the earpiece. Maureen gave him a sharp look. Was he playing for time—did he have something to hide—or was he just marshalling his thoughts?

''Well, Superintendent, I suppose you could say we're the, er, general dogsbodies of the company. Every firm of any size has a department to provide service facilities— cleaning, moving furniture, photocopying, telephones, telex, post, and so on. Keeping the wheels turning smoothly without actually producing anything.'' He sighed. ''People grumbled, of course—but believe me, Mr. Trewley, if we all went on strike, this building would come to a standstill in a matter of hours!''

''Minutes, you mean.'' Maureen, to the detectives' great amusement, had been vigorously nodding her head as Amos spoke. ''Talk about unsung heroes—that's us! Undervalued and underpaid, we are, what's more. . . .''

Mr. Chadderton chuckled. ''When Tesbury's first began to expand, there was just myself and a secretary (not Mrs. Mossley) and a handful of, well, of runaround types who'd pitch in to help with whatever needed doing. A clerk might file documents in the Archives, or sort the post, or deliver it—anything. None of today's, er, specialisation. When I say *today*, of course, I don't mean that, er, literally. I'm talking about years ago—nothing to do with Ken Oldham.''

''It would have been, if he'd felt like it,'' muttered Maureen. ''If it hadn't happened already!''

Amos coughed. ''Yes, well, it had. Because we gradually came to understand that it wasn't, er, efficient to chug on in quite such a casual way—so we recruited people to take over certain areas of responsibility. First, someone for office cleaning—and because the cleaners were mostly women in the old days, we've tended to keep a woman in that job, though it soon expanded to include wastepaper, and furniture moving, and storage of equipment—which in those days meant mainly typewriters—and somehow she collected general maintenance, as well.'' An unhappy expression crossed his face. He braced himself.

''Our, er, Ms. Halliwell—you won't have met her yet—has been doing that job for the past four years—and most competently, too.''

Stone, who prided herself on being liberated whether or not she used all her vowels, tried not to show surprise at anyone's being willing to stay in the same job for four years. Granted, she knew nothing of the day-to-day excitements and crises and challenges of House Services; but she preferred variety, and a real chance to get on. She had no idea, of course, about Amos's suggestion that Sadie might take his place when he retired.

Trewley, who knew his sergeant very well, suppressed a chuckle as Amos continued:

''My other Deputy Manager is Mr. Slack. His job developed naturally, as machines like photocopiers and microfilm cameras became more complex, and I was unable to keep up with the, er, technology. And, with microfilmed documents saving so much space, he—or rather one of his predecessors—took over the Archives as well. Mr. Slack,'' he added, before they could ask, ''has been with us over two years now.''

''What sort of documents does he film?'' For Stone, management of paperwork and the saving of space were matters of some concern.

''Oh. Well, anything, er, valuable—important, perhaps I should say,'' as she and Trewley looked as if they might have found a clue, ''because we have no signed first editions of *The Mysterious Affair at Styles*, or anything like that.'' Amos smiled rather sadly. He'd had daydreams, in the past, of secondhand bookshops and ignorant owners. . . .

''The law, you see, requires us—the Company—to keep, er, certain items for certain periods of time, although it doesn't insist they have to be kept in their, er, original paper form. Invoices, delivery notes, receipts, and so on—lease agreements, insurance policies—and besides the legal requirement, you know, and the space saving, there's the, er, safety aspect. We take diazo duplicates of every film, and if a fire should break out . . .''

Amos coughed again. "Yes, well, that's how the jobs are divided in House Services, Mr. Trewley. We have an organisation chart somewhere—Mrs. Mossley will make you a copy, if you'd like it."

"Thanks, we would." The superintendent's eyes lost some of their habitual gloom. "For one thing, Mr. Chadderton, it might help us to find out what *you* do all day long!"

"My word, yes, how silly of me." Amos blinked and took off his spectacles again. "Well, I've kept responsibility for the Post Room—internal and external mail, you know—and telephones, telexes, that sort of thing. . . . But it's a young person's job now," he said, thinking of Sadie. "I'm not going to be altogether sorry when I retire—it isn't easy to understand these newfangled notions. Ken Oldham made me realise just how out-of-date I've become."

"Umph." Trewley made a mental, Stone a discreet pencil, note. "How much did Oldham try to interfere with the way you run things? I mean—you've been doing it for years—you must know the job backwards. Did he let you and the others just get on with it, or did he have lots of bright ideas for improving things?"

"Bright ideas were, well, *his* job, Mr. Trewley."

It wasn't, as an answer, very helpful. "Any particular bright idea you can tell me about? Give me a feeling for what the chap was like—how his mind worked." And, though Trewley addressed this query ostensibly to Amos, it was Maureen Mossley he looked at. Her expression as she stared, first at her typewriter, then at her filing cabinet, hinted more than enough even before Amos admitted:

"I'm afraid I've never read any of his reports—modern, you see. Jargon—rather above my head, I thought. Maureen is the one to ask, because she typed them—and there's his clipboard, of course. He always took his clipboard with him so that he could make notes of whatever, well, he thought he ought to. . . .''

Stone was already leafing back through her notebook as

Trewley turned to ask. She shook her head. "No, sir. No clipboard found by the body."

Amos and Maureen gaped. Amos said: "But—but you could hardly miss it—black leather, tooled edges, a bit flashy—he always took it with him when he went anywhere. . . ."

"Went *snooping* anywhere," amended Maureen—which remark was duly noted by Trewley and Stone. The superintendent sat and thought for a moment.

"I reckon it would help me and my sergeant here quite a lot if we could only get a proper feel for this place, Mr. Chadderton. How about you letting us borrow your secretary for half an hour or so, and she can show us all the sights?"

Amos tried not to frown: he almost succeeded. Trewley and Stone wondered whether he was simply worried about being deprived of Mrs. Mossley's services during her absence—or whether he was more concerned with what she might, when he wasn't with her, reveal of the Company's—the department's—secrets.

"Of course, Mr. Trewley." Amos knew he could reasonably say nothing else. "But it is, er, extremely odd—that you didn't find Ken's clipboard, I mean. He always had it with him. And his notes—the ones he was making just before he . . . he died—they'd be important, wouldn't they? A clue!"

"They would," Trewley agreed. "Leastways, they would have been, if we'd found it—but we didn't. So perhaps I could ask you if you'd be kind enough to lock Mr. Oldham's desk before we go, and give me the key? Because we don't want anything else that's—really important—to go missing, do we? Not now Mr. Oldham's dead. . . ."

———— Fifteen ————

DICK AND SADIE, of course, had sat with their ears flapping throughout the entire interview. No sooner did Maureen lead her little party past their desks for the start of the guided tour than they leapt to their feet and came hurrying in to discuss the whole affair with Amos.

Nobody pretended a grief they did not feel, though they voiced appropriate expressions of shock. "But let's be honest about it," said Dick, speaking for them all. "He's no great loss. Nobody liked him—and we certainly won't miss him. We managed perfectly well before he came, didn't we? And I should think we'll manage just as well now he's gone."

"I wonder," said Sadie, "if they'll replace him."

There was a thoughtful pause. Amos sighed. "I suppose, in due course, they must—but as he was directly appointed by the Board, they might not find it easy to get someone else with similar qualifications and experience in too much of a hurry. I believe it was a sheer fluke the headhunters came up with him at exactly the right time."

"Let's hope they don't," said Sadie. "*One* Ken Oldham was bad enough. The idea of another makes my heart sink."

"I shouldn't worry, Sadie—you're pretty safe, I should say." As she stared at him, Dick grinned. "Come on—would *you* apply for his job if you thought you might end up . . . if you thought the same sort of thing might happen again? Once the news gets out . . ."

"Oh, dear." Amos slumped on his chair. "I'd forgotten how people are bound to talk about . . . well, about *things*." Which, from one so devoted to gossip, was surely proof that the shock he'd suffered was genuine.

"They'll do more than talk, if you mean just among themselves." Dick shook his head. "Newspapers, radio, television—they'll have a field day. And with eight hundred likely witnesses . . ."

"Oh, dear." Amos turned pale, then braced himself. "We must try to—to curb their enthusiasm, I suppose. At least—no, a tannoy Call is hardly . . . Well, House Services most definitely ought to be given the fullest possible details, to prevent the, er, wildest rumours spreading. . . ."

Nobody cared to remark that the spreading had almost certainly already started, or that *wild* had to be the understatement of the year. Amos sighed again. "Dick, would you go to the Archives and, er, have a word? Sadie, if you'd deal with your Lads and Mrs. Hiscock and the Maintenance people—when Maureen comes back, I'll ask her to speak to the Switchboard and the Post Room—Dick had better talk to his Reprographics as well. . . ."

Sadie's tone held a tinge of malice. "But if Maureen's only just gone off with those detectives, and Dick and I are disappearing, too—what about you, Amos? You'll be left all alone to face the music. Which at a conservative guess will be the *1812 Overture* with knobs on—just for starters." She looked pointedly at his telephone and smiled.

Amos turned even paler. Dick hurried to the rescue—and not only of Amos. "You can count me out for spreading the glad tidings! Have a load of women go hysterical all over me? No fear! I'll stay here with you to man the fort and answer the phone—if Sadie doesn't mind doing the rounds by her own sweet self." He smiled his most persuasive smile. "Please, Sadie? Have a heart—take pity on us poor suffering males."

"Poor weak males, you mean." Sadie tossed her head, and hid a smile for the way he'd caught her conversational ball. "In this particular instance, I *am* prepared to agree— but don't take it as a precedent—that a woman's touch might be better than the way a man would bulldoze through everyone's finer feelings. You can leave everything to me, Amos. And try not to worry!"

She was just preparing to leave when a movement at the office entrance caught everyone's attention. Steven Bamber, postbag in hand, stood looking in on the intense little group. His eyes were bright, and his mouth was stern.

"The Post Room are saying, Mr. Chadderton, that there are policemen in the building. Such talk may be harmful, leading to all manner of rumours. But these voices are loud and insistent, Mr. Chadderton. Is it true?"

A quick and silent consultation between the three managers ended in Sadie's admission that yes, it was. Steven's gleaming gaze turned slowly upon her.

"Is it in order for me to . . . ask what has happened? It is nothing to do with—no harm has come to—to . . ."

"Veronica's fine, Steven." Sadie's reassurance came quickly. "She's safe—nothing's happened to her. But—it has to . . . someone else. It seems that Ken Oldham was found . . . dead . . . over in the Warehouse, and that his death was—was not accidental. And the police are investigating."

"Ken Oldham is dead?" Steven seemed turned to stone. "He . . . has been killed?" Then he drew a deep breath. "The Lord is known by the judgement which He executeth. The wicked is snared in the work of his own hands. He was a sinner—a blasphemer, an adulterer. I will not play the hypocrite and mourn his passing. Indeed, I would be glad to shake the hand of the man who rid the world of him."

A lesser woman than Sadie would have goggled at him. Ms. Halliwell merely stared, speechless. Dick swallowed, and in his turn could find nothing to say.

It was Amos who finally broke the uncomfortable silence. "You're . . . rather later than usual with the post this afternoon, Steven. Anything, er, particular to delay you?" The first shock had abated, and the years spent reading Wimsey and Poirot and Appleby and Fen now clamoured to be fulfilled. Not (Amos told himself) that he seriously suspected Veronica's husband of having killed the man who'd flirted with her—he had no such idea. Of course he hadn't! What he *did* have were his daydreams—the desire to act out in real life the role of the ratiocinative superman who, initial appearances to the contrary, triumphed fantastically over adversity, red herrings, and the stupidity of Scotland Yard. "Any particular reason to be late?" he asked again, and reached for a stick of barley-sugar to stimulate his brain.

Steven frowned. "Everyone has seemed to want to *talk*—and more than idle conversation. I see now that there must have been some inkling of what happened already in the air, and that they were making attempts"—his frown deepended—"to ask news—even of me. I, of course, knew nothing. But if, Mr. Chadderton, the tidings generally rumoured are true, should those rumours not be brought under control by the telling of the truth?" He glanced at the black bulging mailbag he still held. "It would perhaps be seen as my duty to inform the Post Room, for instance."

Sadie intervened while Amos was still busy trying to analyse Steven's state of mind from his demeanour. "That's just what we were saying as you came along. I was getting ready to go and let people know—but if you don't mind telling the Post Room, that will be one job the fewer for me." Her glance flicked to Amos, who nodded. "Right, then. Shall we be on our way?"

Talking it over afterwards, Dick and Amos agreed that Ms. Halliwell had shown great foresight, and skill equal to Ken Oldham's, in the way she absented herself from the House Services department at that time. It was, they said, very well planned—though they would, of course, have expected nothing less of Sadie. No sooner had she disappeared than the telephones began to ring. Dick and Amos snatched them off their cradles and left them on the desks. They hadn't quite regained their breath when (they afterwards found) Steven Bamber began to break the news to the Post Room: and every female member of the staff promptly went into hysterics, with not a few of the males joining them.

Dick and Amos—paler than ever—sent at once for the two nurses, who arrived armed with sharp words and smelling salts and brisk slaps to the face—the latter a treatment neither of the male managers had dared to apply, fearing ramifications from the Sex Discrimination Act. Nurse Joan and Nurse Jane had no such scruples. They smacked and shook the Post Room back to sanity, issuing instructions concerning strong, hot, sweet tea, and the necessity for the girls to take cups round to everyone in the department and stop acting like idiots.

"Not a genuine case of shock among the lot of them," said Nurse Joan, as Amos stuttered everlasting thanks and Dick almost grovelled at Nurse Jane's feet. "Silly young fools—now if they'd actually seen him, like poor Ted . . ."

Which led to further discussion and speculation about what had happened. Amos, an interested listener, relished every syllable, and longed for Maureen to return from her guided tour so that they could swap notes: he was fairly sure the police would have learned from her things he might have preferred they didn't, but he was also sure it would not have been a one-way exchange. . . .

When Mrs. Mossley eventually did come back, it was with Ms. Halliwell not far behind. Sadie had dispensed information and gloom as briskly as possible in the circumstances, and couldn't wait to be in relative safety once more. They all assembled in Amos's office, drinking cups of Post Room tea and talking eagerly together.

"Something Steven said," remarked Sadie, "makes me wonder a bit—no, of course I'm not saying he did it! But he did call Ken a seducer and an adulterer, didn't he?"

"*Cherchez la femme*," said Amos. "You think there may be a—a lady in the case? A jealous husband—not Steven, of course. He has very firm principles. But I haven't heard of anything like that—have you?"

As he turned to Maureen, and she shook a regretful head, Sadie managed to look portentous. "Actually, I was thinking more of a jilted lover. Men, after all, often behave very badly. Remember last week—Friday—the car blitz when we had the fire alarm, and that girl from Accounts kicking up such a fuss until she spotted Ken? You were all here—you saw her." She grinned at Dick. "She passed out cold on the floor, like an old-fashioned heroine who's been betrayed. And goodness knows, from her clothes and hairdo she's old-fashioned enough—precisely the type to work herself into hysterics, and then . . ."

There was an impressed and thoughtful silence as everyone considered this. Amos took more barley-sugar and pushed the tin across to his colleagues so that they might help themselves. Before they could do so, however, he was struck by inspiration.

"You know, Sadie, you've had a very stressful time of it this afternoon—repeating the same shocking story over and over again. It must make it worse for you, coming back to the office and seeing Ken's empty desk. I think a change of scene would do you good. Why not go off now on one of your walkabout tours and check if any maintenance work needs doing around the building?"

The twinkle in Sadie's eyes matched that in Mr. Chadderton's as she lifted her teacup to him in a toast. "Starting, of course, at the top floor. Perhaps in Accounts? It certainly is a long time since I was last there."

"That, my dear Sadie," said Amos, "is the best idea I've heard for a long time," and he beamed at her with approval.

Maureen said: "I don't know why I didn't think of it before, but we could always try having a word with Dorothy, in Personnel. If she's in the right mood, she just might spill a few beans about—certain persons of our acquaintance. . . ."

And her reward was another approving beam.

Ms. Sadie Halliwell, duly armed with tape measure, notebook, screwdriver, and lightweight hammer, made her purposeful way up to the second floor. She first inspected the state of the ladies' cloakroom (for a change it passed); she then marched into the Accounts department in search of what needed to be put right. It was not long before she had the first complaint.

"That carpet tile ought to be replaced," the Accounts Manager told her, sounding aggrieved. "It's very worn—it could trip someone up quite badly one day."

Sadie followed his accusing finger and frowned. "How long has it been like that? And just how"—in suspicious tones, as she peered more closely at the damaged tile and its neighbours—"did it happen, anyway?"

"Oh, well . . . I really couldn't say. Does it matter?"

"It does if it's your fault." Sadie turned to glare at him. "You've been moving the furniture about, haven't you? Your desk never used to stand here." Her quick eyes had spotted the giveaway indentation where stubby metal feet had once stood—next to the worn tile.

The manager mumbled something about the light not

having been right for his eyes, which his optician had advised him should not be exposed for too long to fluorescent glare. The desk had accordingly been moved nearer the window—

"And *where* did that lamp come from?" Sadie made an ominous note in her little black book as he mumbled again, then set him straight on the nature of the Furniture Store, the system for requisitioning equipment therefrom, and the importance of following proper procedures at all times.

She also, without fuss, fixed the tile. "Just lift that corner of your desk while I shift this potted palm—yes, fine, hold it there. . . ." Some judicious juggling contrived to banish the offending tile from sight. "Well, that should do it for the moment." She dusted her hands. "What? Oh, yes, you can put the desk down again—and is there anything else while I'm here? How about the notice board—that corner looks a bit shaky. . . ."

With the occasional tap from her hammer and note in her book, Sadie gradually worked her way closer to Angela Farnworth's desk. The young accountant, head bent industriously over piles of papers, did her best to ignore the newcomer. No doubt she was embarrassed by memories of Friday's faint and preferred to foster the pretence that Ms. Halliwell was invisible.

She may have been invisible, but she was not inaudible. Sadie edged toward the window nearest to Angela's desk. "Could do with a lick of paint here—someone's given this ledge a real scrape with something. Moving another desk, no doubt. Oh," before the manager could think of a suitable reply, "I'd never realised before what a good view you have from up here. Right into the Warehouse—the entrance, anyway—and all the police cars, as clear as anything!"

"Police cars? What's happened?"

The voice of the Accounts Manager rose above the general clamour. "More pilfering, I suppose." He had never reconciled himself to the appearance of *Natural Wastage* on the balance sheets as an official euphemism for *Warehouse Perks*. With all the rest of his staff except Angela, he moved to a window. "Good gracious. That's a lot of coppers just for a—a little thing like that." Possibly, after the matter of his anglepoise lamp, he was more inclined to view with sympathy certain aspects of the irregular.

"Oh, no." Sadie was watching Angela as she answered. "Didn't you notice Maureen Mossley showing a couple of detectives around earlier? They wouldn't want a tour of the office block just because of the Warehouse—although that is, of course, where the body was found." She paused to let a surge of exclamation die down. "But I expect they'll end up investigating the whole firm, Warehouse or no Warehouse—they couldn't do anything less, in a case of . . . murder."

The outburst after she uttered the final word was deafening. She waited until they were ready to listen to her again. "A man," she told them, still watching Angela, whose face was pale, whose fingers gripped her pencil, whose knuckles were white. "Dead—underneath a crate of frozen fish fingers dropped on top of him from a forklift truck. . . ."

"Fish? Thank goodness it's not Friday!" It was a weak joke, but it served to lighten the atmosphere—for everyone except Angela. "Who was it?"

Miss Farnworth's fingers tightened on the pencil as she felt Sadie's gaze still on her. "Someone," said Sadie, "who works—worked in our department. A man called Ken Oldham."

There came a loud crack as Angela's pencil splintered in her grasp. Sadie nodded, and only then turned away. "Poor Ken—battered to death, you might say."

Her own little joke earned a ripple of nervous laughter before more questions were hurled at her from every direction save one. There were so many she couldn't answer them, and stood listening, and watching, turning again so that she could see Angela from the corner of her eye.

"When did it happen? . . . Who found him? . . . What was he doing in the Warehouse, of all places?"

"Out moving his car from the traffic wardens," someone suggested, "and got waylaid somehow—by something pretty important, too. As soon as *I* heard that Call I was out of here like a rocket, straight down to the road! And anyone with a car's bound to have done the same." Which was fair enough comment, though the speaker's view was not unbiased. He had honeymooned in a renowned tourist spot and been wheel-clamped three times during one week.

"Haven't seen an office empty itself so fast," somebody else said, "except for a bomb scare. Angela, you must have broken the record for starting from a sitting position! If you wanted to enter in the Olympics, we'd be sure of a gold medal, no question."

With all eyes upon her, Angela tried to stop her voice betraying her as she replied: "Of course I did. After what happened to my car last week, I had no intention of taking any more risks. Would you?"

And Sadie silently applauded the way the girl had pulled herself together after receiving such a shock. She must be sure to tell Amos. . . .

"I told Mr. Chadderton the same thing," continued Angela, making Sadie jump. "On Friday, after that idiot ran into my car—I said enough was enough, and that I wasn't prepared to take risks with my no-claims bonus again—not for all the traffic wardens in Allshire. So of course I was in a hurry to leave the office. I meant every word I said!"

Sixteen

"PAPERWORK! I HATE it." Detective Sergeant Stone staggered into the Incident Room with her arms full of files and dumped them on a table. "If I had to check every single one of these myself, I think I'd go mad."

The two uniformed constables in front of whom she'd done the dumping sighed, but said nothing: they were too much in awe of Detective Superintendent Trewley, who looked up from his own labours and managed a very faint chuckle.

The police had not been idle since the discovery of Ken Oldham's body. They had established a discreet presence on Tesbury premises (the Training Department had been persuaded to relinquish a lecture room for their particular use), and had unobtrusively, yet methodically, been beavering away at their various tasks ever since. Progress was slow: but it was, none the less, progress. They asked questions, particularly of the Warehouse; they checked facts.

One of the first facts they'd checked had been Ken Oldham's Personnel file. Stone had suggested that, since he'd only been with the company a matter of months, it could be that a personal (as opposed to professional) motive for his murder had come from a pre-Tesbury connection. Accordingly, Trewley placed a complete embargo on the files of the entire department until they'd been searched—which, as they were not yet computerised, would take many man-hours—and had strictly forbidden any of the staff to breathe one word of what was going on. The Personnel Manager had been minded to protest, babbling of confidentiality. Trewley, at his most bulldogish, said that in a case of murder, nothing had any right to be considered confidential, and swore considerable oaths as to Stone's honesty, probity, and discretion.

He got the files.

"Then you shouldn't have brain waves," he now re-marked, as his sergeant dropped into a chair and flexed her arms, muttering of cramp. "I'm not saying I hadn't thought of it anyway—I'm not in my dotage yet, girl—but *you* were the bright one who came right out and said it. So of course I wanted you to have a share in the glory. I'm not selfish."

"Of course not, sir," murmured Stone. "I should say it's terribly *un*selfish of you to check all the statements from House Services and the Warehouse by yourself, instead of joining in the fun we're having with these files. . . ."

He chose to take her remarks at face value. "So it is. How many men work in that warehouse? And the House Services lot—they've all got to be eliminated before we can start on the other departments—that's why it was their files you checked first, remember. Nothing helpful in them, of course—but there might have been. And once you and your friends have finished with the rest, why, then we start the next round. So the sooner you stop moaning and get back to work, the better—even though," with a yawn, "it's a horrible hot day for this sort of thing. . . ."

When Old Jem Tesbury, founding father of the firm which bore his name, realised that he had a glorious marketing success on his hands, eyebrows were raised at his decision to plough back as much of the profits as advisers deemed wise into building a custom-designed Head Office complex at some suitable location. But Jem ignored the eyebrows. He had sense enough to know that a happy work force means a contented company—and a contented company is a profit-able one.

The site, on the outskirts of Allingham, county town of Allshire, was as well laid out as anyone could wish. Set back from the road behind a graceful and artistic screen of now-mature trees and shrubs, the three-storey office block shielded from casual view the massive warehouse area to its rear. Access to the Warehouse was along one of the two side roads which flanked the office block: the second led to the car park. Both roads were bordered by landscaped banks of sloping grass, dotted with flower beds and bushes.

At the very bottom of the site, sheltered by the Warehouse, was a picturesque open space intended by the planners as a picnic place for such members of staff who chose not to eat in the excellent (subsidised) canteen on the top floor. Outside, rustic benches, tables and chairs of hard-wearing plastic were plentifully positioned where, in fine weather, anyone with sufficient energy to walk a few hundred yards might relax and enjoy an alfresco snack in the sunshine.

"Don't you go putting the tables right under the trees, mind, whatever you do," Old Jem warned the planners. "I'm not having my people sitting down to eat off birds' business—it looks horrible, and it'll turn their stomachs. I don't want 'em off their feed and not fancying work in the afternoons!"

Any impartial observer of a psychological bent would have noted with interest how the large heavy-duty parasols, fitting as required into central holes when sunstroke might affect those eating at table, had remained in their allotted places from the opening day of the new site until the last few months, untouched by anything save the vagaries of the English weather. Then, as Tesbury's slowly stopped feeling like Tesbury's, canvas and ribs had been torn, bent, and broken, and entire fixtures were somehow removed—a vanishing trick which exasperated Sadie Halliwell, whose Maintenance responsibilities were deemed to include the tables and other attractions of the picnic area.

Nevertheless, it was still a popular place to eat, or even just to sit, during the free hours and minutes of an otherwise busy day. Many of the office staff, despite the disruption caused by the rubble and lorries and dust of the new computer block, would make their way along the road to enjoy a short spell in the open air, ignoring the various hazards of the route—hazards which included the "Ordeal by Ogle." The Warehouse men had appropriated for their own that bank which bordered the road and which, by a happy chance, faced due south. In summer, the sun shone full upon the bank at those times when the Warehouse took its breaks; and a daily baring of muscular torsos and tanning of masculine skin was the result. Modest young females walked by with lowered gaze and blushing speed; the immodest sauntered past the broiling brown ranks with disdainful noses in the air and hopeful eyes alert—just in case.

By teatime, the Warehouse had grown more than weary of the murder, frustrated in their efforts to get on with their work. A cordon of ribbons and an eagle-eyed constable made it very plain that, productivity bonus notwithstanding, nobody would be allowed back in the building until some hours had elapsed. Those would-be workers not being interviewed by the police banded together to drag young Ted—his inner man already full of strong, sweet tea—out to the aforementioned bank, where everyone stripped gleefully to the waist and prepared to foam at the mouth should any candidate worth the effort of effervescence elect to leave the office block—doubtless seething with hysteria—for a breath of fresh air.

Most of the people who escaped into the relative sanity afforded by the sunshine and greenery of the picnic place were plainly in no mood for the usual interplay of whistles and tossed heads. They were subdued, and shaken: in rumour, Ken's death was made even more bizarre than it had been in fact, and only the strongest-minded—and thus best-equipped to deal with Warehouse admiration—remained indoors to swap gossip and stoke the fires of speculation. The weaker ones, with their insistence that they didn't want to think about it anymore, could hardly wait for the tea break to get away from it all, no matter how unsuitable their habitual flirtatious pastime now seemed.

There were, inevitably, those who disagreed with such puritan opinion. ''What about her, eh?'' A hip-swaying nymph with a retroussé nose paraded her charms before the watchers on the bank, high heels clicking, bare feet slapping on plastic sandal soles, bosom bouncing as she wiggled along. Ted found himself grinning for the first time since he'd found—

He shut off that awful thought, drew a deep breath, and whistled shrilly. The girl giggled, glancing sideways at her admirer.

''Hardly out of the egg,'' growled one of the older oglers,

"and a right little tart already—I'd hate to think how many
blokes she's dropped 'em for. Better not go after *her*, son—I
mean, who's to say you wouldn't catch nothing, neither?"

"Oh," said Ted, as a general mutter of agreement greeted
this grim warning. "But she don't look that sort," as the girl
tittered and tittupped her way out of earshot.

"The ones as don't look it are usually the worst." His
mentor shook a doleful head. "I could tell you things'd
make your hair curl about a couple of convent girls I used
to know. . . ."

He'd told the story before; but it was good, if unprintable,
and nobody minded hearing it again. Try as they might not
to dwell on what had happened, it was harder than they'd
expected. When the punch line was delivered, the appreci-
ation came louder and more forced than usual, followed
promptly by impossible anatomical suggestions from an
audience dredging up boastful (and equally impossible)
memories of its own, as other girls passed by to an
accompaniment of whistles, catcalls, and friendly banter,
countered by the bolder spirits with mock-indignant squeals—
squeals which, like the accompanying guffaws, seemed
somehow stifled.

But a relatively good time was had by all, even if little
was achieved beyond mutual encouragement; sunshine and
hormones could not completely banish the dark shadow that
had fallen—but it could not be denied they did their best.
Ted, indeed, was starting to think himself, as Ernie Oswald
had earlier intended, the hero of the hour; he flexed muscles
he'd never realised he possessed, and his whistle came clear
and shrill. But as one small group of girls drew near, he
was surprised when his colleagues did not join him in a
suitable response. Instead, there came a considerable muting
of their admiration, an embarrassed murmuring rather than
an exuberant outcry—yet one of the group, delicately pale
and being supported by her friends as she was, had to be the
most gorgeous girl he'd ever seen. A stunning figure—hips
that, no matter how fragile her state, still swayed as she
walked—long, shapely legs . . .

"Wow!" breathed Ted, lost for further words. Those
eyes—were they blue, or green, or grey? And her hair—that

shining tumble of gold-red curls about her generous bosom—
her creamy skin, her warm, welcoming mouth . . .

"You can forget about her, too," said his neighbour, as
he at last dragged his goggle-eyed gaze away from the girl's
retreating form. "She's married, is Veronica—and don't
nobody forget it!"

"Lucky devil." Ted sighed. "Must be a pretty special
sort of bloke, getting a bird who looks like that. . . ."

"Looks aren't everything, son, as you'll find out—but, as
to *special*, depends what you mean. He's a funny one all
right, is Steve Bamber. Used to work in the warehouse, but
there was an accident shifting some crates. . . ."

Everyone coughed, and eyes shifted to the ground. Ted's
informative neighbour cleared his throat.

"An accident," he said firmly. "Not his fault, and he
could've took the company for thousands, except he didn't.
He just got 'em to find him an easier sort of job—
physically, like—and he does the post now."

"Why didn't he sue them?" In Ted's short time with
Tesbury's, he'd seen how the Union flourished; it seemed
an odd omission on the part of the unknown Steven.

"Umph." His neighbour rubbed a thoughtful nose. "If it
was to happen now, the way things've bin since the
Takeover, I dare say he might just think about it—but this
was a year or so back. Said it was against his principles, him
being a religious bloke, having to forgive everyone their
sins—leastways, that's what he said then. Too soft for his
own good, our Steve. The silly beggar could do with the
money all right, but he's not the sort to go asking for it, and
the Union can't rightly start demanding compensation on
his behalf if he don't want 'em to."

"I would, if it was me," said someone else, and the rest
agreed. "Lucky not to have bin crippled, he was, maybe
even killed—and Christian forgiveness is all very well when
you ain't got a wife and a baby and two homes to
support—"

"Two homes?" Ted was startled. This seemingly righ-
teous and God-fearing Steven had a mistress—had committed bigamy? "Why two, for heaven's sake?"

"Honouring his father and mother, son, like the Bible

says—or his mother, anyway. His dad's bin dead these ten years, and Steve, he lived at home right up till he married, only then his old ma said she'd not have Veronica under her sacred roof. One of the hellfire lot, she is, preaching and texts and a double dose of damnation if a fallen woman comes into the house, even if your son's married to her.''

Somebody snorted. ''And maybe she's not so far wrong, at that. Up the spout when he married her, weren't she? And not his kiddie, neither. *I* wouldn't stand for it.''

Ted was still puzzled. ''If it's not his kid . . .''

''Oh, he acknowledged the little basket all right, treats it really well, you'd never guess it's not his own, though we all know it ain't. Nobody knows *whose* it is. Not even Veronica, except he must've bin one of the ones as spiked the drinks at that party. He could've left Tesbury's by now and be miles away—and if he ain't, and Steve ever runs him to earth, he'll wish he was! There's not many blokes with tempers I'd watch out for, but for all his Bible business Steve Bamber's one of 'em—as far's Veronica's concerned, anyway. Talk about jealous!''

''Worships the ground that girl walks on,'' someone else said. ''Talked her out of having an abortion—all life is sacred, see. Offered to give her his name—and the baby too, poor little bee—and still lets her come to work, when any decent woman'd be ashamed to show her face, parking the brat with her ma all day because she says they need the money. . . . But Steve lets her do just what she likes!''

Ted pulled a face. ''Sounds a funny sort of do all round—I mean, why marry her at all, apart from the baby? These religious types, they'd surely never go for the sex bit—and upsetting his mother as well, that's not right, is it?'' Ted was not married and still lived at home.

''Son, you ever seen a cat with a bird? The bird'll just sit there—can't fly away, even when the cat's not touching it, poor beggar. Fascinated, that's what the bird is—and it was the same with Steve. Couldn't take his eyes off her the first time he saw her, no more than you could. Course, he'd never dream it was the old sex thing, same like the rest of us poor mortals—if you was to hold him at gunpoint he'd never admit it, because his sort don't. But you got to hand it to him, when the girl was in trouble he didn't back down—he wasn't just a load of hot air and hormones. Saw her right, he did—so there really must be something in it, at least on his side there must. Wouldn't like to say about her, mind.''

"She's still got that old look in her eye," said someone who had once been snubbed badly by Veronica at a party where the drinks hadn't been spiked. "With a husband to make it respectable, she's the same little baggage now she ever was—thinks she can get away with it, I reckon. Give her half a chance, and . . ."

"She'd best watch out, if she tries anything—and so had anyone else," with a warning look for young Ted. "Ought to be grateful for the way he stood by her, she did, not be thinking to rub his face in it—and then, maybe she's learned her lesson and she won't. If she's got any sense, she won't, because if she ever pushed him too far—"

"If *anyone* pushed him too far," amended his neighbour; and nobody disputed this. The point had been made, and very clearly: it would be a foolhardy man who interfered in any way in the marriage of Steven Bamber and his wife, the delectable—and out-of-bounds—Veronica.

Seventeen

ON WEDNESDAY MORNING, it was clear that Angela Farnworth had spoken no more than the truth when she announced her resolve to run no further risk with her no-claims bonus. Amos Chadderton, who had sat up half the night thumbing through his crime fiction library in search of suggestions and hints for solving Ken's murder, arrived at work later than he'd ever done before . . . to discover, in his personal bay, a car, defiantly parked. It was a white BMW.

"Oh. Oh dear, oh dear. I'd better have a few words with Miss Farnworth. . . ." Words, however, would come after actions: he had first to find somewhere to park. He rolled down his window, almost as if by doing so he would obtain not only a clear view, but clear parking places, too: yet as he glanced round the other reserved bays he saw, as he'd feared, that every one was full. Even Ken Oldham's place had been appropriated by—

"Sadie's Astra," said Amos, recognising the bright red GTE and mentally noting that Ms. Halliwell harboured no superstitious nonsense about dead men's shoes—or their parking spots. He made a bet with himself that when she'd found her own space stolen, she'd refrained from encroaching in turn upon his. He must thank her once he was in the office.

"But when will that be?" He looked round again, wondering where all the other cars had come from. He stared and frowned. Surely most were unknown to him? And, as far as he could tell, none of these unknowns carried authorised windscreen stickers. . . .

A jingling of keys caught his attention. "I told the Switchboard to let me know when you arrived," Sadie said, as she waved towards the plate glass windows. "You won't mind parking in Ken's bay, will you? Not scared of ghosts?''

"Er, no. No, indeed, of course not. That's very kind of you, Sadie—but, er, what about you?''

"I'm not, either. Oh, I see—silly of me. Don't worry about that.'' Sadie grinned. ''I'm going to box our friend Angela well and truly in, which should teach her to pinch an allocated space—if the road's good enough for everyone else, it ought to be good enough for her.''

She manoeuvred her GTE deftly over the white lines, then jumped out to wave Amos with competent hand directions into the space she'd just left. As he watched, she backed up as near to Angela's bonnet as she could go, while still leaving an exit—tight though it was—for others. ''And I think,'' she remarked, as the two then made their way indoors, ''that I might well join you in The Spice Trader for an hour or so this evening. Nobody'll find me there, will they?''

Amos was still chuckling as they reached House Services, to find Dick and Maureen gossiping over coffee. Dick shook his head at Sadie, continuing the argument they'd been having before Mr. Chadderton's arrival.

"It's your car, not mine, I know—but I'm blowed if I'd run the risk of some idiot scratching the paint when I hadn't had the thing a month! Or denting it—or worse.''

Sadie shrugged. ''Risks are there to be taken—especially in a good cause.'' She smiled toward Mr. Chadderton. ''It's the principle of the thing, quite apart from the fact that Amos had nowhere to park—''

"Oh, yes.'' The caffeine had stirred his weary brain into action. ''And why didn't I? Those cars—I'm sure not all of them are ours. Where have they come from?''

His three colleagues groaned, and Dick tore ineffectually at his hair. ''Blame Radio Allshire, not us!''

The local broadcasting service had become gleefully aware of its homegrown scoop at around teatime the previous day. It was with great pride that the station informed the world of the outrage committed, by person or persons unknown, upon the hitherto dignified premises of one of the county's best-known employers. The bizarre nature of Ken Oldham's demise had sizzled over the airwaves and been picked up by the national networks. . . .

"You must have come in the back way and missed them," said Dick, who'd come in the front way and hadn't.

"They've been waylaying everyone coming to work with a load of damn fool questions," said Sadie, scowling. She had thought it a gross insult to have been asked whether she, as a woman, feared for her safety on Tesbury territory while A Menace Stalked the Streets. She reminded the reporters that said Menace seemed to prefer Tesbury's Warehouse to Allingham's roads, and suggested they should try pestering Charley Marks and his mates instead. "Goodness knows what will be in tomorrow's papers—today's were bad enough."

"Half the cars out there"—Dick nodded through the wall in the direction of the car park—"belong to the press, and the rest to a lot of broadcasting types. I'd have chucked them out for trespassing, but the superintendent said not to, because then they'd cause an obstruction out in the road and have the traffic wardens in hysterics."

"You'd think," said Maureen, brooding on Amos's little black book, "they'd be grateful for the money. They're quick enough to fine *us* whenever they feel like it!"

"Yes, but Trewley said we shouldn't annoy them, or we'd run the risk of unfavourable publicity—well," as the reaction of his hearers to this innocent remark made him realise what he'd said, "worse than what we've already got. Remember how Radio Allshire were so decent about those dodgy tins of corned beef? We could have been in real trouble then, if they'd felt like it."

Everyone shuddered. Memories of that time were still vivid. "Yes," said Amos, fumbling in his desk drawer, "better the devil you know, I suppose. Things could really be so much worse—but I have to admit," and he sighed, "that I'm starting to see what Ken meant when he said we were old-fashioned." He looked at the barley-sugar, shook his head, and replaced the sweetmeat in its wrapper. "If we'd only had proper, up-to-date security, they'd never have managed to find their way on to private property in the first place. But as all we've got is Old George . . ."

Everyone knew Old George, a Tesbury legend in his own lifetime. He had been a Warehouseman, injured long ago in the days before such things as claims, liability, and damages had entered management consciousness to any great extent. Decades (so it was rumoured) past the official retirement age, Old George pottered about the place, dozing in a little shed during the day, keeping a watchful eye (in theory) on everything during the night.

"Odd, isn't it?" said Dick, grinning. "You'd have thought the new Board would've axed him first thing, and put a team of muscle-men in his place, or a pack of Rottweilers. Old George must know where the body's buried, all right. . . ."

There was a pause. Maureen nerved herself to mention the name they'd all been reminded of. "No doubt Ken would have written one of his reports about security, once he knew how things were—but it would've taken a while for him even to find George, if you ask me. He's a cunning old devil. You won't catch him easily."

Sadie giggled. "I wonder whether it's true he uses this address for his entry on the electoral roll. If his voting card ever turns up in the Post Room, Amos, do tell me!"

"I'd never put anything past him," said Amos, as everyone smiled. "He's a born survivor—he'll see the rest of us out, I expect. He was at school with my older brother Joel, you know, and had the reputation even then of being, er, resourceful. Not that he just lived by his wits, mind you—he could pack a good punch if he—"

"Oh!" Maureen's squeal made everyone jump. "I'm sorry, Amos, but—talking of punches—guess who's got a black eye this morning? I saw her in the loo just before she went on duty. She tried to hide her face, but you could still see, because she hadn't finished doing her makeup. . . ."

"Not Angela Farnworth?" Dick's eyes gleamed. Sadie's report yesterday of her visit to Accounts had interested him greatly. Anyone silly enough to faint when she saw Ken Oldham was certainly silly enough to enrage someone into hitting her, deplorable though such an action might be.

"No, not Angela—Veronica!"

A pause for contemplation. Then: "Veronica Bamber?"

enquired Amos, though from Maureen's tone and meaningful looks there could be little doubt about it.

"Of course Veronica Bamber—and what d'you reckon it
was Steven who hit her? You know what a state all the girls
were in yesterday afternoon—"

"Not Janice," put in Sadie.

"Well, no, not Janice—but only because she's too slow
to have taken it all in at once. I don't suppose she
understood what had happened until she read it in the paper
this morning. But Veronica got herself in a real tizzy, didn't
she—hysterics and skiving out of the office and, well,
everything. You know she did!"

"I'll say we know." Dick glanced at Amos, who was
busy unwrapping his "old-fashioned" barley-sugar again.
"Veronica came charging out of the Switchboard straight
after you'd left them to go to the Archives, Sadie. She and
Tracy began carrying on like a pair of lunatics, and the
others joined in. We were sending them outside in relays, by
the end of it, just so we could get some peace and quiet!"

"Sisters in misfortune," remarked Sadie sourly. "Just
what was it, I wonder, that made Ken so attractive to a
certain type of idiot female?"

"Sexist!" snapped Maureen, for the first time in her life,
and was gratified when Amos chuckled through the calories.
"Heaven knows, we can't all be as strong-minded as you,
Sadie—and Veronica certainly isn't. My guess is, she spent
most of last night at home in hysterics, too, until Steven
couldn't stand it any longer. Remember—oh no, Amos
hadn't come in then—but when he brought today's post, I
thought Steven looked a bit sheepish—very stiff and uncomfortable. And doesn't that mean a guilty conscience?"

Sadie muttered of hindsight, but when Dick showed
every sign of agreeing with Mrs. Mossley she allowed
herself to be persuaded that there could be something in the
theory. Amos did not join in the discussion. He couldn't
help recalling how late Steven had been with the post
yesterday afternoon, and coupling this rare event with the
unusual treatment (or so it seemed) of the wife he'd
heretofore patently adored. He felt uneasy. Was real life
about to encroach on his secret and long-held detective

fantasy? Was he going to have to finger one of his staff to the police? Or was it all no more than coincidence? . . . And he remembered those words of Gervase Fen which he'd quoted on the topic of coincidence and felt even more uneasy.

Fen, however (he told himself sternly), would first make sure the evidence under consideration was reliable. He sat up and coughed. Maureen, Sadie, and Dick fell silent. "I don't think," he began, fiddling with his spectacles, "that we ought really to, er, speculate without knowing, er, the facts. It's so unlike Steven to be, well, violent—there may be a perfectly simple explanation. Perhaps I should have a quiet word with him? Just a friendly sort of chat." Then he sighed. "But it does rather seem like, well, prying. Interfering in people's private lives. . . ."

"You can't, anyway," Maureen told him. "For one thing, he's still delivering the post, and for another—well, if he *is* in a mood to thump people, it might be you he thumps next. Tell you what, though. You'd never get anything out of Veronica in a month of Sundays—but Janice is another kettle of fish. How about having your quiet word with her?"

Sadie choked. "Unless Steven's been indulging in wholesale assault and battery, what use is it talking to Janice? Besides, even if she did know anything, she wouldn't think it was polite to discuss her cousins' home life at work. She's almost as bad as Steven for disapproving of gossip."

Amos looked pained. "My interest for the welfare of my staff surely can't be construed as gossip, can it? I only want to ensure that, well, everything is as it should be."

Maureen glared at Sadie as she hastened to say that she didn't see any harm in it, and if Amos wanted her to slip into the Switch Room and ask Janice to come through to have a friendly chat sometime, she would. Janice, she reminded Mr. Chadderton, would be unnerved by a telephone request from the seat of operations: a face-to-face invitation would be less likely to throw her into a panic.

Sadie swallowed a remark concerning the slowness of Janice's wits precluding the likelihood of panic—which is by nature swift and unexpected—and suggested aloud that it might be awkward for Mrs. Mossley to invite Janice anywhere, with Veronica sitting right beside her at the Switchboard. And if phoning the girl wasn't a practical option . . .

"Eureka!" cried Dick, as Amos was coming to the reluctant conclusion that the life of a would-be sleuth wasn't as easy as the books made it seem. "I'm a genius. When Sadie and I go back to our desks, we can see the door of the Switch Room easily enough—so, the next time Veronica goes to the loo, we tell Maureen—and *she* goes in and tells Janice that Amos wants a word. Brilliant!"

Whereupon Sadie held her peace, the plan was duly accepted, and she and Mr. Slack returned to work.

Eighteen

"OH, HELLO, CLEM. What can we . . . This week's Circular? Er—surely Maureen sent you an advance copy?"

Mrs. Mossley nodded energetically. She had brandished it angrily—at a safe distance—under Mr. Chadderton's nose just before putting it in the internal post yesterday.

But Amos seemed neither to notice nor to remember, his attention caught by whatever he was hearing on the telephone. "Oh dear—I'm sorry, Clem, but I don't see how we can really . . . Well, yes—I appreciate that Ken, er, isn't here to stop you, but he *did* have Board approval for . . . Oh, dear. But it's gone for printing, I think—it would be, well, difficult to withdraw it now."

"What?" Maureen snatched up her extension. "Now listen to me, Clem Bradshaw! I'm not typing that thing a third time, and you needn't expect me to! Whatever you want will have to wait for next week's Circular. Anyway, like Amos said, this one's gone for printing."

"Hello, Maureen." The Transport Manager's chuckle came along the wire as if he hadn't a care in the world. "You've no need to worry about that—I've just rung Reprographics, and they haven't printed it yet. Which means," as she drew breath to give him another piece of her mind, "there's time for my Mary to pop along to collect it and type it all out again with my amendments—"

"What? *Mary* type the Circular? Why, of all the—"

"Don't worry about a thing," Clem broke in. "She's as good a typist as you—almost—and I'm sure I wouldn't want to bother you with it when I know how busy you—"

"Busy be damned! Not so busy I can't see when somebody else is trying to take over my job—because it *is* my job to type the House Services Circular, as well you know. Look, if your amendment's as important as all that, you just send it along here this minute, and I'll type it out for you, *and* see that it gets printed and sent out on time—and never you mind your Mary, Clem Bradshaw!" And Maureen, flushing, hung up the telephone with a bang.

Another chuckle sounded richly in Amos Chadderton's ear. "There now, Chad, as Maureen seems to have answered at least one of your objections—have you got any others, or can I go ahead?"

"Well," temporised Maureen's boss, watching her as she sat, pink and bristling, "I suppose . . . if you're sure—and if you're willing to accept the responsibility . . . then you pop it in the post, as Maureen said, and—"

"I said this was important, Chad! We want that Circular out on time—and I don't know what's got into your young man who brings our post recently. It was ages late yesterday, and if Mary hadn't chased after him with it this morning he'd have left our bag of outgoing stuff behind him. In a dream, he is—you can't trust him—so I'll send Mary down with it herself."

"Oh," said Amos, still watching Maureen. "Is, er, that really a good idea?"

Clem misunderstood him. "Well you know, Chad, maybe I was a bit hasty in not listening to Oldham. When I read the Circular with his notice in it, I made a few enquiries—and it might not be unworkable, after all, with a few amendments—presented the right way, of course. If you let it go out how he's written it, you'll have a riot on your hands!"

"Oh. Er, yes," said Amos, who hadn't meant that. "Perhaps I should send one of the Post Room girls for it," he suggested. Mrs. Mossley tossed her head and sniffed.

Clem laughed out loud. "Anything to keep Mary and Maureen from tearing each other's eyes out, eh? Whatever you say, Chad—but send her along soon, whoever she is. I want that Circular out on time every bit as much as you do. . . ."

And the sound of his farewell laughter disturbed, rather than cheered, Mr. Chadderton as he set the telephone back on its cradle. What enquiries could Clem have made that had so influenced him he was willing—even eager—to accept Ken's idea of a Tesbury bus service? What answers had the transport companies given him which had pleased him so much?

With Ken no longer around to ask inconvenient questions— was it only coincidence that Clem had suddenly become so amenable to the Oldham parking solution? Or did he now feel secure enough to risk bluffing his way through the tangle of denial and deceit in which the Management Consultant's suspicions had been about to ensnare him?

"But we were at school together," murmured Amos, as he unwrapped a stick of barley-sugar. And he sighed.

Once again, Dick found it politic to avoid the canteen at lunchtime, and hung around Sadie's desk dropping hints she seemed, on this occasion, to ignore. She wanted, she told him, a few minutes' peace and quiet.

"I've already had enough disturbance for one day, thank you, sorting out my Little Lads. They jammed so much furniture into the goods lift they couldn't shut the door, and if I hadn't found out in time they'd have taken a leg off one of the desks to make it fit! They rang to ask if I had a saw, and luckily I asked why they wanted it. So I had to make them take everything out, and supervise them while they put it back—and what with all that, plus interruptions from moaning females saying *Oh dear, poor Mr. Oldham*, I need an hour by myself to give me strength for the afternoon."

"You don't know what *moaning females* means, unless you were in this office yesterday," said Dick, with emphasis. "Floods of tears and fits of hysterics—ghastly! If you ever hear me say the nurses don't earn their money, feel free to kick me. If it hadn't been for them, I don't know how Amos and I would have survived."

He raised his voice as he said this last, and the voice of Mr. Chadderton also rose in heartfelt agreement from the other side of the screen. Dick went on:

"*They* could box their ears, you see, but Amos and I just couldn't." He favoured her with a smile. "Still, I bet if you'd been here they'd never have dared be so silly. . . ."

"Probably not." Sadie stabbed a bean sprout with her fork. "I always think a good strong dose of common sense is worth all the emotion in the world—or flattery," she added with a smile to match his own. "Perpetual pragmatism should be the watchword of one's working career. . . ."

"Oh," said Dick, who wasn't sure whether or not this was a brush-off. "I think," he said, "I'll stretch my legs and see what the world outside is like today before I find something to eat."

"The walk will do you good. Exercise helps to work up a healthy appetite—and people who drive to work every day need it far more than the rest of us." Ms. Halliwell played squash three times a week and jogged in her spare time. "If you're not too long, though . . ."

But before he had time to reply to this (possibly) promising lead, the door of the Switch Room drifted open to emit an excitement of female lamentation. Dick winced. "Yes, a walk will do me good!" he cried, and was gone.

Behind the screen, Amos woke from his doze and began to turn pale as the lamentation increased in volume. He hoped that Sadie might be willing to find out what the matter was; he feared she wouldn't. It was, after all, her lunch hour. He wondered if whoever was howling at the Switchboard was doing so on Tesbury time: but he hadn't the nerve to leave his desk and go to find out.

He heard Sadie give an exasperated sigh. She uttered a short oath, and then there came a click, followed by the sound of dialling. "Hello, Switchboard? Is that you, Janice? No, *don't* start chattering—I can tell there's nothing the matter with *you*—but why on earth is Veronica kicking up all that hullabaloo? . . . Oh, really! Send the silly girl out this minute to have a word with"—Mr. Chadderton turned quite white—"me, I suppose," and she sighed again. "It's thoroughly irresponsible of her, and I'm going to tell her so. Doesn't she realise external callers will hear her? They'll wonder what can be going on. . . . Yes, Janice, thank you. I *know* she's upset, or at least thinks she is, but the point I'm trying to make is that she has no reason to be—which I intend to make very clear. . . . No, I haven't time to talk to anyone else now, Janice. Some of us," very sharply, "are trying to have a break from work. . . ."

In the outer office, Veronica emerged from the Switch

Room with smudged makeup and her face streaked with tears. Her black eye was now all too visible, but for once she was oblivious to her appearance. She sat and sniffled, occasionally hiccupping, as Sadie began her lecture, and seemed incapable of pulling herself together as Ms. Halliwell instructed her to do.

"There's no need at all for this ridiculous boo-hooing, Veronica—we had quite enough of that sort of nonsense yesterday. Besides, it's hardly fair to make poor Janice listen to your racket when she's trying to work."

"Janice? Oh, Miss Halliwell!" Veronica sobbed all the more. "Oh, I'm sorry, but it was—was what Janice said—"

"Something *Janice* said has upset you?" The idea was astonishing: nobody could call the gentle and woolly-minded Miss Blake malicious, never in a million years. Unless, of course, she'd triggered this outburst without realising what she'd done—which (since she was so woolly-minded) wouldn't have been hard. "Now what can she have said to upset you so much? It must have been fairly dramatic to have resulted in so many tears. . . ."

"Oh, Miss Halliwell, I'm so sorry—I know I'm being silly, but I just can't . . . it's all been so awful—poor, poor Mr. Oldham—and Janice—Janice said . . ."

Veronica dissolved into sobs again. Sadie drew in one of her deepest breaths, held it while she counted to ten—and then spoke, in a voice deceptively calm. "Veronica, you must stop this. Anyone would think you'd lost the love of your life, instead of a virtual stranger. . . ."

There was a long pause, during which Veronica sniffed and blew her nose—and Sadie thought hard. In the end, she enquired calmly: "He *was* a stranger, wasn't he, Veronica?"

"Oh, yes, Miss Halliwell—well, I suppose he was. But it was when Janice said—said about how nice and friendly he'd been . . . talking to her about the telephones, and then she said about Tracy's party, and I remembered—"

"If I were you, Veronica, I'd remember nothing at all about Tracy's party. Steven wasn't too pleased about what happened then, was he? Not with you—or with Ken Oldham. Suppose the police heard about it? They could easily get the wrong idea, and then—"

"Oh, Miss Halliwell! Surely they wouldn't think—"

"You never know *what* they might think. If I were you, I'd stop thinking so much about Ken Oldham and start thinking about Steven, and how all this might affect him. If Ken really was a stranger to you both . . ."

"Oh yes, Miss Halliwell, he was!"

Sadie hesitated. "Look, Veronica, you can tell me. You were upset yesterday, weren't you? Most of the other girls were, too. But was Steven—well, cross with you in particular, for being upset? Did he get in a—a mood? And now you've had time to think about it, are you worried he might be suffering from—from a guilty conscience?"

"Oh, Miss Halliwell!" Veronica gaped at Sadie, so horrified she forgot to cry. "Oh, Miss Halliwell . . ."

"I think it would be a good idea if you made a real effort to be nice to Steven tonight, Veronica. Keep him happy and keep both your minds off . . . everything. Cook him an extra special meal—perhaps a bottle of plonk, if it's not against his principles. . . ." She did not leave Veronica time to wonder if Steven Bamber had acted against his principles once already that week. "Get off home as early as you can, and make a proper fuss of him. Forget all about . . . this other business, and—"

"But Miss Halliwell, I'm working the late shift tonight! Steven will be home hours before me. I won't have time—"

"Oh, Veronica." Sadie sighed. "Ask Janice to swap with you! Sometimes I wonder—but never mind. Now pull yourself together, and remember what I said, and don't cry anymore. Concentrate on your work and nothing else until it's time to go home—and then, just concentrate on Steven."

Steven's wife gave one convulsive sob and sniffed monumentally. Then she gulped. "Yes, Miss Halliwell . . . thank you. Had I better go back to work now?"

"Good heavens, yes. Run along—and don't worry about anything—and remember what I said."

"Oh yes, Miss Halliwell!" And Veronica took her leave, going first to the cloakroom to repair the damage to her makeup, then back to the Switchboard. As she hurried through the door, she waved, and smiled gratefully at Sadie.

Sadie smiled a thin smile in response, sinking back on her

chair with a sigh. If anyone had told her she'd have to act as a welfare officer for a young woman with whom she had nothing in common beyond a shared gender, she would never have believed them. On the other hand, she'd probably made a better job of it than Amos, that born bachelor (poor Maureen!), would have done. . . .

But she hoped she wouldn't end up making a habit of such action. Once might be justified, as an emergency: but life in House Services was a regular procession of emergencies, great and small. And once (as far as Ms. Sadie Halliwell was concerned) had been enough! There was, after all, a Welfare section in the Personnel Department: she must ensure that she pointed people in its direction, should a similar problem occur in the future.

And, thinking of the Personnel Department, Sadie remembered Maureen Mossley's acquaintance with Dorothy in Personnel, and Ken Oldham's file; she thought of the rumours even now racing round the building. She wondered what the police were doing. . . .

Nineteen

THE POLICE, DURING the day, had been far from idle.

They had begun by getting their priorities right.

"It's going to be another scorcher," came the greeting of Trewley to Stone, as his weary bloodhound face appeared in the doorway of the Incident Room. He'd reached home late last night and hadn't slept well. "Let's hope they ginger up the air-conditioning, or I'll go mad!"

"No problem, sir—I've already had a word with someone. I didn't really suppose you'd fancy being cooped up in here twice running unable to hear yourself think." Stone's brisk gesture encompassed the busyness of the lecture theatre, in which the two uniformed constables continued to labour amid an ever-growing drift of documentation. From time to time, the telephone would ring; it was impossible to shut out the sound of the tannoy; and by the end of the previous afternoon, Stone had been seriously concerned about her child's blood pressure.

"We've, er, been offered one of the interview rooms, sir," she now informed him, with a wink that hinted at the nature of the offer. Trewley knew his sergeant well enough not to press for details. "It's a bit smaller than this, but much . . . quieter, sir. For, er, interviews."

He looked at her sharply, then grinned. "Thanks, girl. It was like an oven in here by the afternoon. The thought of going through it all again today . . ."

Stone led the way, admitting as they went that the idea had not originated with herself. "Remember how Mrs. Mossley took us on the guided tour and told us about the VDU operators upstairs, and how they're always going on about Sick Building Syndrome and wanting electric fans in summer?" Trewley grunted in sympathy. Stone hid a smile.

"And how she was sure the Personnel people had the best

air-conditioning of the lot in the interview rooms, because it fooled people until they'd signed on the dotted line and then it was too late? Well, I remembered her saying it, sir—and this"—throwing open a door—"is the result."

Filtered air seemed to inspire the superintendent. He reread Stone's notes, and studied the organisation chart, and from time to time summoned various Tesburians to question them with great thoroughness—or as thorough as anyone can be when there is little idea of exactly what is being looked for. With—as he said—no obvious suspect, they should try to eliminate as many people as possible before starting the in-depth investigation. The Warehouse must be ruled out first: everyone had been spoken to yesterday, but loose ends remained. Once these had been tied up, he proposed working at random through each department with which Ken Oldham had been connected since he joined the company. There was a surprising, not to say depressing, number of these, and they had barely begun by the end of the afternoon, when Stone complained bitterly of writer's cramp.

"Eliminate?" Trewley mopped his brow in despair. "It's made things a hundred times worse! *How* many people did this Oldham character get on the wrong side of, in eleven weeks? I don't believe it!"

"I do." Stone tapped her notebook with her propelling pencil. She had refilled it twice. "If even half of what they say is true, he was a regular pest, always poking his nose into things that didn't concern him." She regarded him thoughtfully. "Which gives us endless possibilities for suspects, sir. Eight hundred of them, if you think about it. He *was* a Management Consultant, after all."

Trewley shook his head in silence, looked at his watch, and sighed. The bulldog features creased in a frown.

Stone stopped teasing him. "Well, sir, if you're not keen on that idea—let's adopt a positive attitude, as my old Anatomy tutor used to say. He never could put the skeleton together again once he'd taken it to bits for the demonstration. Everyone hated Oldham—right? So let's say that, *because* he was such an overall pain, nobody he worked with has been any more annoyed by him than anyone else.

And then we can rule out every single one of them, and start looking for a—a completely different reason for wanting to kill him. What d'you say to that, sir?''

"I say you're crazy. Good grief, I never heard of such a cockeyed way of investigating a murder!''

"With respect, sir—short of delving into eight hundred separate job descriptions, what other choice have we got? We do rather seem to have eliminated a lot of people on, er, first acquaintance, sir. Until the Personnel files come up with something . . .''

"If they do. No real reason why they should.''

"And no real reason why they shouldn't, sir. We need a—a starting point—and everyone we've talked to appears to be, well, *normal*—no latent paranoia, nothing to suggest they'd automatically want to brain him if he trod too hard on their toes: we can rule out the passing loony, I think. And as for work—well, like him or not, they agree Oldham was trying to make everything more, er, cost-effective sir, which is pretty harmless, I should have thought, no matter how far round the bend he drove people on a, well, a personal level. And if all he did was work—''

"So far as we know." Trewley sighed. "We've plenty yet to learn about Ken Oldham, if you ask me. And, talk about *asking*—nobody did, did they? For him to come and start interfering, I mean. They didn't ask for him—they were lumbered with him. And if you're stuck working with someone who drives you round the bend . . .'' Trewley glared at his grinning subordinate. "I tell you, girl, it always amazes me there aren't more murders committed.''

"Couldn't agree with you more, sir." Stone sounded positively cheerful about it, and her superior scowled.

"Oh, couldn't you? If you're trying to take the—''

"Wait, sir!" She held up a hand, her head cocked to one side. "Listen! I wonder . . .''

Her younger ears had heard them first: footsteps, hurrying toward the interview room, followed by a cursory rap on the door. It burst open almost immediately to reveal a uniformed figure with a Tesbury Personnel folder in his hand, and a grin on his face.

"Here, sir—I've just found this!''

He held out the file to Trewley, but it was Stone who jumped up to take it. While the superintendent dismissed PC Benson with gruff thanks, accompanied by exhortations to keep up the good work, his sergeant turned to the marking slip of paper; and a slow grin crept across her face as she read. Once the door had closed behind a gratified Benson and the two detectives were alone, she handed the file to Trewley and remarked, staring at the ceiling:

"I always think people who say *I told you so* are really annoying, sir. Don't you?"

"Umph." Trewley was reading, scowling. "Umph," he said again, and slammed the folder shut upon the table. "Women's intuition, that's all! Just because this Angela Farnworth has a history of nervous trouble, and spent several months in Nazareth, doesn't mean she's crazy enough to have killed Oldham. You of all people should know that."

"I never really studied psychiatric illness, sir—but I agree. Nazareth's a very good hospital. If they released her as cured, then as far as I'm concerned, she is." Stone favoured her chief with a sideways look. "Anyway, hadn't I already said I ruled out the passing loony, sir? Which does suggest—as you've evidently found Miss Farnworth's file to be of such interest—that the, er, other little item you, er, haven't mentioned yet is more likely to—"

"Stone! One day, my girl, you'll go too far." But the threat was halfhearted, and Trewley's thunderous glare was soon directed to the pages of Angela's file, which he opened as his sergeant composed herself in a repentant attitude and prepared to listen. He met her watchful eye and permitted himself a faint grin as he cleared his throat and began to read selected snippets out loud.

"Voluntary patient . . . honourable discharge . . . back to work—new company—excellent references . . . normal enough unless working under pressure, or sudden shocks. . . ."

"Then accountancy's just the job for her," said Stone. "Nice and steady—figures instead of people. You can't argue with facts. And pieces of paper—on a small scale, that is—don't often start quarrels, sir—or wars."

"No need to bring history into all this, Stone."

"Except very recent history, sir. Angela Farnworth's—and Ken Oldham's." Stone looked at him. "Farnton Enterprises—where Angela was working just before she cracked up—and where Oldham worked, too. He skipped off to the States around the time, didn't he?" She was leafing through her notebook now. "Yes, it fits. Inference—she cracked up because of him—and when she saw him again . . ."

Trewley grunted. "Another *inference* for you: Farnton. Combination name, maybe? Farnworth and—Bolton? Atherton? Preston? This Angela's the daughter, niece, something like that of the company's big bug—chairman, managing director, whatever. Oldham's an opportunist, makes up to the girl, gets what he wants—in the job line, anyway. No idea about whether he worked his wicked way with her or not, but . . ."

"Sir!" Stone contrived to look shocked by the suggestion, without much success: she'd seen too much of life during her time in the force. "Well, you could be right, sir. Hell hath no fury, and so on."

"You'd know all about that, of course." This was rather naughty of the superintendent, for Stone was attractive, in an efficient way, and the relationship with her close friend in Traffic Division was far from scorned. She made a face, and Trewley chuckled, then grew serious. "For all we know, the blighter loved and left dozens of 'em in his career. If what's left of your perishing Personnel files shows up any more coincidences like this, we could be knee-deep in hysterical women before we know it!"

Stone was rereading her notes, checking them against Ken's Personnel file. "You know, sir, if she did bump him off, I'm not sure I altogether blame her. I don't much care for what we've found out about Oldham so far—that ruthless career type, all out for number one and never mind anyone else—especially," and she grimaced, "the, er, weaker sex. On the other hand, if it *is* a motive like plain old jealousy, it's going to make a very dull crime—almost as dull as those interminable reports he would keep writing."

"Give me dull every day, girl—as you'll find out for

yourself, when you've been as many years in this job as me. The clever crimes are the ones that put grey hairs on your head and give you ulcers—the dull ones are cleared up nice and fast. Let's hope Angela Farnworth's going to tell us this is one of them. . . ."

"We'll have to be very careful with her, sir. If she's put under pressure, remember—"

"I'm not past it yet, Sergeant. I've still got the sense to handle her right, I hope—I'll treat her like one of my own. And if she *does* go into hysterics—well, you can't have forgotten everything they taught you at medical school. I'll leave you to burn feathers under her nose and loosen her corsets. . . ."

Not that Trewley seriously supposed this would be necessary: a man with a wife and three teenage daughters should, he felt, be capable of coping with most eventualities when dealing with the opposite sex. He prepared himself to be avuncular, but firm, with Miss Farnworth; and, for a while, this approach worked. Angela was shocked, she was distressed, but she was (reasonably) willing to talk. In answer to his questions, she admitted she had known Ken before—that she had no great liking for him—that she didn't realise (her voice began to tremble) he had come to work at Tesbury's . . . and that no, she didn't have (her voice rose to a squeak) an alibi. . . .

Then she dissolved into tears. Stone tried to calm her. Angela would not be calmed. She sobbed into her lace-edged handkerchief, then crumpled it into a soggy ball, stuffed it in her mouth, and emitted stifled screams. Stone, sighing, shook her, slapped her face, and sent for Nurse Joan. Angela Farnworth was escorted tenderly from the interview room, leaving two very large question marks beside her name on the list of witnesses, and two thoughtful detectives thumbing glumly back through all the statements they'd so far taken.

"It's no good," growled Trewley at last, looking again at his watch. "I can't get a line on anything or anybody—and you're not coming up with bright ideas either, are you? You weren't wrong when you said we had too many to choose from—the likeliest bet is Farnworth, and she's out of it. For this evening, anyway."

"We can always try again tomorrow, sir. I'm still not sure she wasn't faking it, and we might catch her out if she tried the same trick twice—I doubt if she's got the nerve to carry it off again." Trewley grunted: he didn't. "And don't forget the Personnel files, sir. Something else might turn up there—positive thinking, remember?"

"Wishing thinking, you mean. Those two lads are on the last lap, according to Benson. If I'm right, and they *don't* find anything else . . . where do we go from here?" He sighed, and stretched in a massive yawn. "I'm tired. We both are—it's been a long day. I could do with a drink. Care to come along to the Trader for a jar?"

"The Tesbury local, sir?" Stone grinned. "Thanks, but I wouldn't want to cramp your style—all chaps together, as it were." She tapped her notebook. "I'm going to read through my notes again, maybe take another look at Oldham's reports—the titles, anyway—in case inspiration strikes. If *you* listen and *I* think, between us we could well come up with a new line on all this. . . ."

Which explains why, as Amos sat in The Spice Trader drinking Old Guvnor at a corner table, an unexpected shadow fell across his empty supper plate. He looked up.

"Mind if I join you, sir?" Detective Superintendent Trewley held a half-full pint mug in his hand and looked ready to drain what was left at one gulp. Startled, Amos nodded an invitation, and Trewley, with a groan, collapsed on the nearest chair.

"Been a hard day," he explained, licking froth from the rim of his glass and eyeing Mr. Chadderton's beer with some approval. "Old Guvnor, I suppose. You can't beat it, can you?" Without waiting for an answer, he drank deeply. "Get you another?"

Amos blinked, but remembered his manners and accepted. Five minutes later, he and Trewley were sharing crisps in a companionable (and comparative) silence, from time to time drinking from their mugs, greeting acquaintances as they passed, listening idly to snatches of conversation drifting across the room. It was one of the most remarkable moments of Mr. Chadderton's life.

"I hope," he said at last, as Trewley neared the bottom of

the glass and began to look less harried, "this doesn't, er, mean I'm a suspect, Superintendent? I've read a great many detective stories, you know, and the hero doesn't usually hobnob with anyone unless he harbours, er, doubts about them. I don't believe I have an alibi for the relevant period, for one thing—"

"Nor do most people." Trewley's tone was glum. "Don't you worry, sir—I haven't got my eye on you any more than on anybody else. Yet, that is."

Amos chose to ignore that uncomfortable coda and said: "But no less, either?"

Trewley acknowledged this with a nod and a grunt, then could restrain himself no longer. "The trouble is, *nobody* who worked with his seems to have liked him—and Stone can keep on about thinking positive till she's blue in the face, we've got to narrow it down somehow. Eight hundred people! Now we've got a bit more of a feel for the type of work he did—my sergeant's a good girl—she's still there, going over that list of report titles your Mrs. Mossley gave us—we'll be checking his desk first thing tomorrow." Trewley patted the pocket in which Ken's keys now rested. "But we'd like a look at that clipboard of his, I don't mind telling you. How do we know what he might not have seen and jotted down that could be a clue?"

"I see. Yes. Well . . ." Amos didn't want to accuse any of the Tesbury staff of murder; but, if suspicion had to fall on anyone, he'd prefer it not to be on members of his department. "No doubt this is a foolish comment, Superintendent, but—have you wondered what he was doing in the Warehouse in the first place? It's miles out of his way. Certainly, he had a—a brief to go where he liked and to study whatever he wanted—but the Warehouse was one of the places he'd always tried to, er, invade—and they never let him over the threshold. Ever."

"Oh, didn't they?" This was the first Trewley had heard of such prohibition. They'd kept very quiet about it—and he couldn't blame them—but now it made him wonder why. . . .

Some judicious prompting led Amos to reveal what he knew of the Union anger at Ken's computer-based proposals, though he was careful to gloss over how it was he came to know; and he concluded his slightly flustered narrative by explaining that it was typical of Ken to have taken the first advantage he could of so rare an event as a protest meeting to snoop at Warehouse practices and procedures. Before he'd reached the end, Trewley's eyes were gleaming.

"Loss of perks, eh? And that clipboard of his missing. Makes you think, doesn't it?"

And Amos had to agree that it did. . . .

While her weary boss refreshed himself in the fleshpots, Stone was poring over her notes, rereading them, condensing and refining them, writing what might be salient facts on separate sheets of paper and shuffling them round the table to see if any sort of pattern emerged.

It didn't. She began to feel she'd have done just as well to have gone to the pub with Trewley, and was on the point of calling it a day when there was a knock on the door of the interview room, and in came her two uniformed colleagues, obviously tired of paperwork.

"We've gone right through the lot, Sarge." PC Benson looked relieved it was all over. "Nothing."

Stone raised an eyebrow at his silent companion, who nodded confirmation. She sighed. "Oh, well, trot off home, then. Leave me to my fun and games—unless either of you has any bright ideas?"

PC Hedges lumbered across to the table on which she had spread her Salient Sheets and bent to peer closer. Stone waited while he thought about things.

He straightened. He cleared his throat.

A scream rent the air through the half-open door of the interview room: a scream which, as all three police officers froze in horror and stared at one another, died away into a long, slow, gurgle which seemed to echo round the now-empty building. Stone leapt to her feet; Benson and Hedges came to their senses and turned to run. The door was a crowded jumble of arms and legs as they met. . . .

And by the time they had sorted themselves out, the gurgles had completely died away.

Twenty

"DOWNSTAIRS," SNAPPED STONE, starting to run. "The Switchboard—never mind the lift!"

They were too late. By the time they had dashed along the corridor, turned two corners, pelted down the central staircase, and run through the main foyer to the discreet outer door of the Switch Room, there was nobody there.

Nobody alive.

Benson gave one horrified gasp, and bolted back to the entrance hall, where they could hear him struggling not to be sick. Hedges, more phlegmatic, choked, clapped his hand over his mouth, and sat heavily down on the chair farthest from that on which . . . she . . . was slumped, leaning forward on the table with—something—wrapped tightly round a neck above which her face was blue and breathless.

Automatically, Stone administered what help she could, though she knew it was useless. Benson, shamefaced, spoke from the doorway.

"Is she—really dead, Sarge?"

"Yes. Go and fetch Mr. Trewley, will you? He's probably still in the pub—the Trader. He was hoping to pick up a little local colour. Hedges and I will stay here."

He nodded, and went, only too glad to be out of there. He drew in deep, shuddering breaths as he emerged from the foyer into the early evening sunshine, and headed for the car, hoping he wouldn't have too much difficulty in following Stone's instructions. Everyone in Allingham knew The Spice Trader. The drinks were good—the food was better—and the parking was abysmal. He could spend as much time trying not to cause a traffic jam as it would take to walk—or at least jog—the distance on foot.

Then he thought how that suggestion would go down

with Trewley, and grinned. Car, then, and let the motorists of Allingham take their chances. . . .

"Sir—Mr. Trewley, sir!" He manifested himself in front of the corner table just as Trewley was about to suggest it was Mr. Chadderton's round. The superintendent looked up in some surprise. He frowned as he read the expression on Benson's face. "Could you come back to Tesbury's at once, sir? It's . . . an emergency, sir." His eyes flicked to the listening Amos and back. "Sergeant Stone's already there. . . ."

Trewley rose to his feet and drained his drink in the same instant. "My old bones tell me whatever's happened is pretty serious, Benson—and that Mr. Chadderton's department is tied up in it somehow." The young constable gulped at this unfortunate choice of words. Trewley glared. "Right, Benson?"

"Sir—yes, sir." And he studied his boots as he spoke.

"Something's happened in House Services? Come on, lad," as Benson gulped again, "Mr. Chadderton's in the clear—he's been here with me this past half hour or more!" And Amos, bracing himself for bad news, nodded, and stood up, breathing hard.

"It's—it's the girl on the Switchboard, sir. She's—she's dead." As the memory of her death made Benson shut his eyes for a moment, Amos emitted a little cry of horror. "Dead, sir, and I think—I think she was . . . strangled. . . ."

"Veronica's been strangled?" Amos sat down again. "No, that's not possible! I won't believe it. . . ."

Because that would mean, if it were true, *two* murders in House Services. Murders which reason said had to be linked: and, as the Warehouse went home an hour earlier than the general office staff . . .

Back at Tesbury's, Mr. Chadderton nerved himself to help the police in their enquiries by identifying Veronica's body—and received yet another shock as he fixed a fascinated gaze on that ghastly blue face.

"But—that's not Veronica! It's—it's Janice! . . ."

Stone took one look at the paling Pickwick features and hurried him out of the little room. "Strong, sweet tea's what we could do with,'' she muttered; and he pulled himself together sufficiently to ask whether barley-sugar would do. Stone said it would and escorted him to his office, where she watched for a short while and then left him, with instructions not to stir until she and Trewley returned.

''. . . the life out of me,'' Benson was saying as she went back to the Switchboard. He had recovered from the first shock and was now in the garrulous stage. ''She must've knocked against the switch on that loudspeaker thing while she was trying to fight him off.''

''Poor girl.'' Trewley shook his head. ''Never really stood a chance, did she? Sitting down—concentrating on her job—he jumps her from behind and wraps the microphone flex round her neck and pulls. . . .''

Stone had joined them. ''At a guess, he was standing up. The extra height would have given him enough leverage, force—whatever you want to call it. She hadn't a hope, once he put that wire round her neck. . . .''

At last, the formalities were over. The doctor had confirmed Stone's diagnosis, the forensic team and photographers had done their duty, the body had been removed, and Janice's parents were being notified of their daughter's death. Now Trewley and Stone were on their way to talk the matter through with Amos Chadderton. His inside knowledge might be invaluable: and he had, as Trewley said, an alibi for this murder, at least. Even if he'd committed the other, what he said (or didn't say), and the manner of his saying it, could just give them the lead they were looking for.

''It's got to be something to do with Oldham,'' Trewley said, as the three sat together in Mr. Chadderton's office. ''Something she knew that she hadn't told us, perhaps. . . .''

''Something she'd seen,'' suggested Amos, as Stone sighed and said nothing. ''Something incriminating to, er, Ken's—Ken's assailant. When you recall that the windows of the Switch Room look out on the road—oh, no. They overlook the main road, not the one leading to the Warehouse. Still, she *could* have seen something—somehow. . . .''

Stone jotted down a note to the effect that Mr. Chadderton seemed keen—understandably so—to link the two killings so thoroughly that the fact he had an alibi for one would rule him out for the other. She frowned, and remembered the layout of the House Services main office.

"Something she'd seen," she said. "Oldham's desk is in full view of the second door to the Switch Room, isn't it? Hadn't we better take a look, sir?"

"We should never have left it for tomorrow," muttered Trewley with an oath, as thirty second later they stood, dismayed, staring down at that view of Ken's desk invisible to anyone merely walking through the office, as they had done not ten minutes before. "He's beaten us to it—with a chisel, if I'm not mistaken."

"Sadie—Miss Halliwell—keeps the toolbox over there," Amos told him, pointing to the nearby potted palm. "She says you never know when you're going to need a spanner or something—oh, dear."

Stone had darted across to check even as he was speaking. "And nobody thought to keep it locked, of course," she said. "Haven't any of you people heard about opportunist thieves and crime prevention?"

"Everything is clearly marked and labelled," began Amos, then blushed, and fell silent, as Trewley and Stone stared at him in disbelief. Trewley nodded to Stone.

"There *was* something in his files we weren't meant to see—and ten to one, now we never will. Good job you've got those report titles written down, anyway. But—"

"Oh, no." Amos was blushing again, but for a different reason, as he broke in. "The reports are kept in Maureen's cupboards, Superintendent, and nobody's broken into them—I would have noticed, you know, with her desk being so close to mine. I'll check, of course, if you like."

"Yes, please." Trewley was frowning as he examined the plundered desk. "Whatever was on that clipboard *must* have been a pointer to why he did this—either it said too much, or not enough. Either way, he needed to get something out of this desk—but what?"

"And Janice," said Stone, gazing from the desk to the Switch Room's other door, "could have looked out and seen him at it. It's near enough for her to have heard the noise—she'll have wondered what was going on, and . . . and why,'' she demanded of nobody in particular, ''didn't he kill her at once, right here in the office? Why give her time to raise the alarm? Not that she did, but . . .''

Amos, having checked Maureen's cabinets and found them secure, had rejoined the two detectives. At Stone's words, he coughed. ''I expect—I'm afraid, you know, she wasn't a terribly bright girl. Neither of them is—I mean was—oh, dear—well, Janice was good at her job, but—to be honest, you could tell her almost anything plausible about anything else, and she'd swallow it. She found life in the Post Room too much because of the teasing,'' and he explained.

Trewley grunted. ''So when she saw him breaking in, he fobbed her off with a story she believed at first—and then he got nervous, and thought even she would smell a rat, and he knew she had to be silenced. . . . Ah. Changed your mind, have you?''

For Stone was shaking her head. ''No, the dumbest person—with all due respect to Janice—isn't going to let some chap kid her a crowbar's an acceptable way of breaking into anyone's desk, not for a minute. She probably slipped out to powder her nose, or something. Is this door closer to the loo than the door leading into the foyer?''

Amos told her there was little difference, but that the telephonists hung their coats on House Services pegs rather than inside the Switch Room, because it was less cluttered. Stone nodded.

''She needed something out of her coat pocket—we'll see what's in there presently—and she saw him *near* the desk, but not actually doing anything to it at the time. So he was able to bluff his way out of it and only realised later that when news of the burglary came out next day she'd be bound to remember what she'd seen.''

Trewley, with a few routine grumbles, announced himself willing to accept her version of events, adding: ''But what could he have wanted so much it was worth taking that risk?'' He turned to Amos. ''Look, do you know of *any* other projects Oldham had in mind that might not go down well with people—apart from the Warehouse thing and the computer? Do try to think, Mr. Chadderton. This bloke's already killed twice.''

At first, Amos was unable to meet the superintendent's eye, as thoughts of Clem Bradshaw came unbidden to the forefront of his mind—indeed, hadn't been far from it since the discovery that Ken's notebooks and rough files all seemed to have disappeared along with his clipboard. Surely the suspicions Ken had voiced had been proved groundless, though? Hadn't Clem agreed to let the bus trial go ahead, just as Ken had planned? Would a man taking bribes, or touting for them (if that was the accusation), be prepared now to change his tactics and be so open about everything?

Unless it was all an elaborate charade. Maybe Clem had already made up his mind which bus company was to be awarded the contract—maybe this talk of a fair trial for each was no more than a bluff.

"I—I'm afraid I can't . . . think of anything," said Mr. Chadderton in desperation; and was thereupon dismissed with thanks—and with the uncomfortable knowledge that he hadn't fooled the superintendent one little bit.

"We'll get him later," promised Trewley, as, late in the evening, they left the Tesbury premises. "He's hiding something—he *knows* something, even if he doesn't really know he knows it—the man reads detective stories, for heaven's sake! Told me about it in the pub," he added, as his sergeant fixed him with a wondering eye, then chuckled. "Quite a fan, it seems—so he damned well ought to know better than try to act clever with the likes of us! In his precious books, that sort of thing never pays, in the long run. And if he's hoping to pull some daft amateur stunt and show the thickheaded coppers how to do their job, and goes rampaging round the place destroying evidence . . .''

As he paused to draw breath while he thought of the most bloodcurdling fate he could devise, Stone chuckled again. "Do you really see him running about being a sleuth, sir? I'd have said he was far too lazy for anything of the sort—oh, he'll daydream about it, but nobody as—as tubby as Mr. Chadderton's going to do much more than dream, surely."

"Stone, if that's yet another hint about sugar, I—"

"Sir! As if I would. Your, um, avoirdupois is entirely a—a personal matter, sir—although, since you've chosen to raise the subject, I must admit—"

"Stone! Just because my wife's had one of her little chats with you—oh, don't try to look surprised. You can't fool me—I'm a detective, remember? And so," becoming serious again, "are you. Amos Chadderton isn't. But he's got an eye for detail, all right, and a pretty good memory for what goes on—in his office, at least. We could do a lot worse than have a long talk with him sometime—once," he added, sighing, "we know what the hell to ask him about."

Stone stretched and yawned. "Let's sleep on it, sir. You know what they say about things looking better in the morning. . . ."

On Thursday morning, however, things were far from better: they were much, much worse than on the previous day. When news of the second, even more grotesque, murder broke, media invasion—or (thanks to police warnings) siege—of Tesbury's made earlier efforts look like practice runs. Those members of staff who hadn't opted to stay safely at home had to brave the cameras and microphones of scores of reporters and other journalists; they also had to fight for parking spaces which should have been theirs by right, but which had been taken over by vehicles displaced from the road by the besieging busybodies. The car park was full—the streets were crowded—and in House Services, everyone was praying that there wouldn't be a fire alert.

Amos's department, having lost two of its members in as many days, was now experiencing the inevitable result. Post Room hysteria had reached an all-time high; the Switchboard was in chaos. Veronica Bamber hadn't come to work at all. Steven, who'd been sent for by Janice's parents the instant the police officer had left their house, insisted that no wife of his was to be exposed to the same risks as his late cousin. The hastily acquired temporary operators were having their minds blown by a Switchboard which flashed incoming calls at an almost impossible rate: they kept rushing out of the door into House Services to throw tantrums and to demand tranquillisers, throat lozenges, and danger money.

Mr. Chadderton cowered in his corner, two distraught even to crunch barley-sugar. Maureen could spare no time from trying to talk sense into the telephonists to worry about him. Sadie and Dick were their usual selves in the outer office. Sadie threatened to box a few ears; Dick tried to jolly the girls along with a few feeble jokes. If the situation did not improve out of all recognition, it did, nevertheless, at last improve—but very, very slowly.

It wasn't helped by the fact that Trewley and Stone, interviewing again, were concentrating their attentions—for obvious reasons—far more noticeably on House Services than on any other department. Mr. Chadderton was informed that, unlike the practice of the previous two days, there would be a complete in-depth grilling of every member of his staff at work that day—starting, if he didn't object, with himself. Having made his own statement—less helpful, he feared, than anyone else's would be—Amos looked so miserable that Maureen dug the departmental brandy out of the emergency drawer and tipped a double measure into his morning coffee.

"I could do with some of that," called Dick, who'd seen what she was doing. "Dutch courage for the ordeal to come—whenever that is."

Sadie muttered something about spineless males, but her heart wasn't in it, and when Mrs. Mossley felt constrained to invite both deputy managers "for discussion" she accepted with as much alacrity as Mr. Slack.

"Get yourselves outside of that," said Maureen, pouring brandy into three more mugs, and giving herself the most generous slug with the remark that, after the Switchboard temps, she needed it more than anyone else.

"They all egg each other on," said Sadie in disgust. "Look at the ridiculous way the Post Room's been behaving! The only people who've stayed remotely sane are Biddy Hiscock and my Little Lads—"

"As far as you know," Dick reminded her; but Sadie did

not smile. Amos could see a squabble developing, and he wasn't in the mood today.

"Talking of temps," he said quickly, "and the Post Room, I've, er, been thinking."

"We couldn't have any temps in the Post Room," Maureen said. "They'd take too long to learn the job, what with all the abbreviations and the destination codes—it isn't like the Switchboard, where it's standard equipment."

"Er, yes—that is, no, it wasn't the Post Room I meant exactly. It was the Switchboard. It had never really occurred to me before how, er, vulnerable we are—with Janice, er, gone, and Veronica not coming in—we'd be really in trouble if we didn't have those temps. But if there were a couple of bright Post Room girls we could, er, train up in case of similar emergencies—"

"Good heavens!" Sadie stared in horror at her boss, and Mr. Slack took the words out of her mouth.

"How many more murders are you expecting, Amos?"

"Oh, dear. None, of course—but we *are* rather, well, haphazard about things sometimes. It was a sheer fluke that when Julie, er, left us there was somebody already trained who could take over. . . ."

The thought of what had happened to Julie's successor filled everyone's thoughts, and there was an uncomfortable pause. Dick was the first to break it.

"A sort of official substitute system, you mean?"

"They'd have to be paid extra for being trained," Sadie was quick to point out. "Extra qualifications merit more money—that's how they do it in the Warehouse, and Steven used to work there. He'd remind them, if we forgot. You know how very . . . honourable he is. He'd think it was the only fair thing to do."

There was another pause, while they all thought about Steven Bamber, husband to Veronica—who'd flirted with Ken—and about Ken, who was dead. . . .

Dick said: "Perhaps we could even extend the system. Suppose Sadie learned to type, then she could cover for you, Maureen—and I could take a bodybuilding course so that I could help shift the wastepaper and the furniture when any of the Lads were ill or on holiday—"

Sadie rounded on him. "Don't be ridiculous! You'll be suggesting next that Amos learns to service the photocopiers and the offset litho printers! And why should *I* be the one to type, just because I'm female? Why should it be the Post Room *girls* who are trained to use the Switchboard? Why not my Little Lads?" Then, before anyone could reply, she hurried on: "If you ask me, we ought to stay exactly as we are. If we continue to bring in good-quality temps from an agency the way we do now, there can't be any possible hint of discrimination about it—"

Ms. Halliwell was clearly set to do battle on behalf of Women's Lib, and Amos blinked at the hornets' nest he seemed to have stirred up without meaning to. He might prefer, on the whole, warlike females to hysterical ones: but at the moment he didn't want either. He shot an anguished glance at Mrs. Mossley . . .

Who, though she could think of nothing very helpful to say, was about to hurl herself nobly into the breach—when another furious female voice suddenly made itself heard, and Angela Farnworth came storming into House Services with a very angry look upon her face.

Twenty-one

SHE FIXED MR. Chadderton with a glittering eye. "Well, *you* may be in your office—but where is Mr. Bradshaw, I should like to know?" She gave him no time to reply. "In hiding, that's where—because you and he and your *friends*," with a scowl for Sadie, Dick, and Maureen, "have looked after yourselves, as usual, and found places to park while the rest of us have to put up with the inconvenience *again*! Where has Mr. Bradshaw gone? I want to tell him what I think of him!"

Brandy and desperation made Amos bold. "Why should I know where Mr. Bradshaw is? This is the House Services department, not Transport. And my *colleagues*"—indicating Sadie, Dick, and Maureen with one all-embracing flash of his spectacles—"and I are having a staff meeting."

Angela was oblivious to hints. "I've told you before that I won't be fobbed off, and I meant it! Last night I had to hang around for hours here because somebody's car was blocking mine in—and of course I couldn't find Mr. Bradshaw to make him do anything about it. This morning, I couldn't even drive down the road because it was full of parked cars! If I can't make an official complaint to Mr. Bradshaw, then I insist on making one to you. What are you going to do about it?" She waited. "Well?"

Amos shook himself, his spectacles glinting. "Oh, yes, the car park. You, er, will be pleased to know that this week's House Services Circular—"

"Huh!" Mrs. Mossley emitted a monumental sniff.

Amos gulped, but rallied swiftly. "Er, yes—the Circular will, er, explain the solution that has been, er, proposed— thanks in part," he added, as she opened her mouth to argue, "to Ken Oldham." She shut it again, and licked lips that had suddenly gone dry. Amos took heart and spoke more firmly, though he still kept a wary eye on Maureen.

"The Circular will be distributed later today. It contains full details of the bussing-in system we will be trying for a test period of three months. . . ."

When Angela had gone, there came a gratifying chorus of admiration (though Maureen's was noticeably muted) from all who had witnessed that little exchange. Amos beamed modestly and allowed himself to bask in the praise of his colleagues to stop himself thinking . . . thinking how Angela Farnworth had been delayed last night by Sadie's car, and had gone to look for Clem Bradshaw—and hadn't found him. And Amos didn't remember spotting him in The Spice Trader, either, though he generally dropped in after work for a drink. Nor did he appear to be around this morning. . . .

And, without asking Maureen for permission, Amos poured another tot of brandy into his coffee.

It was a long, hard, tiring day for everyone at Tesbury's, whether or not they had legitimate cause to be on the premises. Old George disturbed a surreptitious pair of reporters near his hut and chased them away with a broom. A formal complaint was registered (by the reporters) and promptly capped (by Old George). Both sides claimed a moral victory.

The weather didn't help tempers remain steady. July is generally the hottest month of the year: this July had been no exception. A pitiless sun raged down upon the heads of all who waited to catch sight of the police going grimly about their business—Trewley, of course, cocooned himself in the coolness of the interview room and was never seen—or of stray Tesburians going about theirs. The Spice Trader, which was within walking distance, did a roaring trade in Off Licence sales. Stone, observing signs of mirth among the thirsty hordes, sent a quick message to her friend in Traffic. It would be a considerable feather in his cap if he could book an entire column of journalists for drunken driving, though it was preferable, in the interests of public relations, that he should give them a friendly warning first.

By the time people began to go home, most of the reporters had already departed, sped on their way by Stone's tactful and persuasive colleague. People who popped wary heads out of the main door began to hope that they might escape without further questioning. They'd had enough, they grumbled, from the police.

"I've had just about enough of all this," said Sadie Halliwell grimly. "One more sob, and I swear I'll massacre whoever it was, inch by inch!"

"They were fond of Janice," began an indignant Maureen, but Dick's indignation was louder.

"You won't be able to, because I'll have done it first. Heaven knows, I'll have had plenty of practice with the offset service people. . . ."

Amos shuddered. "I'm only thankful I didn't know about the delay this morning, when I spoke to Miss Farnworth. Why didn't anyone from Reprographics think to tell you—any of us—that the printer had broken down?"

"Rather a lot's been happening recently," said Dick, who might enjoy sharing a moan about his staff but preferred to keep their major errors, as far as possible, to himself. "You should be thankful for small mercies, Amos. Once that Circular *does* go out, the phones will be ringing like the clappers all day long with people complaining about these buses of yours—"

"Not mine," interposed Amos, with another shudder. "They're Ken's basic idea, as I told Miss Farnworth—and now they're Clem's. He's more than welcome to them!"

He gulped a large mouthful of brandied coffee. Maureen had kept him well-supplied throughout the day: she had never seen her boss in such a state. Not that anybody was particularly cheerful, of course—but with Amos, the contrast between his present and his normal mood made the lack of cheer far more noticeable. Maureen told herself that the replacement brandy—the last drops had gone into Mr. Chadderton's seventh cup ten minutes ago—must come in a full, rather than a half, sized bottle. She could hardly wait to get to the shops and get away from the telephone. . . .

Which rang again. Mrs. Mossley sighed as she picked it

up, then frowned as she clapped a hand over the mouthpiece and turned to Amos.

"The police," she hissed. "For you!"

Amos jumped, blinked, hiccupped, blushed, hiccupped once more, and reluctantly reached for his extension. Having heard what the disembodied constabulary voice on the other end had to say—he put it down again; and the look he directed towards Maureen was almost reproachful.

"They want me to—hic!" One plump hand briefly covered his mouth, and he muttered a quick apology. "They want me to go and talk to them a—hic!—gain. Another statement, or some—hic!—thing, I suppose—and just listen to me! How can I help the police with their en—hic!—ries when I can't string two words together? You shouldn't have made me dri—hic!—quite so much brandy. . . ."

"Drink a cup of water backwards," came Dick's suggestion from the other side of the screen, since Maureen was rendered too speechless to reply.

"Breathe in and out of a paper bag," called Sadie, above the sound of rummaging, and a few moments later she appeared around the screen. "Here, have this. The carbon dioxide you exhale suppresses the hiccup centre in the brain, or something—whatever it is, it works. Go on," as he opened his mouth to question this remarkable advice.

But as what emerged in place of a question was another hiccup, with an embarrassed grin Amos shrugged, took Sadie's paper bag, buried his face in it, and began breathing in and out with great fervour. Mrs. Mossley watched him doubtfully, Ms. Halliwell absently, her attention focussed more on the clock above his desk.

"See? I told you it works—two minutes, and all your hics at the beginning. Doctor Halliwell, take a bow!"

Amos emerged, pink-faced and flustered, from the brown paper bag. "Thank you very much indeed," he gasped. "Could I, er, keep this, do you think? In case of, well, a relapse—I mean, I know how keen you are on recycling, but . . ."

Maureen was maliciously amused to observe Ms. Halliwell flinch. Mrs. Mossley wondered whether she, in similar circumstances, would be as sensitive about wrapping a whole-food lunch in paper so well and truly breathed on—but, being honest with herself, supposed her reaction would be much the same as Sadie's—though she hoped she'd manage to hide her feelings a little better.

With a nod, a rather forced laugh, and a wave, Sadie was gone, leaving Amos to fold the bag, a little untidily, into his pocket before heading for the interview room. He pushed back his chair, gripped its arms, and rose to his feet, shaking his head to clear it. But his step was almost steady as he passed Mrs. Mossley's desk, and—his hiccups in thorough abeyance—he beamed down at her, murmuring proudly:

"Helping the police with their enquiries, you know—the way they always do in books!"

And he had trotted merrily away before she could point out that this would be the third session he'd had with Trewley and Stone—whereas everyone else, as far as she knew, had only spoken to them twice, at the most. Amos was still muzzy from the brandy and perhaps couldn't be expected to have noticed; and she wondered, as she watched him weave his way between the Post Room tables towards the door, whether he was so muzzy that he might say rather more than he should when the police began asking their questions.

The first question came from Stone, five seconds after Mr. Chadderton closed the door of the interview room and began his cautious advance to the waiting chair. "How about a cup of tea?" she said, as the brandy fumes reached her side of the table. "The superintendent and I were about to have one—with plenty of sugar. Weren't we, sir?" as Trewley spluttered. "I'll see to it now," she promised, and set off quickly on her sobering errand.

Ten minutes later, Amos was sipping from a steaming cup, and chatting away with the two detectives as if they were old friends. With very little prompting, he was prepared to expound on the workings of House Services, the changes proposed by Ken Oldham, or anything else about which he might be asked. When Stone began to speak the words of the caution, he had joined in, nodding and smiling. He'd read this sort of thing so often—and now fiction was turning into fact. And it could just be that, without his help, the case would never be solved. . . .

"No, Mr. Trewley, to be honest with you"—Amos blinked at the superintendent through his spectacles—"I can't honestly say that anyone liked him. Though they all liked poor Janice, of course. But Ken Oldham—honestly, he annoyed us all. All of us!" He leaned forward, waving a plump forefinger for emphasis. "The list of suspects, you know, is endless—stands to reason. Everyone in the building, you see. Eight hundred people!"

Trewley nodded. "Yes, sir, we'd noticed. See how far through her notebook my sergeant's got with taking all their statements? But I must say, not many of 'em have been as helpful as you—not that I'd expect it of them, of course, seeing they wouldn't have the chance to be. If I've understood the workings of this place, if anyone's likely to know what's going on around here, it's House Services. And with you being the boss . . ."

"Pretty well everything, that's true, Superintendent." Had he slurred the last three words, or not? Amos frowned, then smiled. "Pretty well everything—because I'm interested, you see. I listen when people tell me things—listen most of the time, come to think of it. Finger on the pulse, you might say."

"Ken Oldham jealous of you, was he, by any chance? With him being so keen on finding things out, and you always one to know them, I should have thought . . ."

Trewley allowed the sentence to tail off invitingly, and Amos accepted the invitation with glee. "He might have been—he might have been, Mr. Trewley. I can't honestly say I'd ever considered the point before, but when you, er, point it out, then yes, I suppose he might have been. But not much," he added, with a wink. "He was very sure of himself, that young man. *Too* sure, sometimes—a cocky young snirp, someone called him, and I couldn't have put it better myself. He never liked admitting he didn't know things—but," with a chuckle, "sometimes you could catch him out—as Dick did last Friday, I remember. . . ."

Amos, on his way back from responding to a call of nature, had seen Dick engrossed in a complicated graph plotted in red and blue which proved, to his acute dissatisfaction, that (despite his every endeavour) the amount of photocopying on Tesbury premises was increasing remorselessly, month after month, year after year. Not a blip or dip or hiccup could be seen on those relentless felt-tipped lines . . . and Dick frowned as he programmed the next set of figures into his calculator, divided them by twelve, and inked the next, inexorable dot on the paper. Mr. Chadderton, shaking his head in sympathy, trotted on without a word.

Ken, still smarting from his encounter with the puritanical Steven Bamber, was obviously spoiling for a confrontation he could be more confident of winning—the charge of blasphemy had pricked his Welsh Methodist conscience. "You look busy, Dicky boy," he said. "I never realised you went in for so much calculation in your job. Hard work, is it?"

"What makes you think I'm working? I'm only passing the time of day. I do so enjoy making pretty coloured patterns on squared paper—I find it soothing. I mean, it's not as if I've anything better to do, is it?"

Amos smothered a chuckle at Dick's tone. It was the first time he'd ever heard Mr. Slack really on the defensive: but it was the first time (so far as he knew) that Ken had in any way intruded into the other's work. Until now, Mr. Oldham had elected to interfere with other departments than House Services, reorganizing and making suggestions and instituting surveys without, it seemed, concerning himself with that area with which he was most closely associated. Now, however, it appeared he must feel sufficiently confident to charge in and start upsetting his colleagues to his heart's content—relying, no doubt, on his Board backing, on the apprehension (if not outright fear) of his . . . his *opponents*, thought Amos, for their jobs. He was throwing down the gauntlet: it was to be a matter of survival: and Mr. Chadderton commended Dick highly for not allowing himself to be bullied.

He'd missed the opening salvoes. ". . . hardly cost-effective, Dick, surely you see that?" There came the sound of rustling paper. "From the prices in these lists, I think it would be far better to do away with all the small copiers there are around the building and replace them with more machines in Reprographics—bigger, faster machines, Dick. But I suppose you've always been too busy coping with the day-to-day logistics to think of the wider solution. . . .''

Amos marvelled that Dick could hold himself back from kicking Ken Oldham where it hurt. It was the height of impertinence for the newcomer to suggest that the more experienced Mr. Slack didn't have the wits to run his department efficiently. . . .

''You think so?'' And Dick's tone made Amos offer up a silent cheer: he might have known the Old Guard could rely on Mr. Slack. ''As a matter of fact,'' said the Deputy Manager cheerfully, ''I haven't—been too busy to think it over, I mean. Three months after I joined Tesbury's, I looked into exactly the sort of scheme you're suggesting— but it never got off the ground because it was, ahem, hardly cost-effective. Care to take a look at the figures?''

More paper was rustled, with considerable enthusiasm. Dick spoke slowly and clearly, as if to a small child. ''You see, most people only want to take one or two copies at any one time. Now, the bigger machines you're talking about are geared to runs of five or more—they may well look faster on paper, but that's only for bulk printing, which is what the smaller, casual copiers don't do so well. And if you add the cost of time wasted in sending or taking the material to be copied to and from Reprographics, plus the increase in Post Room staff for extra sorting and collection and deliveries . . .''

Ken, after a pause, rallied. ''Time wasted, Dicky boy— that's the trouble! Think of how people just stand about, waiting and queueing and gossiping by the copiers, instead of being at their desks where they belong. Do these figures of yours take *that* into account?''

There was an eternity of weariness in Dick's voice as he replied. ''Look here, *you* can hop about the building trying to cut costs and save time, if you like—be my guest! But *I* gave up all hope of doing any such thing ages ago. You've just got to accept that if the machines are there, people are going to use them. Oh, I suppose if they'd never had the facility in the first place we could have stopped them getting the habit—but they were, and we didn't—and now we can't, believe me. And the very best of British luck to you if you fancy trying to take it away from them now!''

Mr. Oldham was not giving up yet. "Look here, Dicky boy. Suppose the copiers were *slower* than they are now? Then people who didn't have access to word processors, people who only wanted to save themselves the bother of making carbons—call it the Lazy Typist Syndrome—well, they *would* take carbons, wouldn't they? Rather than hang around by the copier for ages?''

"Yes, well, that one's got whiskers on it, too." Dick sighed. "I tried renting smaller, slower copiers as an experiment a few months ago. . . .'' It had been when Tesbury's financial problems were becoming acute, with everyone loyally buckling down to cost-cutting where possible. Dick's effort—despite having first been discussed in depth with Amos, Maureen, and Sadie—had failed dismally: customer demand for the service as usual had evicted the trial machines within days, if not hours. "The lazy blighters just won't wait. They complain so much you wouldn't believe it—the phones didn't stop ringing until we'd put the old machines right back where they'd come from, and fast.''

"But, Dick—''

"Then," Mr. Slack pressed on, evidently enjoying himself, "I took away all the plain white copying paper and put in coloured, instead. We'd had a wrong delivery of some ghastly bright pink stuff which should have put anyone off using it unless it was really urgent. Which is why I was fool enough to think they'd be more likely to take carbons, or send it to Reprographics—but I was wrong.''

He sighed and seemed set to say nothing more. Ken was unable to refuse the bait. "Why?''

Dick chuckled. "Why? Easy. The Financial Director's secretary went to copy the minutes of a Board meeting— some graphs and charts she couldn't print on her word processor—and his lordship didn't like the way they turned the damn things piebald. He was on the phone moaning that we had to change the paper back to white—but only in their department. So we did—he's one of the bosses, after all.

And you can guess what happened next, knowing what this place is like. Especially as it's open-plan offices. . . .''

Ken weakened again, though he hated admitting his ignorance. "What happened?"

"Everyone else found out in ten seconds flat there was white paper in that one machine, so they started queueing to use it, and causing traffic jams miles long—so the bigwigs complained about the queues—and we ended up swapping all the other machines as well. At which point, I decided to stop bashing my head against the brick wall of photocopying costs and settled simply for keeping the machines working and the customers happy. . . . Still, like I said, Ken, if *you* fancy a go, be my guest. Just remember that saying about immovable objects and irresistible forces. . . .''

Ken loathed having to ask; but he did. "Why?"

"Because on the one hand I'm supposed to reduce the number of copies and, as a result, the copying costs— right?"

"Well, yes, of course."

"Says you! The Board, on the other hand—I assume this new lot's no different from the old—insists that normal service must be maintained—for them, at any rate. But try treating the rest of this place as second-class citizens and see what happens! It'd make the French Revolution look like a—like a Scout jamboree. . . .''

There came a snort from Sadie Halliwell, an amused spectator of the little scene. Amos chuckled again, and Maureen—who had likewise been gleefully eavesdropping— sniggered.

Ken must have heard them. Babbling about user needs and time-and-motion studies, he scraped the feet of his chair on the carpet, trod heavily across to his desk, and hurried off on what he announced was to be a tour of the entire Tesbury building to find out what, and how, the company's employees thought of the photocopiers. . . .

Dick rushed to tell Mr. Chadderton in gloating detail how Ken, frowning horribly, had almost forgotten his personalised, black leather clipboard in his haste. "And the best of British luck to him," he concluded, laughing out loud. "Photocopiers, indeed!"

"That young man's a glutton for punishment," remarked Mrs. Mossley, sniggering again, then frowning. "Unless, of course, he's really gone somewhere else—another of his snooping expeditions. . . ."

Amos stopped chuckling. "Wherever he's gone, I'm afraid that at long last the attentions of the Tesbury Management Consultant are to be directed toward House Services—and I suppose we've been very lucky it hasn't happened before. It had to come in the end. . . ."

"He'll be after you next, Sadie, now I've shut him up for a bit." Dick grinned as Ms. Halliwell looked across in some surprise. "If you're in need of any moral or physical support, just let me know. I'll sort him out for you."

"What makes you think I can't take care of myself—and my department—perfectly well without anybody? There's no need for Ken Oldham to interfere with *me*—with any of us, really. I'm sure that if we all stick together and keep squashing him—though I doubt if we'll manage such a good job as you did, Dick—he'll soon get tired of snooping round House Services and go back to annoying somebody else. We've all done these jobs for years, and done them well—and this is hardly the sort of department where you can afford to make experiments." She smiled at Mr. Slack. "Look what happened when you tried it, after all."

Dick muttered something which made Maureen gasp, though Sadie Halliwell only laughed. "Language, please! But if we make it clear we don't want, or need, Ken Oldham, then he might start looking for places where *real* improvements could be made."

"He's looked at enough of them while he's been here," said Maureen, evidently thinking of the many reports she'd typed for him. "Places, I mean. It's like Amos said—it's our turn now. More's the pity."

"He'll be on at you about the word processor again, mark my words," Sadie warned. "You'd better be ready with the facts and figures to shut him up, the way Dick did—the only way that seems to work, with Ken. I intend to blind him with so many when he tries it on me that he won't dare to *breathe* anywhere I'm in charge of!"

Dick preened himself, but remarked that in all honesty

he'd been lucky, because he'd worked out the figures fairly recently just in case there was an angle he'd overlooked—which there hadn't been. "So I knew exactly what to say to our know-it-all friend—but nobody'll have a hope of getting him out of their hair unless their figures are as up-to-date and double-checked as mine were."

"I can assure you there's nothing wrong with *my* paper-work. . . ." And as Sadie bristled, Amos's heart sank. She'd reminded him of what he'd so far managed to overlook: the plan Ken Oldham had suggested for the car park—and his insinuations against the Transport Manager, Clem Bradshaw. . . .

Twenty-two

THEN AMOS GASPED, gulped, and made a frantic grab for his cup of tea. Trewley chose to ignore this sudden loss of enthusiasm on the part of his witness and uttered a sympathetic chuckle.

"Yes, the car park. My word, we could tell you a few of the choicer things the Traffic people have said about Tesbury's over the past few months—couldn't we, Sergeant?—except we wouldn't want to shock you, Mr. Chadderton. Very, er, ripe, some of 'em were."

Stone winked at Amos, glumly peering over the edge of the teacup he still held in a tight grasp. "Very ripe," she agreed, thinking of the vast sums recently expended by her close personal friend on indigestion remedies and headache pills. Amos saw her smile, and found to his surprise that he was smiling back. Stone nodded cheerfully.

"But then, from what you say, Mr. Chadderton, it seems we could be over the worst. If, that is, Mr. Oldham really did manage to think up a solution. . . ."

On the morning of his death, Ken had bounced into House Services even more full of himself than usual. He greeted his colleagues in ringing tones, but did not stop to drop his briefcase—black tooled leather, to match the clipboard—at his desk before marching past Mrs. Mossley into Mr. Chadderton's office and commandeering the visitors' chair.

"Well now, Amos—take a look at this, will you?" He produced from the briefcase a sheet of paper, which he brandished triumphantly in front of Mr. Chadderton—just out of easy range. "I want this to go into this week's House Services Circular, Amos."

No *please*, no *if it's not too much bother*. Maureen glowered: she'd just finished typing it. Amos blinked.

"I spoke to the Board last night," went on Mr. Oldham in a decided tone, "and everything's been agreed, right down the line. We really couldn't wait any longer, Amos, for you and Clem Bradshaw to make up your minds—so this," and he brandished the paper again, "is the way it's got to be. I'm sorry if you feel I've overstepped your authority"—Amos was of the opinion he wasn't sorry in the least—"but it had to be done. Maureen"—he'd condescended to notice her at last—"you ought to be able to fit these few lines in for me, eh?"

Not for me, but for the Board, whose backing I've quoted so often, whose support I know—and you know—I've got. Mrs. Mossley took the paper he held out to her and studied it. "I suppose," she admitted, "I could squeeze it in on the end somehow—"

"Oh, Maureen, that won't do! On the first page, if you don't mind. This is important, remember—approved by the Board? And we all know how many people bother to read the House Services Circular through to the last page!"

Maureen looked as if she could have brained him: Amos blinked behind his spectacles. Of course nobody read the Circular right through. It was a fact of life that it was easier to find things out by word of mouth, or the tannoy—even by means of the local newspaper, on occasion . . . but there was no need to make the point with such relish.

"You want this on the first page." Maureen's struggle not to scream the words at him was evident.

Ken smirked. "The front page is the only place for something as important as this, Maureen. And it had better go right at the top of the page—we want to be sure that as many people as possible see it before they throw the Circular in the bin."

"At the top of the front page," Maureen said, casting a wary eye at her boss, who could not meet her gaze. This was a battle she'd have to fight on her own—but he knew, in his heart, it was no contest.

Ken smirked again. "Ah, if you'd only agreed to have a word processor, Maureen. . . ."

He would normally have gone on scoring points for some time, but Providence now arrived, in the form of the morning post—brought by Steven Bamber. Even Ken's bumptiousness collapsed beneath that stern and accusing eye, and, with a few more muttered instructions, he hurried from Amos's office, leaving the House Services Manager sighing in despair, and his secretary scowling as she read through the addition Ken Oldham wanted to make to that week's Circular.

She peered round the screen to check that Ken was out of earshot. As she'd expected, he had disappeared from view. Having thanked Steven and said good-bye, she turned to Amos.

"You'd better read this—may as well know the worst. He's going ahead with the buses, all right—even mentions the trouble with the car park as . . . as 'an emergency reason for such controversial corrective measures'—huh! And not a word of apology—not to the staff, not to you, not to Clem, even, for jumping the gun like that!"

Mr. Chadderton didn't feel he could bear to read the jargon-infested memo: Maureen could give him the gist of it, he knew—and that would be more than enough. "Which firm has he chosen?" he asked, feeling he had to say something.

She scanned the notes again. "He doesn't say—in fact, he doesn't go into too much detail at all. I suppose with it being such short notice, he didn't want to start muddling everyone. He says the scheme will start in the first week of August."

Amos sat up. "But it's almost the end of July!" And a horrid suspicion seized him. "Maureen, he must have been looking into things more closely than he led us to believe. Saying it was only a suggestion, indeed!"

Maureen shrugged. "Deceit's his middle name, I've said so all along. He's been fooling you and Clem right down the line, Amos—if you ask me, he'd already made up his mind, and everything else was him pretending, and playacting, and being two-faced—which is all Ken Oldham's good at, in my opinion!"

"I can see," remarked Trewley, "why nobody much cared for the chap. He wouldn't be one of *my* favourite people, carrying on the way he did, trying to teach everyone their own business. You and Mr. Bradshaw must know the workings of this place backwards, you've been here so long. . . ."

Amos had bumped into Clem Bradshaw on Monday evening, in the pub where they so frequently shared a packet of crisps and a burst of Tesbury gossip. Mr. Chadderton greeted his friend with a rueful smile.

"This round's on me, Clem. My goodness, it's certainly been one of those days today!"

"Thanks." The Transport Manager grinned. "But when was it ever *not* one of those days in House Services? You should try working in *my* department if you really want to know what life's all about!"

"Not more BMWs," pleaded Amos, as they took their drinks and headed for a corner table. "I've had a word with Insurance—"

"Don't mention those idiots to me! Remember that young fool from Grocery Buying who tried to swim his car through a river? I'd never have believed how much trouble they could create about that if I hadn't seen it for myself. I'd dock the money from his wages if he worked for Transport, let me tell you—I haven't the time to waste with paperwork!"

So that emergency telephone call which had so conveniently drawn Mr. Bradshaw out of House Services and back to the safety of his own department had been genuine.

Or had it? Did Amos have the detective daring to talk to the Insurance people again and ask a direct question? He was very much afraid he hadn't. . . .

"Is that," he enquired, burying his nose in his mug so that his old friend wouldn't think he was staring at him, "why I couldn't reach you on the phone this afternoon? I had an idea that, er, Ken Oldham was coming round to see you, so I thought I'd, er, warn you before he arrived."

"About his blasted buses—I know." Clem's snort was followed too closely by a drink from his mug, and it was a while before he stopped coughing long enough to curse Ken Oldham's name and tell Amos why he was so angry.

After the indignities (as he no doubt saw them) heaped upon him on Friday by Steven Bamber and (to a lesser extent) Dick Slack, it seemed Ken must have been brooding all weekend. He had thrown his weight around a great deal during Monday, and descended upon Mr. Chadderton to harangue him yet again about the car park, quoting his bus calculations and saying that if Amos was unable to make any decision without consulting Clem Bradshaw—who was never there to be consulted—then he, Ken Oldham, Board-appointed Management Consultant, would go in search of Mr. Bradshaw to confront him with the full facts, and to insist on a speedy decision.

"Mary told me," ventured Amos, "that you weren't in the office—but I, er, gather she passed on my message."

"She's a good girl. Yes, she mentioned you'd rung, but by the time I got back he'd gone—*after* he'd bent the poor girl's ear about those bloody buses. . . ."

"Maybe," said Amos, watching Clem's face closely— was that scowl really one of anger, or was there a hint of fear as well?—"maybe it *could* solve part of the problem— for a while, anyway. Running buses, I mean."

"Maybe. But the last thing I want is some young snirp who wasn't even born when you and I started work telling me, or anyone else, how to do my job. Improvements—modernisations—that blasted computer changing everything—change just for the sake of it. Look, Chad, we—you—mustn't let the likes of Ken Oldham kick you around—"

"I don't! He doesn't! That is . . . well, not really." Amos remembered the bleeper, and the reserved space in the car park, and . . . "Not about anything important."

"*Important* depends on where you're standing, Chad. That cocky young beggar's in a very convenient corner right now—convenient for him, that is. All out for himself and to the devil with the rest of us, that's Master Oldham—they tell me he's been promised a bonus, and higher grading, and gold-plated wheel nuts on his company car, for all I know, if he gets us *modernised* how the Board says it wants, whether it's the right way or not. But he needn't think he's going to get it from Transport without a fight!"

He drained his tankard, stood up, and scowled again. "My round, right? Same again?"

Amos watched as Clem made his way through the Tesbury throng to the bar, nodding a greeting here, making a quick joke there. How could a man whose authority was under threat—whose honesty had been impugned—be so cheerful? Wasn't he worried—or didn't he know? Had Ken dared to voice those earlier insinuations again to Clem's loyal Mary? The Transport Manager was making no secret of his hostility toward the Management Consultant. Was this carelessness—bravado—or a double-bluff as devious as anything Ken Oldham could dream up?

"Clem, I've been wondering." Amos had nerved himself to speak while Clem had been buying the drinks and plunged in as soon as his friend returned. "About, er, those buses—it was, well, something Ken suggested—hinted at, really, I mean . . ."

"Hints and suggestions be damned! Why can't he come out with it like a man? And why, Chad, can't you?"

"Oh, dear. . . ." Why couldn't he, indeed? In that comfortable world of detective fiction where Amos spent so much of his spare time, interrogation never seemed so—so embarrassing. He sighed. Clem looked at him. He gulped.

"Clem—you *could* make up your mind about those buses, if you wanted to," he blurted out at last, trying to study his friend's face for signs of guilt or innocence, but unable even to meet his gaze. "But you don't—you won't. Why won't you?"

Mr. Bradshaw seemed to sense that Amos was really suffering as he asked his disjointed questions. He frowned, and stared, and fiddled with the handle of his tankard. Amos wished he'd kept quiet—the suspense was terrible. How people survived to become series characters, instead of giving up after just one book, he'd never know.

"Chad, old friend," said Clem at last, taking a deep breath. Amos froze. A confession?

Clem glanced around, noticed as if for the first time that they were in a crowd of Tesbury employees, and said . . . what Amos was almost sure he hadn't intended to say a few moments before.

"Look, Chad, you've got to admit there's nobody knows my job as well as I do. And what I'm not having is anyone—I mean *anyone*—waltzing in telling me how to do it, and saying I'm for the chop if I don't."

"He didn't!"

"Didn't he? A misunderstanding, then, if you say so— but what *I* say is that so far as I'm concerned, there's no room for the likes of Ken Oldham in Tesbury's—there never was, and there never should be. I don't like threats, and I don't like nosiness. So if that young man keeps poking his nose into my affairs . . ."

And he stoutly refused to utter another word on the topic of the car park, the buses, or Ken Oldham. He urged Amos to drink up because it was his round, demanded salt-and-vinegar crisps, suggested a game of darts. In short, he acted in every way as if the subject was closed. . . .

But Amos was very much afraid that it wasn't.

Twenty-three

TREWLEY RUBBED A weary hand across his face. "Wonder how much of all that has anything to do with this affair?" he said, as the door closed at last behind Amos Chadderton.

Stone flexed her wrist and closed her notebook with a sigh. "Total recall," she said, "has its drawbacks, sir. The man's obviously longing to play the Great Detective. . . . Goodness knows if the beans he was spilling were useful or not, but there were a great many of them—I'm whacked!"

"We could take a leaf out of our friend's book and nip down to the pub for a jar," suggested Trewley, daring her to remind him that alcohol contained calories. "I couldn't face another cup of tea, but a nice, cool beer . . ."

"Tea!" She pulled a face. "The cup that cheers, but does not inebriate—and works the other way, if you drink enough of it. Nobody could say we took advantage of him, could they? And it isn't as if he was even tipsy—just a little . . . out of focus, at the start."

"Well, you sorted him out nicely. I sometimes think," Trewley told her, with a chuckle, "that was the only reason I let you into plainclothes—your training's come in handy a good few times now. He's not fit to drive yet, though—and he said he was off to the Trader for his supper. With us still around, he'll be walking there, of course. Just as well. . . ."

The Tesbury local was The Spice Trader, formerly The Three Crowns. One of the earliest casualties of the Takeover had been the head of Sauces and Seasonings, whose department had been forcibly joined with Pickles and Preserves to form Consolidated Condiments. The former S&S Supremo, being some twelve years older than the P&P Principal, had accepted his redundancy money with a sigh of relief, and embarked on a new career as a licensed victualler and publican.

His erstwhile colleagues were happy to assist him in his endeavours. Every day, and most evenings, they would assemble in the pub at the end of the road to enjoy company gossip, lament the good old days, and generally set the world to rights. They could eat a proper meal of meat and two veg, or they could settle for pie-and-pint snacks: there was a cribbage board, and darts, and shove-ha'penny—this latter pastime being much in vogue among the Grocery Buyers, who could obtain favourable terms on bulk purchases of the powdered arrowroot needed to keep the board shiny.

Amos Chadderton, that bachelor gourmand, was one of many Tesburians to show his approval of the new regime by keeping a pewter tankard reserved for his especial use hanging above the bar. No sooner did his beaming Pickwick features appear in the doorway than the landlord reached down the tankard and started to pour Rudnam's celebrated Old Guvnor into it, calling an order through to the kitchen as he did so.

"Won't be a minute, Amos, if you're having your usual—the wife's dishing up a lovely bit of steak and kidney tonight, for all it's so hot. Fancy a lemon-and-lime to cool off a bit first, do you? I've mixed a fair number of those since opening time, believe me."

Amos, full of sugared tea on top of brandy, decided he would indeed enjoy the sharper taste of a long, nonalcoholic drink before Old Guvnor helped to wash down the steak-and-kidney pie. "With ice, please," he said, and licked his lips as the cubes clattered into the glass.

The first glass refreshed him so much that he ordered another, and a tray, on which he loaded the Old Guvnor and the lemon-and-lime to carry them across to his favourite table. Here, he sat for a long time by himself, sipping, eating—and thinking. Thinking about what he had told the police . . . wondering whether he had been of any help—of too much help, perhaps, or even too little . . . remembering other things which might have been of help in the enquiry, if he'd only thought of them at the time. . . .

• • •

Nobody had found it easy to work on the day following Ken's death. The whole building hummed with muted excitement, generated both internally and externally. Telephones rang with specious queries and problems, invariably followed by ultracasual enquiries as to what was known about the case. The rapidly evolved policy of House Services was to tell all Tesburians to read the next Circular, and to hang up—while the Switchboard girls grew hoarse with chanting *I'm sorry, no comment* before putting outside callers through to Public Relations. Under such stressful conditions, it wasn't long before Veronica Bamber, still shaky after whatever experience seemed to have unnerved her last night, retreated from her post to the cloakroom; and Maureen, urged by Amos, was free to enter the Switch Room to drop the right sort of hints to Janice Blake.

Janice had seemed rather alarmed as, ten minutes after Veronica's return, she slipped from the Switch Room and made her way to Mr. Chadderton's office. As she passed through the department, she paused to speak to Dick and Sadie, both busy, for once, at their desks.

"Oh dear—Mr. Slack . . . Miss Halliwell, I was just wondering—I mean, it seems, well, sort of strange . . ."

Sadie was kindly, but brisk. "Now, don't worry about a thing, Janice. Mr. Chadderton won't bite—he only wants a little chat. In you go!"

"Yes, Miss Halliwell. But . . . I don't understand—"

"Run along, there's a good girl." Dick was known to have even less patience than Sadie with adolescent angst, particularly when the sufferer was physically some years beyond adolescence. "He'll explain everything—there's no need to fuss. Be off with you!"

Janice drifted across to the screen, where Maureen took charge of her and ushered her into Amos's presence. As soon as the girl was out of sight, Dick spoke to Sadie in a very firm voice—Amos could almost see him rotating an expressive finger at one temple:

"I think I'll just slip along to Reprographics for a few minutes. I want to know if they've fixed the offset machine that was making those funny noises yesterday. . . ."

Sadie refrained from pointing out that he could have learned what he wanted by picking up the telephone, restricting herself to the remark that if anything, er, interesting cropped up during his absence, she would tell him later. Amos heard the laughter in her voice as she said this, and Dick's spluttered response as he hurried away and left her to her eavesdropping.

Oh, yes, said Janice—wasn't it dreadful about poor Mr. Oldham? Such a nice, friendly man—he'd talked to her once about the new telephone equipment they were thinking of buying (Amos, to whom Ken had *not* talked, was astonished at this, but held his peace) just as if she'd been someone important. Which reminded her—could she ask Mr. Chadderton to put a piece in the Circular about collecting newspapers? Because they needed new equipment, too—only for camping, of course. The Guides. She was a Ranger. And someone had told her you could get thirty pounds a ton! Guides were ever so good at collecting things to make money, only there weren't enough of them for new tents. Last year, they'd collected milk bottle tops for a Guide Dog. Not a dog for Guides, she meant, because they could see as well as anyone, but for blind people. Not just milk bottle tops, of course, but aluminium foil and cans, too. Did Mr. Chadderton know that when she was a little girl the Brownies had saved milk bottle tops for the hospital? It was years before she'd realised they weren't going to melt them down—the tops—and put it in the thermometers when they wore out—the aluminium, that was. How silly of her! Because everyone knew thermometers were made of mercury, though the new sort you stuck on kiddies' heads were plastic strips with numbers. Grown-ups could have the new sort with real numbers that changed like a clock, if they wanted—and it was a pity she hadn't got one for poor Veronica, because she just wouldn't go to the nurse and she really didn't look well—

"What!" cried Amos, amazed that she'd eventually wandered to the point he'd wanted her to reach when he was still trying to break into the stream of words and change their direction.

His outcry was a mistake. Startled, Janice blinked, and

blushed, and fell silent. Maureen shot Amos a reproachful look, and he thought quickly.

"So sorry, my dear—a touch of cramp. An old man like me . . . not like you young people. I'm, er, sorry to hear Veronica's not well. Anything, er, serious?"

"Oh, poor Veronica!" Janice sighed. "She's being so brave, and it must hurt so dreadfully—bruises always do when they're fresh, don't they, and it only happened last night. Poor Veronica! The most dreadful black eye—and all because she walked right into a door!"

"And only Janice," said Maureen, once that innocent maiden had taken her leave, "could possibly believe a story like that!" Mrs. Mossley had abandoned her typing and listened with as much interest as anyone to Miss Blake's babbling.

Amos hesitated. "It's possible, I suppose. . . ."

"Pigs might fly, but they're very unlikely birds!" Maureen shook her head. "You know Veronica. If it was a door, she'd have been playing for as much sympathy as she could get when I saw her in the loo—but she didn't. She kept trying not to look at me. It was Steven, I'm sure."

"Was it?" Dick's eager voice accosted them from the entrance to the office. It seemed he had been unable to spin out his visit to Reprographics any longer—or else could restrain his curiosity no further; and, as Sadie had slipped away on some errand, Amos and Maureen were the obvious people to ask. "Did Janice say so?"

He was as incredulous as Maureen when he heard what they had to tell. "A door? Never! He duffed her up, I bet—"

"Then don't talk so loud, in case he hears you." Maureen glanced at the clock. "The next post is due in a few minutes."

"That's why Janice hopped it, then." Dick grimaced. "She wouldn't want to face him, cousin or no cousin, knowing what a temper he's got and busy gossiping about his private affairs with Amos—"

"But she wasn't," protested Mr. Chadderton. "She really said nothing to which *anyone* could have taken exception. . . ."

"Anyone normal," said Dick darkly, then coughed, as he spotted Steven Bamber approaching with the post, and changed to dark mutterings of his intention to concoct a blistering letter to the external service engineers for his offset litho printers. He wished Sadie was there. Ms. Halliwell's way with words was proverbial in House Services, her memos models of clarity and conciseness; but until she came back, he'd struggle nobly by himself. . . .

Steven departed quietly with the outgoing mail. Maureen turned in triumph to Amos, and said that Steven's silence *proved* a guilty conscience, about something, and what else was there but Veronica and her black eye . . .

"Black eye," murmured Amos now, into the depths of his Old Guvnor. "Black eye. . . ."

He found himself musing on Steven Bamber. Never mind that Janice had been his cousin. If she'd seen him at Ken's desk—perhaps removing some evidence of his guilt he hadn't realised before was kept there—would Steven have killed her? Would he have needed to? Surely Janice would have believed her cousin, if he'd presented her with an even halfway credible reason for needing to burgle the desk . . . and what, in any case, could the desk have contained that Steven would need to clear him from suspicion? What Post Room secrets could he have known—could Ken have discovered he'd known and abused?

Ken Oldham and Steven Bamber—Ken Oldham and Veronica Bamber. Motive for murder there, in that tactless *birthday* kiss unexpectedly witnessed by Veronica's husband. So was the desk break-in simply a blind? A poor excuse for murder, then—but excuse enough for Steven, that religious, strong-minded, honest, and genuine young man—with a hidden streak of violence. Veronica's black eye bore witness to that. . . .

Veronica. Amos had thought, when the news of another killing had been brought, that it was Veronica who'd been killed: he knew the week-long rota the girls worked on overtime rates. But Veronica and Janice had swapped at the last minute. If Steven had been sufficiently roused that he had already struck her once, could he have seen it as only a short step from a black eye to some sort of execution—some sort of punishment for having flirted, and for having mourned the man with whom she'd flirted?

Which meant he'd murdered Janice by mistake. . . .

Which meant—Amos sat up suddenly—that Veronica must still be in danger. What a shock it would have been for her husband when he arrived home from—from work—to find his wife alive and well and waiting for him. . . .

Amos couldn't bring himself to pursue this train of thought any further. He finished his beer, rose hurriedly from his chair, and made for the door.

Whereupon off-duty Police Constable Benson, seated at the bar, slipped from his stool and followed him out into the car park—and thence, with some difficulty, into the Allingham streets. And along those streets as far as the Bambers' little flat: outside which Amos parked his car and sat, silently worrying, watched from the shadows in an unworried, though interested, silence by his constabulary companion.

———— Twenty-four ————

"AND HE JUST sat in his car half the night?" demanded Superintendent Trewley next morning, as a red-eyed Benson, yawning, presented his report. "Why the hell did he do that?"

"No idea, sir—but he must've thought he had a reason. He'd been working himself into a real state in the Trader, muttering to himself about—black eyes, it sounded like—and sort of counting off on his fingers and, well, *thinking* about things, sir, you could tell."

Trewley grunted. "Thinking about the Bambers, that's clear enough, or he'd never have gone to watch their flat. And with you there watching him, you'd have seen if anything had happened, wouldn't you, lad?"

"Yes, sir. And, well, it didn't."

"No axe murder?" enquired Stone, as Trewley frowned and indulged in some thinking of his own. "No midnight screams? No sinister masked figures creeping out with bulging sacks over their shoulders?"

Benson grinned faintly. "No, Sarge. Nothing."

"Both Bambers in this morning?" Trewley glared at his sergeant, but spoke to Benson. "All present and correct?"

"Er—couldn't say, sir. But I could always find out."

"Stone?" But the sergeant shook her head without saying anything: a sudden twinge of memory had rung a faint bell.

Trewley nodded briskly to PC Benson. "Off you go then, lad. Pop your head into the Switch Room and check if Mrs. Bamber's there—you can't miss her, she's a regular looker, red hair and all. Can't be two like that in a place this size—then check on the husband. Don't ask around—if Chadderton knows he's a wrong'un, and hasn't had the sense to tell us, he might do a runner if he gets twitchy now.

Use your eyes, and any common sense you've got, then come back and tell us when you've found him. Them.''

As the door of the interview room closed behind PC Benson, Trewley groaned. ''What does Chadderton know—or at least think he knows—that we don't, to make him act that way? You've read all those statements enough times, girl—what have we missed? What's the use of a woman in the job if she doesn't use her intuition?''

Stone did not reply. The bell was ringing louder now— the memory was coming closer. . . .

Trewley recognised the signs, and knew that one way to pin down the elusive was to concentrate on something else, connected—not necessarily closely—with whatever-it-was you were trying to remember. He said softly:

''Of course, Chadderton might have been mistaken. He evidently thought better of whatever theory he came up with in the pub—otherwise, why didn't he go bursting in there, or call us, or—or something, instead of staying outside while he made up his mind what to do? And then he goes and does nothing!''

''But he *goes*,'' said Stone. ''He *went*—and he must have had a reason. Unless, of course, he's just a dirty old man who wanted to catch a glimpse of Mrs. Bamber in her undies—oh!'' She slapped herself on the forehead with the back of her hand. ''Of course—that might be it—and it's about the last thing you would—could—have noticed, sir. . . .''

''Stone, you're havering. Would, could—what difference does it make? And why are you telling me I'm an unobservant old fool, for heaven's sake?''

''No, listen, sir. It's a bit of a long shot, but if I'm right, it explains last night—we only interviewed Veronica on the afternoon of Oldham's death, didn't we? And she howled her eyes out and enjoyed herself saying how dreadful it all was—and she was in, er, splendid condition then, wasn't she? Some people—not necessarily myself, of course— might have said you were almost foaming at the mouth. Sir.''

''Never mind the manners, girl. Get on with it!''

''Benson reminded me—I bumped into her next day in

the ladies' loo, where you couldn't possibly have seen her, and she was spending ages fiddling with her makeup—well, it seemed ages to me, because I hardly ever wear the stuff, as you know. If only *you'd* seen her on Wednesday, sir—with a wife and three daughters, you'd have spotted it—but Veronica works shut away in that little Switch Room, doesn't she? Where neither of us has any need to go. And I'm prepared to bet that all the makeup business was to cover up a black eye—which means she must have been injured—however it happened—on the same evening Oldham died—''

''And Bamber kept her off work yesterday! Said he wasn't having her work where it was so dangerous—and anyway she was too upset—but *he* came in all right, didn't he? When it was *his* cousin!'' The bulldog wrinkles contorted themselves amazingly in the effort of concentration. ''Stone, I ought to bawl you out for not telling me earlier about this, but I won't, because you were right! Chadderton *did* want to see Mrs. Bamber—''

''But not for the reason I thought—he wanted to make sure she was safe!''

Trewley lumbered to his feet. ''And so do we, girl. Get along to that Switch Room right away, and if she's not there check the l—''

A sudden scream broke into his instructions and caused Stone to freeze halfway out of her chair. It was a triplicate scream, yodelled from the ceiling at an almost painful pitch as the Tesbury fire alarm gave tongue.

Stone unfroze, and sprinted to the door even as Trewley burst out: ''Damn and blast, that's all we need! What the hell do we do now?''

She was reading a red-lettered notice pinned to the wall beside the door. ''It says here that intermittent tones mean Prepare to Evacuate the Building—and only when the tone is continuous should we actually leave, and rendezvous at Point Three in the Warehouse yard—there's a map—''

''Map be damned—we're not waiting! Leave the building? What's the betting our man set it off on purpose—he'll be up to something, mark my words, and using this racket as an alibi of some sort. Leave the building? We're leaving it, all right—now, to make sure nobody else does—and if it turns into a continuous tone, we're going to keep our eyes peeled in case anyone tries to sneak out of the place. Come on, girl!''

He was through the door well before Stone: who thus had no time to ask why, if Steven Bamber wished to run away, the method of flight he'd chosen was so complicated. Surely it would have been better if he'd simply stayed at home, and gone from there at his leisure—creeping out, perhaps, with a bulging sack over his shoulder. . . . Despite her haste, she found time to grin. Then she frowned, as she contemplated Trewley's hurrying back view as it turned the final corner towards the stairs. How were the pair of them, plus Benson if he had the sense to join them, supposed to surround the Tesbury site and prevent any flight—if, by some strange chance, one should really be planned?

As the two detectives hurtled breathlessly through the foyer and headed for the main door, Stone was about to make these observations when the pitch and frequency of the yodel audibly changed.

''Continuous!'' barked Trewley, looking about him in dismay. ''Good grief, the place must be on fire after all. . . .''

''Then it makes a change,'' said Stone, thinking of certain pithy comments reported as coming from Allingham's Fire Chief. ''Wonder how long it will be before the brigade arrives? And I don't see any smoke, or flames—''

''Can you see Bamber? Never mind the rest! Find Point Three, and—oh! What the—!''

A wave of Tesburians, grumbling excitedly at the interruption to their working day, had begun to flood down the steps in an orderly torrent, heading for the Warehouse yard. Trewley had no chance to say anything more, for he was swept away in the stream, and could only gesticulate to Stone to do her best. ''Keep your eyes peeled!'' he cried, above the chattering uproar of speculation that this, at last, might be the Real Thing. ''Don't let him get away!'' he shouted, in a desperate diminuendo. The elbows and handbags of the evacuees were both forceful and insistent: he was being borne along by an irresistible wave of VDU operators. "Stone!"

All Stone could do in response to his final bellow was nod and wave as reassuringly as she could, while pressing on with following his instructions—which wasn't easy. Judo or no judo, she could hardly toss aside the milling crowds to ensure she reached the spot where her suspect might be before anyone else did. But she could, being slight, wriggle; so she took a deep breath, and wriggled, and thus made her way towards the Warehouse yard.

Weaving their way down the road, two-toned sirens wailing, came fire engines with flashing lights on top, and oilskinned passengers inside. The leading engine screeched to a dramatic halt at the main Tesbury entrance, and a squad of helmeted hose-carriers leapt down, ready to pound through the front door and up the stairs, axes at the ready, breathing apparatus fully primed. Orders were shouted, radio receivers crackled, and people moved out of the way.

Two figures appeared on the steps in the wake of the main evacuation. One was tall and rangy, with a beard; the other was short and portly, on the balding side. The tall one carried a megaphone; the short one wore spectacles with gold frames. Both figures looked acutely embarrassed. Dick and Amos, dutiful captains of a sinking ship, had been the last, as usual, to leave the doomed building. . . .

Only, once again as usual, the building wasn't doomed.

"It was that pipe-smoking idiot in Grocery Buying," Dick began, as Amos tried to hide behind his taller colleague from the furious gaze of the Fire Chief. "His desk's right underneath a smoke detector, and normally when he lights up he waves the cloud away before it reaches the ceiling—but, well, this time his phone rang—and the fool went and, uh, answered it."

"Then why did the alarm sound to Evacuate, instead of staying on Alert as usual?"

Dick's attempted grin was, by his standards, feeble. "I'm afraid that in all the excitement he dropped his pipe—into the wastepaper basket. Which was, uh, full."

"But we have Ben Morecambe to thank that the whole place *didn't* go up in flames," emphasised Amos, emerging from Mr. Slack's shade as the Fire Chief's accusing eye sought him out. "He apparently realised at once what was happening—"

"But by that time it was too late to stop the alarm—"

"And we could hardly have called a halt to eight hundred-odd people trying to get out of the building in an orderly manner—"

"But at least," concluded Dick, "we can now be absolutely sure we can empty the whole place inside six minutes. You could say it's rather a good thing to have tested it under real conditions—even if it isn't, uh, quite how we'd normally do it."

"*You* could," replied the Fire Chief. "*We* could not." And the wrangling which ensued, as the full iniquity of the occurrence became clear, was not brief. The top step became a small battleground, with a megaphoned Dick supporting an Amos whose attempts to bargain with the authorities were doomed to failure. This time, the Fire Chief announced in ominous tones, Tesbury's had Gone Too Far. He would be charging them double the usual call-out fee, and more than likely would Take the Matter Further, as well.

The crowded Warehouse yard was growing restive. The roster for each department had been called, checked, and approved. Stone, ensnared by the press of people, stood on tiptoe and observed that Sadie Halliwell and Mrs. Mossley joined together to count off House Services, in which group Steven Bamber (or at least the top of his head) appeared to be present. She also thought she caught a glimpse of Veronica, alive and well, though from such a distance she couldn't be sure, and was preparing herself for another bout of wriggling when Trewley, looking like a bloodhound with acute indigestion, forged his way through to her, and groaned as he drew near.

"Women!" He rolled his eyes and took her to one side, with a wary glance over his shoulder. "Hundreds of them! Like being captured by—by—who were those warrior females who chopped bits off themselves so they'd be the right shape for using a bow and arrow?" He didn't wait for her to supply the answer. "I got away at last. . . ."

Stone felt sorry for him. Clearly, he had suffered—or anyway, believed he had. Nevertheless, she had information to impart and wasn't prepared to wait for him to recover from his ordeal. "*You* may have got away, sir, but our man didn't. Look over there—Point Three, at least I think it is—Steven Bamber, all present and correct. And that looks like his wife, too."

"What?" Trewley was several inches taller than his sergeant and could scowl easily over the heads of several dozen people. "Yes, I see her—thank goodness for that—*and* him. Ugh!" He shuddered expressively. "Whatever else he may be, he's a brave man, Stone, in the middle of all those Post Room girls." He mopped his forehead and squinted up at the blazing sun. "I'm getting away from here—I'll meet you back inside when all this is over."

"But sir—if the place really is on fire, for once—am I supposed to come rushing indoors to rescue you? Heroics are hardly in my line, you know."

He muttered something she felt it wiser not to hear, just as Dick Slack and Amos Chadderton appeared from round the corner of the building. Dick still held the megaphone in a frantic grasp. From behind the two men came sounds of bad-tempered fire engines roaring into the distance.

Trewley first glared at Stone, then grinned. "Missed your chance for the police medal, Sergeant. Another false alarm, or I'm a Dutchman. See you back inside, like I said—you keep an eye on our friend until we can grab him for a little talk."

She had no time to reply. There was a loud popping and a metallic bang, and then the megaphoned voice of Mr. Slack broke upon the shimmering summer air. "The fire alarm is over now—so will everyone please return to their desks as soon as possible? Thank you."

Before Dick had finished speaking, Trewley was well on his way, terrified the hordes of elbowing Amazons would somehow ensnare him again. Stone sighed, shook her head, smiled briefly, and directed her attentions to what she could see of the House Services department, and to Steven Bamber in their midst.

On the whole, it was an orderly return to the office,

though somewhat slower than various supervisors would have liked. No admission had been made that the whole affair had been an unfortunate error, but for those in the know the look on Amos Chadderton's face was sufficient warning. Nobody addressed even one word to him as they passed his plump form standing sentinel at the top of the steps.

Detective Sergeant Stone, wandering back with Steven Bamber never out of sight, was surprised to be joined by Mr. Slack. Sadie Halliwell hadn't said much to Dick so far that morning; Stone, although a police officer, was an attractive young woman. Making sure that Sadie couldn't miss seeing them, Dick ambled along in step with the sergeant and made idle chatter.

"Nothing like a bit of excitement to liven the working day, is there, Miss Stone?"

"I would hardly have thought," she said, her eyes on Steven, "that two murders in one week could be regarded as *un*exciting, Mr. Slack."

"Well, uh, no. But all that's so, er, out of the ordinary it doesn't really count, does it? Though I suppose it isn't so out of the ordinary, for you."

"We have our odd moments of drama, certainly."

Dick observed Sadie catching them up, as House Services drifted in a slow sideways fanning motion towards the building. He was piqued that Stone seemed to be paying him little attention. He said:

"It can be pretty dramatic for us too, you know! Things hardly ever go as smoothly as we'd like—though of course we cope. Take this evacuation. We're always having false alarms, but we haven't actually emptied the place for ages, so it's been good practice, even if it was by mistake. But take last week—everybody stayed indoors then, instead of running about outside for hours, wasting time and money."

"Tesbury's affords its employees a highly varied work experience," replied Stone, who'd been influenced more than she had realised by the jargon of Ken's reports.

They had almost reached the bottom of the steps. Stone held back to make sure Steven went back in with the rest of his colleagues; Dick, of course, hoped it was for another reason, especially as Sadie was now gazing at them with a too-indifferent air. He was rather pleased with himself.

"Oh, yes, what with false fire alarms and those traffic blitzes your crowd are so keen on—look at Tuesday, for example. Never a minute's peace. . . ."

Steven, unremarked, vanished through the double doors to be buttonholed by a Trewley wondering what had happened to his sergeant. For the first time, Stone was paying full attention to what Dick was saying.

"Tuesday? You had a traffic blitz here the day Ken Oldham was killed?" She shook her head. "You mean Tuesday of last week, of course."

Dick stared at her. "No, I don't, I mean this week—of course I do. Four days ago, just before lunchtime. One of your lot rang in to let us know the wardens were on the way, and we had to put out a tannoy Call for everyone to go charging off and move their cars from the road. . . ."

"But that's not possible." Stone spoke with authority: did she not have a close personal friend in Traffic? "There wasn't an official blitz along this route this week. We've just about given up until the single yellow line has been changed to double—"

"Definitely Tuesday of this week," Dick said, with just as much authority. Stone shook her head again.

"There's been nothing official planned since the council agreed last Wednesday to change the lines," she insisted. Then sudden excitement gleamed in her eyes, and she stared at Dick without seeing him. "Which must mean—if you were all asked to go outside and move your cars this Tuesday—it was a hoax. . . ."

And Detective Sergeant Stone turned and bolted up the steps.

─────── Twenty-five ───────

"EXCUSE ME—EXCUSE me! Excuse me, please." Stone threaded her hurried way through clusters of Tesburians reluctant to rush back to work, gossiping in the foyer as they waited for the lift. She was looking for Trewley: but, after several minutes, realised that she looked in vain. The superintendent was nowhere to be seen. She only hoped he hadn't climbed the stairs in his haste to return to the interview room: it was a hot day, and there had been far too many excitements for a man with his blood pressure.

Stone, however, was younger by a quarter of a century than her boss, and certainly fitter. She wasted no more time in looking, but headed for the stairs, where she joined a group of middle-management squash players as they jogged ostentatiously upwards. She outstripped them as they came to the first bend, and had darted away down the corridor before they'd reached the landing, keeping mental fingers crossed that she wouldn't find Trewley's helpless form collapsed and gasping on the floor.

She need not have worried. The weight of the superintendent's personality had cleared a swift path for himself and Steven Bamber through the foyer's chattering crowds to the lift, where they'd been some of the earliest passengers. Even as Stone was starting to brood on heart attacks, the object of her concern was taking his seat in relative comfort at the interview room table, while Steven, puzzled but polite, was drawing out the chair opposite.

The sound of Stone's footsteps interrupted Trewley as he was gearing up to more pressing questions after the briefest of preliminaries. The superintendent broke off in surprise and frowned as there came a rattle at the door, which opened to reveal his sergeant.

"Sir—could I have a word, please? Now," as he rolled

his eyes briefly in Steven's direction. "I think it might be rather important. . . ."

The least observant detective would have recognised that Sergeant Stone was bursting with news: she wasn't simply there to apologise for not having delivered the missing witness in person. With a hasty request to Steven to wait for a few moments, Trewley allowed himself to be dragged from the interview room. Stone firmly closed the door, then checked up and down the corridor in case anyone should be near enough to eavesdrop. They weren't.

"Sir—the day Ken Oldham died—Tuesday of this week, wasn't it?" Before he could say something rude, she pressed on. "I've just found out there was a traffic blitz on the road on Tuesday—but it was a hoax, sir, I'm sure of it. If we check with the station and I'm right, I've got a good idea why, too." She glanced around again, then lowered her voice as she produced the punch line. "To get Oldham away from his desk at the right time to kill him—and to give the killer a good excuse to be away from *his* desk at the same time!"

Trewley scowled. "Have you checked with the station yet? No sense in going off half-cocked. Where the hell's that fool Benson got to?"

"He'll be wandering round the postal routes looking for Steven Bamber, sir. We haven't time to wait for him to come back—I'll slip along to the lecture theatre and telephone from there. Hedges can keep watch in case anyone comes in and hears what I'm saying."

"Umph." Trewley rubbed the end of his nose. "While you're doing that, I think I'll put one or two questions to our Mr. Bamber—even if they won't be the ones I was going to ask him." He gave his sergeant a little push. "Well, what are you waiting for, girl? You're the one who said we hadn't the time!"

"I'm on my way, sir!" And she was, trying not to run against the flow of pedestrians still making their slow way from stairs and lifts back to work. Trewley watched her run round the first corner and disappear from view, then turned and went back to the interview room.

"Sorry about that, Mr. Bamber." He sat heavily down on

the chair he'd left in such a hurry, and saw that Steven did not appear to have stirred an inch from his own. A clear conscience? Or a guilty one, making him extra wary about showing signs of restlessness?

"About your wife, Mr. Bamber." Steven's head jerked up, and his eyes narrowed slightly. The superintendent carried on as if this were a normal bout of questioning. "She's one of the telephonists here, isn't she?"

After a pause, Steven admitted that she was.

Trewley nodded. "And the other was—I'm sorry—your cousin Janice Blake?"

"Yes, she was."

"On the day Ken Oldham was murdered, there was a traffic blitz along this road, wasn't there?"

A longer pause, while Steven—tried to remember? tried to decide if he could deny remembering? "Yes, there was," he said at last.

"And how did you know about it, Mr. Bamber?"

Steven looked surprised, then rallied quickly, and even managed a faint, exasperated smile. "A Call was put out over the tannoy—as there are *always* Calls being put out over the tannoy, Mr. Trewley. You must have noticed that there is all too seldom that silence which lasts about the space of half an hour."

Trewley, who did not recognise the biblical quotation, grunted. "Drive you mad, every five minutes," he agreed. "Still, they get the message across, all right. And can you remember which of the two girls got the message across about the traffic blitz on Tuesday, Mr. Bamber—your wife, or your cousin?"

If there was any hesitation this time, it was so slight as to be unnoticeable. "My poor cousin put out the Call, Mr. Trewley. Veronica, I imagine, had already left for an early lunch." And Steven's frown was one of deep disapproval, tinged with resignation.

Trewley gave a satisfied sigh. Stone, bless the girl, had guessed right—or so it seemed. The sooner she got back from ringing the station, the better. . . .

Steven gazed with some curiosity at the superintendent, who sat with his head to one side as if listening, with an abstracted look on his corrugated face and obviously no wish to ask further questions. Mr. Bamber was starting to feel guilty about having been so long absent from work. People would wonder where he—where the post—had got to. If the police had finished with him, perhaps he could—

"Ah!" Trewley sat bolt upright on his chair. "This might be her coming now. . . ."

It was: and the brightness of her eyes signalled Stone's triumph the instant the door was opened. "I was right, sir," she said cryptically. "It was nothing to do with us!" Even in her excitement she didn't ignore the presence of Steven Bamber and the need to keep secret this new line of investigation.

"Well, thanks, Mr. Bamber. You've been very helpful," said Trewley at once. "Please don't discuss this with anyone else, will you?" And he began to shuffle papers without another look in the direction of the witness. Steven, startled by the abruptness of his dismissal, was too polite to remark on it, and quietly took his leave.

"So it was a hoax," said the superintendent, as the door closed behind him. "A hoax Call put out by Janice Blake—and she's dead, too."

"Though not because she saw who burgled Oldham's desk," said Stone. "That was just misdirection—a red herring, like the missing clipboard. There was nothing to compromise the killer in Oldham's notes *or* in his desk! But Janice *was* killed by the same person—because it was that person who asked her to put out the Call, which she realised was bogus because that Switch Room overlooks the road, doesn't it? She'll have noticed that nobody came along to tow cars away or slap parking tickets on them—so surely that must mean Veronica's still in danger, sir. She'll have noticed the same th—No, sir?"

"No. Leastways, I don't think so. From what her husband didn't exactly spell out, his wife's a bit too much in the habit of hopping out for an early lunch and leaving Janice to do all the work—we'll check that with the others, of course." He pushed back his chair. "In fact, there's quite a bit I'd like to check with the people in House Services, my girl—so let's get down there!"

• • •

Dick and Sadie stared as the two detectives passed through the department in a surge of excitement and headed for Amos Chadderton's desk at top speed. Without even nodding to Mrs. Mossley, Trewley strode in, thumped the desk, and demanded:

"Which of you authorised Janice Blake to put out that Call on Tuesday—the one about moving the cars?"

Amos, startled, blinked. "Well, I—really, I can't remember. We're *always* being asked to move the cars—it's a miracle to me the fire engine managed to get through safely just now—"

"Never mind the fire engine," barked Trewley. "It's the bogus Call I'm more bothered about now—the one that had Ken Oldham tearing out of here to move his car, and then he never came back. Which was what whoever authorised that Call had meant to happen. . . ."

"Oh, no, Superintendent—I'm sorry," said Amos, blinking rapidly, "but I'm afraid you must be mistaken. Why, Ken has—had—a reserved parking space. Anyone who knew him would realise he had absolutely no reason to go out to move his car. . . ."

"But," broke in Maureen, eyes bright, "that's what he said he was doing, wasn't it—don't you remember? I heard him as plain as I hear you now!"

"He must have had a reason." Trewley glared at Amos for not having mentioned, among so very many facts, the one fact that would have been of greatest help. "He pretended he was going to his car—where was he really going? He ended up in the Warehouse, but did he go anywhere else first?"

"It—it must have been to the Warehouse," said Amos, after a few moments of desperate thought. "Yes, of course—I told you they'd never let him inside—he knew they'd be having their protest meeting, so the place would be deserted—and in all the confusion about moving the cars . . ."

"Cars!" Stone, who'd been so excited she hadn't even opened her notebook, pointed to the wall through which, had there been a window, they could all have seen the car park. "Who's that out there carrying on as if this place is Brands Hatch?"

Amos and Maureen were unable to answer her; but Dick, a shocked expression on his face, came running to join them. "That—that must be Sadie," he gasped. "When you came in, she—she listened for a couple of minutes—you can't help hearing everything everyone says in this office—and then she jumped up from her chair and went storming off without a word—and she took her handbag with her—"

"With her keys!" snapped Stone, as Trewley cried:

"What kind of car does she drive?"

After a horrified pause, it was Maureen who managed to remember.

"A red Astra, I think—but I don't know the number—"

"Doesn't matter, if she goes on driving it like that—there won't be two of 'em. . . ." The sounds of a gunned engine, of screeching tyres, of squealing brakes, were audible now to them all. Trewley would have gestured to Stone, but she had already swung round and was sprinting for the police car.

"You won't catch her," Dick called after them, as Trewley charged in his sergeant's wake with a turn of speed surprising from one with his bulk and blood pressure. "She drives like the devil—good old Sadie," he couldn't help adding, quietly.

"So do I!" came Stone's farewell cry, and the whole department seemed to fall silent as the running footsteps vanished into the distance.

With a shaking hand, Amos removed his spectacles and set them on his blotter as if he'd never seen them before. Dick and Maureen regarded each other in a silence broken only by the roar of a second gunned engine and the squeal of further tyres. Amos drew a deep breath.

"There's the canal—and plenty of brick walls, and the factories—electric fences—they won't take her alive. . . ."

But they did.

Twenty-six

"BUT THEY ALWAYS do the decent thing in books," lamented Mr. Chadderton as, with Dick and Maureen, he joined Trewley and Stone some time later for the statutory summing-up. "A gun in the library—a poison capsule—they always do!"

Stone shook her head. "*They* are usually men—women have a far stronger instinct for survival."

Trewley, still suffering the aftereffects of the car chase—Stone's driving, he always claimed, made him nervous—said sourly:

"Well, that's women's liberation for you—leads to all sorts of trouble. Sadie Halliwell, now," as Stone was about to protest. "What good did it do her?"

"Taught her to think on her feet, for one thing," retorted Stone. "She very nearly got away with it, too!"

Amos sighed. "If only I'd remembered—I tried so hard to tell you everything I thought might be of help"—Trewley and Stone were unable to meet each other's eyes—"but it just never dawned on me it could matter. That Sadie had been so unaccountably thick with Ken, I mean, that morning, before she came back from looking at the coffee machines and told him the Warehouse was out protesting—and Ken went out to move his car—and Sadie had already gone off to fix the ladies' lavatory, she said . . ."

He turned to Maureen. "Remember how she was breathless and a bit untidy, when she came back after . . . afterwards? You told her she needed to powder her nose!"

"Oh, dear, so I did." Maureen sighed. "I still can't really believe she killed Ken. I know she did, but . . . a woman—it doesn't seem, well, possible."

"Sadie found it perfectly possible," said Amos, recov-

ering his spirits as he heard Trewley chuckle at Stone's
snort of exasperation. "Just think about our, er, Ms.
Halliwell for a moment. Quick-witted, practical—liberated—
and mechanically-minded. It wouldn't have taken her very
long to work out how to drive a forklift truck. . . ."

"Car Maintenance classes!" cried Dick.

"Liberated," scoffed Mrs. Mossley. Amos turned to her,
his spectacles gleaming.

"Oh dear, yes. And I ask you, is it the action of a
liberated woman to suggest to another woman that she
should make a special fuss of her husband just to get him in
a good mood?" Detective Sergeant Stone suddenly choked,
but (with an effort) said nothing. Trewley's chuckle was
louder this time, as Amos continued the explanation he
seemed, with the tacit agreement of the police, to have taken
over. "Wouldn't anyone who knew her expect Sadie to tell
Veronica that Steven would simply have to stop his nonsense and pull himself together? But Sadie wanted poor
Janice to be the one on late duty that evening, so that she
could . . . well, she wanted Janice to be on late duty,
which means Veronica had to be induced to swap with
her—and to believe it was her own idea, in case she
wondered about it afterwards, the way Janice must have
begun wondering about that hoax Call. . . ."

Maureen frowned. "Why didn't she ask Janice to swap,
instead of Veronica? If she knew—intended—the poor girl
wouldn't be around, er, afterwards, to say what had really
happened. . . ."

This was too much for Dick. "Oh, come on. Even Sadie
wouldn't have been that callous. Setting up someone she'd
known for ages? Ken was different—but Janice . . ."

"Sadie had her squeamish side," Amos agreed. "Remember how she hesitated about coming to help when
Angela Farnworth fainted in here? Dick, wasn't the first
thing she asked you whether she knew the girl in question?
It was only when you said she was a stranger," as Dick
nodded, "that she offered to assist Maureen in providing
first aid."

Maureen, whose recollection was somewhat different,
gave a quick sniff, but had no time to say anything as Amos

went on with his story. "Miss Farnworth had her part to play on the day poor Janice died, too, because blocking her car in and disappearing for so long gave Sadie just the excuse she needed to be around the building late. . . . And she wasn't so squeamish by then. Not that she was too squeamish after she'd disposed of Ken—in fact, she was rather keen to talk about it. Establishing her alibi, seeing how well she could keep her nerve—and she kept it very well. Really, the only times I've noticed her being at all jumpy were when Ken was discussing his plans for the future of House Services. She always tried to squash him, or pick a quarrel, or start raising objections of one sort or another. And not just with Ken—with anyone who, well, looked as if they might interfere with the status quo."

Suddenly he dragged his spectacles from his nose and began to polish them. "Oh dear, I'm sorry, Superintendent. This is really . . . I mean, I shouldn't be interfering when it's the job of you and your sergeant . . ."

"Oh, don't mind us, sir." Trewley managed to grin as he mopped his forehead. "Makes a nice change for someone else to do the hard work wrapping up the case—especially after the sort of day we've just had. You carry on, Mr. Chadderton—tell your friends now why she did it."

A delighted smile lit Amos's face as everyone prepared to hang on his words. This, then, was how it felt to be Poirot—Wimsey—Sherlock Holmes—Gervase Fen!

Dick couldn't bear it and burst out: "For goodness' sake, Amos, tell us! I've worked at the next desk to Sadie for over two years. I can't think what she can have been doing that was so crooked she needed to kill two people to cover it up!"

Amos looked even more smug. "I should have guessed, you know, when I spoke to her last week about—I'm sorry, Dick—about what will happen when I retire. I thought of Sadie as a likely successor . . . but she didn't seem at all keen. She tried to pretend she wasn't sure she wanted the bother of dealing with a lot of, er, male chauvinist pigs," with a cautious look in Stone's direction. Her shoulders gave a little jerk, but she said nothing, though Trewley clapped a hasty hand over his face to smother a laugh.

"But it was all," said Amos firmly, "fluff. Bluff. Because what Sadie *really* didn't want was anyone coming in to take over her old job, to look into it in detail and learn exactly how it was run—the way Ken had been saying that he was going to do. When she asked me how much more the manager's job would pay, I suggested a likely increase of around twenty percent—but now we know she was making as much in one week from her, er, illicit activities as we paid her in a month—and tax free, too!"

Sensation. When it had died down, Amos continued. "No wonder she didn't want my job. She wanted a new manager to be brought in from outside, someone who'd leave her alone where she wanted to stay—but Ken was a different matter. Even if he didn't uncover her fraud, his longer-term plans for Tesbury's would have meant she'd lose that extra money fairly soon in any case—and, with it, the style of life to which she was accustomed."

"Her divorce," faltered Maureen. "The alimony . . ."

Amos shook his head. "It could never have been as large as she made out—we should have realised she was protesting too much. Dick, you're on the same salary, but you don't live half as well as Sadie, do you? Always smartly dressed—a new car every year—foreign holidays—why didn't we guess she was up to something?"

"Because," said Maureen, rallying, "she was cunning and devious and as two-faced as Ken, and if you don't tell us what she did to bring in all this extra money, I'll scream."

"She stole wastepaper," said Amos in triumph, and sat back to watch the expressions on the faces in front of him. Trewley and Stone nodded, unmoved; Maureen and Dick frankly goggled. Dick at last found his voice.

"Wastepaper? Is that all?"

"All?" Amos had spent an instructive half hour, once he had recovered from the initial shock of Sadie's flight, on the telephone, while Maureen and Dick dealt with Post Room hysteria, PC Benson's bewilderment, and a flurry of activity among the Switch Room temps as the reporters outside the building realised that Something was Going On and demanded enlightenment. "I've had a talk to our buyers, you know. Stock Control alone must throw out getting on for five tons of computer paper a week, because that's certainly what they buy in—and it isn't all stored in the Archives, is it?'' Dick, listening intently, shook his head. Amos smirked. ''If you add to that amount the usage of our other departments—and if you know that any paper merchant will pay around ninety pounds a ton for high-quality paper of this type—and if you multiply the weekly total by fifty-two—and you don't tell the tax man . . .''

''No wonder she didn't want your job,'' Dick agreed, while everyone else murmured. Trewley, who'd had time to brood, raised the objection which hadn't occurred to him earlier.

''Why didn't anyone notice how much paper was coming in and out every week? I'd have thought even one ton of the stuff'd take up a fair bit of room.''

Amos shrugged. ''They probably did notice, but without any particular interest—who would have expected it to be interesting? Why should anyone have bothered to keep check? Ken checked, though. He was planning to microfilm some of the computer records and needed to know how much space it would save. He signed his death warrant when he told Sadie how thoroughly he always researched his projects . . . and she was quick to act. She acted the part of a helpful friend, told him about the Warehouse walkout, and . . .''

''She was a cool customer,'' said Trewley. ''Just her bad luck my sergeant happened, er, to have specialist knowledge about that Call to move the cars. So she was able to work out why Miss Blake had to be killed, and then . . .''

''But I had specialist knowledge too, Mr. Trewley.'' Amos was now quite carried away. ''It wasn't simply because she'd put out that Call poor Janice had to die—she was a credulous young woman, and Sadie would probably have been able to pull the wool thoroughly over her eyes if she'd started asking about it—''

Stone snorted. ''Miss Blake wasn't safe from the moment she put out that Call, Mr. Chadderton. Sooner or later, Sadie Halliwell would have had a severe attack of twitching nerves—take it from me.'' And Trewley nodded beside her.

Amos nodded back. "I'm sure you're right, Miss Stone. But I think Janice was a still greater threat because she knew that even newspaper sells for pulping—she told me so herself, when I was trying to find out . . . er, something else, and she rambled on about how her Girl Guides were collecting for their camping equipment and different ways they raised money. She asked me to put a notice in the House Services Circular—she had a very limited intellect, poor girl, and once she had an idea fixed in her head . . . If she kept on and on about it, somebody was sure to notice in the end. Then they'd start to wonder what happened to *our* wastepaper. Not so much the routine rubbish with staples and carbons, but the top-quality computer printout . . ."

"She'd have pretended it was chucked away with the rest of the rubbish," said Dick, who still had a soft spot for Ms. Halliwell. "We need never have known she'd been helping herself, if she didn't let on she knew—"

"Oh, Dick! Who would have believed she didn't know? Sadie Halliwell—who eats health food, reuses paper bags, puts cans and bottles in the recycling banks, warns of the dangers of pollution? She wouldn't have fooled anyone for a second if she'd tried denying she knew!"

Dick gasped as a sudden memory came to him. "That day we had lunch together—when I told her I'd been a Boy Scout and mentioned collecting newspapers . . ." He shuddered. "She choked me off pretty smartish—I'd forgotten. But I reckon I've had a lucky escape. . . ."

Stone took up the story. "Once we knew where to look, thanks to Mr. Chadderton, it was fairly obvious what she'd been up to. Those three young lads who do nothing all day but collect wastepaper and move furniture—she'd got them trained to do exactly what they were told, so when they had to load the computer paper on a separate van they thought nothing of it. They're a pretty stolid bunch—we had to pull a fair bit of rank to make them spill the beans, but when they did . . ."

"Of course!" Dick sat up. "Oh, they were well-trained, all right. When she was on holiday, I never had to say anything to them except Hello and Good-bye, and give them their bleepers every morning—and I thought what a good job she'd done with them! If only I'd known!''

"If only," said the superintendent, "you'd all known, Mr. Slack. The security in this place isn't what anyone could rightly call good, you have to admit. My sergeant's made a few notes," he added. "We'll be sending our Crime Prevention Officer along for a chat in a day or so.''

Amos looked glum. "I suppose Old George will have to be pensioned off at last, although . . . and as for myself . . ." He sighed. "But we must certainly sort something out before we recruit Sadie's replacement. I daren't think what the Board would say if the same sort of thing happened again.''

"Oh," said Maureen, with a saucy look. "I can assure you Sadie's replacement won't be playing the same tricks as she did, because I'm applying for her job myself. Nobody can say I wouldn't be capable of doing it! Dick and I work very well together—and we'll find a nice sensible secretary for you, Amos. Unless''—as he looked started—"you have other plans for me, Mr. Chadderton, sir? Talking about being pensioned off sort of put the idea in my head that you might just have another position you'd like to, er, propose me for. . . .''

Amos blinked. Dick grinned. Trewley chuckled; and his sergeant nodded her approval of this liberated approach to matrimony. Mr. Chadderton blinked again, looked round at the smiling faces . . .

And realised what Maureen had meant. "Oh," he said; and took off his spectacles, and scratched the tip of his nose. "Well . . .''

That evening, in The Spice Trader, Amos was thinking over recent events and wondering just how he felt about it all. He was deep in thought, and on his third pint of Old Guvnor, when a voice he knew well accosted him. "Chad! There you are." Clem Bradshaw sounded as if he hadn't a care in the world. "All set for the big day, are you? When the House Services Circular," he enlarged, as Amos looked decidedly startled, "finally goes out. A bit of bad luck, having to wait—still, good news doesn't spoil with keeping.''

"I—I suppose it doesn't." Amos took a deep breath. "You're really happy to go ahead, are you? You've made all the relevant enquiries yourself, and everything, er, works? I don't understand," as Clem grinned, and nodded, and drank from his tankard in a toast. "You were so against it before—I thought you'd only agreed because, well, Ken pulled rank and kept going on about the Board. . . ."

Clem continued to drink for a moment, then suddenly choked on his beer, and set the tankard down with a clunk as he started to laugh. "Take that worried look off your face, Chad!" he gasped, as soon as he could. "That's what's been eating you, is it? You've been worried I was on the take—playing off one firm against the other, trying to get one of 'em to bribe me?"

Amos gaped, blushed, and buried his nose in his mug of Old Guvnor. "Ken Oldham . . . well . . . hinted. . . ."

"Oldham!" Mr. Bradshaw's tone held nothing but scorn. "Yes, and that young know-it-all tried *hinting* the same sort of thing to me—and even to Mary, when I wasn't around to clip his ear for him. But what the hell d'you take me for, Chad? After all the years we've known each other?"

Amos gaped again, his blush even deeper than before. He tried not to stutter as he replied. "But—but why wouldn't you even talk to him about it? Why weren't you ever in the office when he—when anyone tried to see you? I was starting to think . . ."

As he broke off, Clem began to laugh again. "Trouble with you, Chad, is that you *don't* think, not right through. And you never could." He aimed a friendly cuff at his old schoolmate's head. "You've not changed a bit from being kids, have you? And neither have I. Bribery and corruption—I ask you, Chad, is that me? No!" as Amos tried to speak. "Don't answer—I can see Oldham at least got you worrying, and that's bad enough.

"But if you'd just use your loaf, Chad . . . I didn't care for Oldham, didn't care at all—but even I have to admit he came up with good ideas sometimes—and sometimes with god-awful ones, as well. Know what his first two suggestions for the car park were?"

As Clem paused to savour the moment of revelation,

Amos said: "No, I don't. He stayed out of House Services rather a lot at first—well, most of the time, really."

"I'll tell you, then. I couldn't stop myself laughing when he tried it out on me. . . . Car park attendants, that was the first idea. Some fancy American notion he'd picked up while he was abroad. Now I ask you, Chad. Can you see Tesbury folk handing over their car keys to someone who's going to cram 'em all together like sardines? He kept trying to tell me it would save half the spaces, but I knew nobody'd ever wear it, and I told him so. Any more than they'd wear his second daft idea. . . ."

Amos recognised a cue when he heard one. "Which was?"

"Compulsory lift-sharing! Did you ever?"

Amos didn't even bother to comment on that one. Clem began to laugh. "So you can see why I was a bit doubtful when the silly young snirp came bouncing along with *another* solution to end all solutions, because solutions like his we can well do without, thanks very much." He raised his mug and drank. "Anyway, cheers—to the memory of Ken Oldham, wherever he is. Because fair's fair, and I'll give him his due—the third time, he came up with the goods, and no question, if only he'd not been so full of himself he didn't think to ask for a spot of advice. Buses!" And he drank again.

"Buses? But—I don't—"

"As soon as I clapped eyes on that notice of his in the Circular, I could see he'd got the answer—but it was the daft way he'd put it, Chad! Making it compulsory—getting everyone's backs up before the thing had even started. That young man and his kind have already got too many backs up around this place—redundancy, compulsory early retirement—you know what I mean." Amos, as close to the end of his working life as Mr. Bradshaw, nodded and sighed. Mr. Bradshaw also sighed. "Tell the truth, that was another reason I wasn't so keen on Oldham—had some notion if I could only fend him off long enough over the car park, the Board might run out of steam and get rid of him, then things would be like they used to be. But I should have known better—you can't go back, Chad, and no use trying.

You've got to move with the times, even if you don't like them. . . .''

"Even if it's on buses," said Amos, with a twinkle.

"Buses—right! That notice would have got rid of him, all the fuss they'd have kicked up—but if he'd put it in the right way, he'd have been made for life. . . .''

"Your way," said Amos, wishing he'd had the nerve to ask Maureen to show him Clem's amendment as she typed the House Services Circular for the third time, before it went to the Reprographics Section. But Maureen had been so very haughty about the whole matter, he'd thought it safer not to ask. . . .

". . . compulsory, the way he wrote it," Mr. Bradshaw was saying, with a smirk. "Like some sort of . . . penalty for not having a high-enough graded job. That's what everyone would have thought, no question. But—here's the beauty of it all, Chad—if you let them see it as a *privilege*— tell 'em how much money they'll save by not using their cars—make sure they know the buses will be free—let them choose the routes and work out the pickup points . . .''

"They'll fight for places!" cried Amos. He knew Tesburians as well as Clem Bradshaw knew them. "We'll have to hold ballots to choose who'll be allowed to use the buses— they'll say we aren't running enough—it's brilliant!"

Mr. Chadderton looked at Mr. Bradshaw; Mr. Bradshaw looked at Mr. Chadderton. They laughed together, and nodded, and raised their tankards in a silent toast to the shade of Ken Oldham, and to the three months' trial of Allshire's two largest coach-hire firms, and to (they were now confident) the eventual solving of the car park problem. . . .

"Odd, isn't it, sir?" said Stone, as they sat in Allingham police station and pondered recent events. Benson and Hedges were in the canteen, the Incident Room duly dismantled; but Stone had returned with Trewley to his office, and had been studying her notes and listening to his comments on the case as he drank copious cups of tea at his desk and slowly recovered.

"Odd," said Stone again. "That it wasn't really us who worked out what was going on, I mean. Of course, we did—but so did Mr. Chadderton, even if it was from a different point of view, because he knew things we didn't. It doesn't seem, well, right, somehow.''

"That's what barley-sugar does for you, girl." Amos had revealed the secret of his hoard when, flushed with success, he'd hunted in his desk for the little black book to confirm beyond doubt the dates of the fire alarm call and the traffic blitz. "*And* reading detective stories in your spare time— not that we were too far behind him, Stone. *You* weren't, anyway. Perhaps, if the weather'd been a bit cooler . . . But why not let the man have his fun? Isn't that the way it happens in those perishing books of his? The gifted amateur puts one over on the police. . . .''

"Especially when it impresses the gifted amateur's lady friend. She, er, certainly was impressed, wasn't she, sir?'' Stone grinned, wondering what response would be elicited if she tried the same stunt as Maureen. Not that she saw any need for marriage, at this stage in her career—a career she was enjoying too much to abandon it for domesticity.

"Umph.'' Trewley eyed her cheerful countenance with suspicion. "I hope you aren't getting any daft ideas, my girl. Not that you're any better at your job than anyone else, mind''—he hoped he'd be forgiven, but he didn't want her getting a swollen head—"but I'm used to you, and I don't like unnecessary changes. Even,'' with a grin, "the way you drive—which reminds me. You weren't going all that fast, by your standards—how did you manage to lose Benson and Hedges so easily on the way back here? I'd better send 'em on a refresher course, if—No?''

For Stone was shaking her head, smiling. "I'd quite forgotten about it, sir, but now you've reminded me . . .'' She hurried across to her desk, rummaged in the top drawer, and brought out a small pocket whose identity the superintendent could not, at that distance, make out. "They were, er, running an errand for me, sir—and for you, too, though you didn't know it at the time. I thought, you see, that it might come in useful. If you'll promise not to tell your wife. . . .''

And she handed him, with a wink, a bag of barley-sugar.

──────── About the Author ────────

Sarah J(ill) Mason was born in England (Bishop's Stortford) and went to university in Scotland (St. Andrews). She then lived for a year in New Zealand (Rotorua) before returning to settle only twelve miles from where she started. She now lives about fifteen miles outside London with a tame welding engineer husband and two (reasonably) tame Schipperke dogs, and is a fully paid-up, though nonparticipating, member of the British Lawn Mower Racing Association. Under the pseudonym Hamilton Crane, she continues the Miss Seeton series created by the late Heron Carvic.